Apprentice Fool

Book One of the Nobody's Fool Quartet

Aldred Chase

DEDICATION

To my wife, Barbara, for all her love and support

ACKNOWLEDGMENTS

Cover Design by www.ebooklaunch.com
Editing by www.firstediting.com

Thank you to Keith Stevenson for the help and inspiration he provided in writing this book through the New South Wales Writers' Centre mentorship scheme.

.

CONTENTS

1 MOTTLE

"Keth has seen thirteen summers," my mum announced as she gave me a shove towards the shafts of the cart.

It was late afternoon and we had just finished harvesting the last field belonging to our village of Mottle. The final load of wheat, tied in golden bundles, was piled high on our village cart.

The tradition was that this last load was hauled home by the young men of Mottle, although my mum had whispered to me that this only became a tradition when Mottle became too poor to own a horse.

Gannett, Stropper, and Taggle, who were all a few years older than me, had already taken up position between the shafts. Gannett, tall and lanky, was in the lead. Behind him slouched Stropper, scrawny and sour. He drummed his fingers on the shafts. Taggle was last of the three. He was short and the shafts of the cart rose above his shoulders.

My position would be behind Taggle. I was about his height so we would look like two headless bodies tugging the cart along. Of course, that assumed I would be allowed to pull the cart.

I plodded towards the front of the wagon. This was going to be embarrassing, mostly for me, and I resented it.

Scour, the village elder, bent double with age and scuttling like an enraged spider, ran in front of me and whacked his bone-tipped stick across the shafts. The ringing thwack made the three lads already in position jump. Scour's stick blocked me from taking my place.

"I don't think Keth is ready this year," Scour said. His head was bald and pink except for the clumps of white hair that grew out of his ears. Mum said he had been old and bad-tempered when she was a little girl, and his temper had only grown worse.

"Keth has seen thirteen summers, Scour," Mum said. "You're not the only one who can count or who can remember our traditions."

"Cheeky young scamp," Scour said. This was aimed at my mum, whose red hair was now streaked with gray.

"Keth's a bit small for his age," Chivel said. He was a thin, stooped, saggy-faced man who tried to keep the peace. "Perhaps Keth could do it next year, Ailsa."

"All the kids are small for their age because none of them ever gets enough to eat," Mum said, "and this isn't about size, is it, Scour?"

"True," Scour said. "Keth has not shown the responsibility expected from him to deserve his place between the shafts."

I was annoyed by the way these grownups were talking about me as though I was not there. I was standing right in front of them. I decided to remind them I could speak too.

"If the greatest honor you can achieve in Mottle is dragging a cart then we're the saddest village in the kingdom and, to be honest, I don't need it."

Scour's jaw dropped, displaying his two remaining stumps of teeth. His pink scalp turned red then purple as the outrage built up in him.

"Did you hear that?" Scour ranted. "He has dishonored his mother."

"No, he hasn't," Mum said, loud enough for the whole village to hear.

"He has dishonored the village of Mottle." Scour ignored her. "He has dishonored our traditions."

I turned and walked to the back of the cart. Every day, I managed to do something to upset Scour, and most of the time, I did not mean to. This was why he was bellyaching about me being irresponsible.

"The weather's starting to turn bad," Chivel said. "We should get this wheat stored before it rains."

We were in the top field of the village. We all looked down the valley and saw where gray clouds had formed. The breeze was picking up and bringing them our way.

All arguments stopped. Once harvested wheat gets wet, you have hard work trying to dry it, and if you don't do it properly then it can go rotten.

The lads hauled on the shafts, and the cart rolled forwards. The track from the top field sloped down to the river so we kids hung off the back of the cart and dragged our feet in the dust to stop it running out of control. The last thing we needed was to be in such a rush to keep the wheat dry that we sent the whole load careering into the water.

At the bottom of the field, the track turned left and ran beside the river. We dropped off the back of the cart and ran along behind it. The wind was getting up, and the rain clouds were scurrying across the sky towards us. The young men strained between the shafts and the old men and the women hauled on the sides of the cart and pushed it from behind. The cart bounced and jolted along the rutted track, and the sheaves of wheat crackled and rustled.

I trotted along beside Arky. He was a summer younger than me and my best friend. His face was pitted all over with small craters. His mum said he had a lucky face because he had caught the pox when he was a baby, and it had marked him but not killed him.

"Faster," Scour shouted, hobbling along and waving his stick in the air.

"We'd be home already if Scour hadn't made such a fuss about me hauling the cart," I said.

"Are you upset about it?" Arky said.

I thought about it. "I'm more upset that my mum is upset."

I was not that bothered about hauling the cart because I had more important things to think about. They were dangerous things, so dangerous that I would not even tell Arky about them.

For the last two years, I had danced the spring dance and the harvest dance, and it was a matter of life and death. When Prince Dorian came to power ten summers ago, he had announced that anyone caught doing these dances would be executed.

The track swung away from the river and we entered our village. We hurried the cart through the cluster of huts where we lived and into the village square.

"Stop," yelled Scour.

Men and women strained to bring the cart to a halt before it crashed into the one stone building in the village, our barn.

Scour lifted the timber bar that held the barn doors shut. The men formed a chain between the cart and the barn and unloaded the bundles of wheat. The first drops of rain began to fall as the last of the wheat was stored, and Scour shut the barn doors, dropping the bar back into place.

"A good harvest," Scour said, and he gave a rare smile.

"Be nice if Prince Dorian's grain collector lets us keep some of it," our neighbor Meg said, with her arms folded. She had a thatch of gray hair and kept a small clay pipe clenched between her teeth. Whatever she smoked, it always smelled foul.

"It's still a good harvest, whatever happens," Scour said.

He hobbled across the square to his own hut, the elder's hut, which was the largest in the village. He turned at the entrance to his hut and rested on his stick.

"Someone needs to be keeping an eye on the cows," he said.

"I'll do it," I volunteered.

"Good lad," Scour said. "Keep it up and next year you'll be between the shafts of the cart."

I did my best to hide my total lack of enthusiasm at this prospect.

***

Our village had six cows: Myrtle, Parsley, Rosemary, Sage, Thyme and Willow, as well as a bad-tempered elderly bull called His Lordship. The cows were placid creatures and easy to keep an eye on. During the day, they grazed close to the village but at night they were shut in a wooden pen on one side of the village square, to keep them safe from wolves. His Lordship had his own field, and no wolf had ever been foolish enough to attack him.

We also had hens that were kept in a small wooden

shed attached to the cattle pen, but as long as they were fed, they tended to look after themselves.

I walked the cows along a track through the wood that emerged into a grassy clearing. Scour had told a story of how a manor house had stood here once, but the villagers, including his great grandfather, had burned it down and chased away the lord. A few traces of the house remained; some stones marked the outline of the walls and there was a depression where the hearth had been. Grass had long since taken over, and it provided good grazing.

The rain was heavier now and in the clearing, I had no shelter from it. I slapped the cows on their haunches and chivvied them until they had taken up a position between myself and where the track from the village entered the clearing. If anyone came from the village, I would be warned of their approach and I could stop dancing before they saw me.

I took a deep breath, ready to start the dance. The hairs on the back of my neck prickled. Was I being watched? I surveyed the edges of the clearing. It would be turning dark soon; perhaps a wolf made bold with hunger was already prowling.

The sooner you do the harvest dance, the sooner you can drive the cows back to the village, I told myself.

I held my arms out, either side of me, and danced: kick, step, cross and stamp; kick step, cross and stamp. As I stamped my feet, mist seemed to rise up from the ground.

I stopped. I was sure I had heard a rustle in the trees at the edge of the clearing.

Rosemary trotted over to where the sound had come from. She would not have done that if it was a wolf.

"Who's there?" I called out.

"Just us," Arky said. He emerged from where he had been concealed in the trees, followed by Gumber and Jenna.

Rosemary nuzzled Gumber and he petted her. He was three summers younger than me and he was a bit slow on the uptake but the cows loved him. When he was little, Gumber had assumed His Lordship, the village bull, would be just as affectionate as the cows and he now had a permanently squashed nose and twisted lips to show for that mistake.

"What are you up to, Keth?" Jenna called as they made their way across the clearing to join me. Jenna was Gumber's little sister. She was always with him and she did the thinking for him; she was so smart she often did the thinking for all of us. Her mother plaited her hair and it was always pulled tightly back, so you noticed how much forehead she had.

"I wanted to be alone," I said.

"We thought we could be alone with you," Arky said.

"All of us alone together, like we always are," Gumber said.

"Were you dancing just now?" Jenna said. She had this way of getting straight to the point.

"Might have been," I said.

"But you weren't," Arky said. "It's cold and wet, and we should get home before the wolves start prowling." He looked uncomfortable.

"How do you know the steps?" Jenna said.

"My dad taught me," I said.

"But he's dead," Gumber said with great honesty and no tact.

"I've seen thirteen summers and Dorian came to take our land ten years ago," I said. "My dad taught me the steps of the spring dance and the harvest dance as soon as I'd learned to walk."

"What were the dances like?" Arky said. He was just too young to remember.

All I remembered were fragments, like pictures from a dream.

"At harvest time all the villagers danced," I said. "Everyone linked up, arm in arm, until the whole village became this huge laughing chain weaving in and out of the huts, and Scour headed the chain, throwing his stick in the air and catching it."

"Did you dance?" Jenna said.

"In a kid's chain," I said. "I was between Stropper and Taggle, and then my dad whisked me up and put me on his shoulders."

"Was the spring dance the same as the harvest dance?" Arky said.

"Different," I said, sorting through my memories. "The harvest dance was just one evening and it took place in the village but the spring dance went on for several days out in the fields, after we'd finished sewing the seed. My dad said it scared the birds away and stopped them eating all the seed."

I had a picture in my mind of a windy spring morning when I was two. The village top field had been cut into stiff, straight ridges of dark earth that came up to my waist. Large black birds had settled among the ridges and pecked at the seed we had planted. My dad and I and the other villagers spread out around the edges of the field. Scour raised his stick, and we danced. The birds took flight in a big black cloud that headed over to the other side of the river.

"Teach us the harvest dance," Gumber said.

I snapped back into the present.

"We could all be executed," Arky said, taking a step

back.

If I'd opened my mouth to speak, I would have said Arky was right, and we should all go home, and I would have done the dance another day or maybe not at all. Instead, I moved my feet: kick, step, cross and stamp; kick, step, cross and stamp.

Gumber moved behind me. I glanced over my shoulder; he was following my steps. "It's easy, Jenna," he laughed.

Jenna watched our feet go kick, step, cross and stamp. As though in a trance she moved beside Gumber and began dancing the steps.

Mist seemed to detach itself from the trees and float across the ground towards us.

Arky looked as though he was going to burst into tears. Rain streamed down his pock- marked face while tendrils of mist seemed to prod at him like fingers. For a moment, he stood still then he moved beside me and joined in the steps.

Without even thinking about it, Arky and I linked arms, shoulder to shoulder. Jenna and Gumber linked up with Arky and with me in the lead, we became a chain dancing in a circle around the ruined manor.

I was in a trance until the loud mooing of the cows broke through. I looked at them as they parted like a curtain to reveal a figure, watching us. I stopped dancing, Arky stumbled into me, and all four of us toppled over still linked as a chain. The figure walked towards us through the mist and rain.

With a mixture of relief and alarm, I recognized the figure was my mum. I was in big trouble but it was a trouble I understood. Mum's face was framed by the dripping hanks of her gray and red hair. She stood over us. Her eyes glowed and flicked from left to right. She looked alert, excited, and a little scary.

"We'll never do it again," I blurted out. "We promise."

"Glance sharp out of the corner of your eye, Keth," Mum said, smiling at me.

I did. For an instant, the mist was a face with holes for eyes and a gaping mouth then it became just whirling mist.

"You can't leave the dance unfinished," Mum said. "It won't do to upset our friends."

"Friends?" I shivered.

"Up you all get and on with the dance," Mum said.

We struggled to our feet, slipping on the slick wet grass, damp and shaken.

Mum danced the steps: kick, step, cross and stamp. Our feet moved without our thinking about it. We linked arms again with Mum leading the chain and me next. I felt her warmth and confidence flowing through me and the dance became joyful. We danced three whole circuits of the ruined manor before we stopped, breathless and laughing. The mist had faded.

Mum gathered us all together in a huddle.

"None of us must ever speak about this," she said. "If word of this got out, we would all be killed by Prince Dorian."

We nodded, and each of us promised to be silent.

"We'd better get the cows back to the village," Mum said.

It had turned dusk, and the light was draining from the sky.

"I'm glad the mist has gone," I said.

"What mist?" Arky said.

"It's just rain, Keth," Jenna said.

I didn't argue but I knew what I had seen, and it frightened me.

10

***

That evening, after we had finished our supper – a thin vegetable gruel with berries and stale bread – Mum and I stood in the entrance to our hut. The rain had passed and the night was mild. The sky was clear and we saw the splinter, a narrow golden rip that ran the length of the sky. You never saw it during the day but at night, if it was not covered by clouds, it spilled a little drizzle of light onto the ground and made the outlines of the huts stand out.

"What was the face I saw in the mist, Mum?" I asked.

"Best come inside, love," she said, glancing around the silent village.

We moved back inside the hut and she pulled the sacking across the entrance and the window. The room was lit by the glow from our cooking fire in the center of the room. The smoke from the charred sticks of wood curled up to the ceiling and reminded me of the tendrils of mist.

"You saw a wraith," Mum said. "The gift of seeing them runs in my side of the family. You inherited it, along with your red hair." She smiled. Unlike other mums, my mum still had all her own teeth.

"The others didn't even see the mist," I said.

"We can catch a glimpse of things that other folk don't even know are there," Mum said. "Mind, we don't talk about it because no one would believe us."

Mum was right. I imagined explaining to Scour that I saw things that he could not. That would earn me a hard whack from his stick.

"Do you dance, Mum?" I said.

"Twice every year," she said. "Once when we finish sowing the crop and once when we finish harvesting it."

"I wish you'd invited me," I said, feeling a twinge of resentment. "The dance had more fun in it when you joined us."

"I wasn't sure you danced," Mum said, "but I half suspected it; that's why I came to the clearing. How long have you been doing it?"

"For a couple of years now, after ploughing and harvesting," I said. "I was a bit surprised I still remembered the steps."

"Some dances don't like to be forgotten," Mum said. "Have Arky, Gumber and Jenna danced before?"

"I think this was their first time," I said. "They followed me. I didn't mean to teach them the dance but it just happened."

"The dances are like that," Mum said.

A stick snapped in the fire and I jumped at its sharp retort. I was getting a bit spooked by the way Mum kept talking about the dances as though they were living things.

Something else was nagging at me; I had seen a bit of mist the last time I danced the spring dance but not before, and I had never seen a face in the mist until this afternoon.

"How come I saw a face and so much mist this time?" I said.

"You're growing into a man, Keth, and your gift is quickening," Mum said.

"Just like going between the shafts of the cart." I said, feeling a bit gloomy. It wasn't that I minded growing up, it was just I wanted more control over it. All these things were happening to me, without me having any say in them.

"We should get some sleep," Mum said. "We'll have hard work tomorrow."

I kissed Mum goodnight then I hung up a piece of cloth to separate the corner of the hut where I slept from the rest of the room. We had only begun doing that since last winter. It was another part of growing up.

I lay awake for a long while, thinking. Why had I begun dancing two years ago?

I had thought the answer was simple. Ten years ago, Prince Dorian arrived in our land and claimed it as his own. My dad and the other men in the village not too old to fight joined a large army to persuade Dorian that he was mistaken. Now, we only had old men and young men in the village; all the men who would have been between them in age never came back from the battle with Prince Dorian, except for my dad, and he only came back to die.

I was now old enough to want my revenge on the Prince. My doing the dances that the Prince had banned was my first small act of rebellion. I'd thought I was in charge of the dances, but now I wondered if the dances were controlling me.

It was a comfort to hear my mum's gentle snoring from the other side of the cloth.

2 THE GRAIN COLLECTOR

For the three days following our completing the harvest, the weather was fine and everyone in the village worked hard, threshing the wheat.

In the center of the village square was a flat surface of paved stones laid out in a circle, with limestone mortar filling the cracks between the stones. The wheat was carried from the barn and laid out flat on the stones. Gumber was in charge of walking our cows in pairs, round and round in a circle on the stones, crushing the wheat with their hooves. This separated the grains from the stalks.

The women of the village tossed the mixture of grain and stalks into the air while the men beat blankets to create a breeze. The heavier grain fell straight back down but the lighter stalks blew a little way away. We kids were responsible for scooping up the grain and putting it in sacks while the men raked up the stalks to use as feed for the cows over the winter.

It was late in the afternoon of the third day after the harvest when we finished threshing the final batch of grain. All the bending and lifting had left me so sore that I was hobbling around like Scour.

"KWAA, KWAA, KWAA." The air was split by the raucous cackling of ravens.

I straightened up and watched as a swarm of them flew into the village square. Every year these miserable flying rats heralded the arrival of the grain collector on the following day.

The ravens settled on the roof of the barn making macabre silhouettes, with the setting sun behind them. The biggest raven, sleek and fat, flew down to the stone circle where we had threshed the wheat and pecked at the one or two grains we had missed.

"They always seem to know when to arrive," Chivel said.

"When the ravens call, the grain collector will not be far behind," Scour said. "I think he will be here tomorrow morning."

Scour made it sound like a piece of ancient wisdom handed down from father to son over hundreds of years, but actually the grain collector had only been coming since Prince Dorian had taken over our land ten years ago.

"Last year he took so much of our grain, we almost starved over the winter," Mum said.

"Every year he takes more," Meg said, puffing hard on her pipe and sending up little clouds of smoke.

I had edged my way behind the raven that was pecking around our stone circle. I picked up a stone, weighed it in my hand then tossed it. My aim was good. At the last moment, the raven hopped to one side and the stone hit the spot where it had stood. It turned and eyed me balefully.

The ravens took off from the roof of the barn with a

great creaking of wings. The raven I'd tossed a stone at launched itself straight at my face. Its beak was like the blade of a knife. I ducked and fell over backwards. The blast of air from its wings struck my face as it flew over me.

"You shouldn't have thrown that stone at it, Keth," Mum scolded me.

"Why don't we hide some of our grain from the grain collector?" Jenna said.

"Behave yourself, girl," Jenna's mum snapped.

It was normally my job to ask the questions people wanted to remain unspoken. I already knew the answer to this one because I'd asked my mum years ago.

"They tried that in the village of Ratcheth," Scour said. "The ravens found the grain and pecked out the eyes of all the villagers."

***

Next morning we woke to a drizzling rain; the kind that soaks its way through your clothes without you noticing it. Mum and I joined the other villagers waiting in the village square for the arrival of the grain collector. People stood around in little groups, muttering and looking worried. No one raised their voice.

Scour and Chivel sat on the wall of the dead garden, looking washed out and faded as though they had been stacked there for burning.

The dead garden was on the opposite side of the square to the cattle pens. In spite of its name, it was the most colorful place in the village. It was a piece of ground enclosed by a waist-high, dry-stone wall. When a villager died, their body was burned and the ashes were sprinkled in the dead garden. At the moment, white, yellow, and pink flowers, growing as tall as the wall, were blooming.

Gannett, Stropper, and Taggle didn't sit but stood looking serious, with their shoulders hunched and scuffing their feet in the dirt. A few years before I would have been able to provoke a playful scrap with them, especially Taggle, the youngest of the three, but now they were adult, solemn and miserable.

My mum stood with Meg, they were talking in low murmurs. They had their arms folded and lips pursed.

No one was doing anything or going anywhere until the grain collector had been. He took a count of everyone in the village and used that to calculate how much grain to leave us, so you had to be there.

Arky, Gumber, Jenna, and I were flicking pebbles against the wall of the barn, seeing who could get their pebble closest to the wall. We did not talk about the dancing. I wondered if we ever would.

I was bored.

"Let's go to the edge of the woods and run back and tell the villagers when we hear the grain collector's cart approaching," I said.

"What if we miss it, and we're not in the village, and we don't get counted?" Arky said.

"How do you miss a cart?" I said. "They're big. They make a lot of noise. What do you think, Gumber?"

Gumber looked at Jenna to tell him what to think.

Jenna was no good at flicking pebbles so I knew she would be happy to do almost anything else.

"The cart isn't going to sneak past us," Jenna said. "Let's do it."

We slipped away from the village square and we were soon marching up the track leading to the town of Brackford, from where the cart was coming.

***

When we reached the edge of the woods, we stopped. We sat down and waited, getting bored again, but in a different spot.

"We could climb a tree," I said.

"Any one you had in mind?" Arky asked, looking at the woods.

"The tallest one," I said. "Then we can see the grain collector approaching."

"You'd just see the tops of the other trees," Jenna said.

I was the oldest kid there and it was my duty to take the lead. "I'll climb the tree and you all wait below," I said.

We found a tree with a wide trunk, next to the road. Arky and Gumber boosted me up; I got hold of the lowest branch and swung myself up.

Tree climbing is easy as long as you don't look down. I swarmed up the tree. I only noticed how thin the branches were getting when one snapped beneath my feet. As I clung on, the tree moved in the breeze. I regained my foothold. The drizzle had made the branches slippery.

I looked around. I saw lots of green, with flashes of orange where the leaves were beginning to change color. I had a grand view of the other trees but little else. I looked down but I could not see the ground, just more leaves and branches.

"Are you okay, Keth?" A distant shout from down below reached me.

"Fine," I shouted back.

A clamor of voices bubbled up from below.

"Did you hear that?" Arky said.

"Hear what?" Gumber said.

"Shut up and listen," Arky said.

"Shut up yourself," Gumber said.

"Shut up both of you," Jenna said.

Their voices fell silent. I listened as well. I thought I heard a jangle of harness carried on the breeze.

Once more the voices rose up from below.

"They're here," Arky said.

"We've got to tell the village," Jenna said.

I heard rapidly retreating footsteps as my comrades ran back to the village.

The smart move would have been to stay where I was. I can always spot a smart move by the way it occurs to me long after I've done something dumb. I decided to climb down the tree. This was when I remembered that getting up a tree is the easy part; getting down is when things get tricky.

The technical term for the quickest way to get down from a tree is falling. Initially, I tried to avoid using this technique but halfway down, I slipped from a branch. What saved me was that rather than a single, big, bone-breaking fall, I made a series of smaller falls, dropping from branch to branch, taking a thump from each one, but collecting no more than bruises and grazes.

I landed in a heap at the foot of the tree. I looked up, amazed at being alive and saw two soldiers pointing loaded bows at me.

I was lucky that my fall had numbed me so I was unable to make any sudden movement.

I heard the plod of hooves and the creak of an approaching cart. I stared at the men. They didn't stare back but darted glances around the wood.

"I fell out of a tree," I said, wanting to be helpful. "It's not an ambush."

The word ambush seemed to make them even more

jumpy, and they peered hard into the trees.

A procession came into view. It was headed by the grain collector, a hook-nosed man wearing a black woolen cloak, with a hood that fit tightly over his head. He sat astride a strutting black horse. Next came a high-sided wooden cart hauled by a huge, shaggy, gray horse. Sitting on the cart holding the reins was a gray-haired man dressed in a gray smock. On a rail at the back of the cart perched the ravens, each one eyeing me. Bringing up the rear were two guards, one fat and red-faced, the other thin and pale.

"Ambush," one of the bowmen said.

The grain collector looked at me and scowled. As ambushes went, I was a disappointment.

"Welcome to the village of Mottle," I said and smiled. I tried to stand up and bow but sat back down again, still dizzy from the fall.

"On your feet, Red," the grain collector said.

I guessed he was referring to my red hair. I stood up, this time with more success.

"Mottle is famous for its rain and many different colored mosses," I said, wanting to give him some local color.

"Walk in front, Red," the grain collector ordered. "In silence," he added, before I could continue with my description of the village.

***

I led the procession along the road to Mottle. When we arrived in the village square, Scour rolled his eyes at seeing me at its head. I cast a hard look at Arky, Gumber, and Jenna, who had just remembered they had left their comrade in the lurch. I ignored them and went over to stand by Mum and Meg.

The grain collector dismounted. He was tall with broad shoulders that tapered down to a narrow waist and long spindly legs. He wore black tights, which made his boney knees stand out, and black leather boots with sharp pointed toes. With his black hood fitted tight over his head, he looked just like one of his ravens. He swiveled his head slowly, examining us all.

Scour hobbled over to the barn door and pushed it open. The grain collector stalked over and peered inside.

"I trust this is all the grain and nothing has been hidden?" the grain collector said. He stared hard at each of us in turn, as though he saw right through to the back of our heads.

The ravens launched themselves into the air. We waited in silence, and the only sound was the flapping of their wings as they flew among the village huts. One by one, they returned to perch on the rail at the back of the cart.

"Are all the villagers present?" the grain collector asked.

"All of us, even the village idiot," Scour said, flicking a glance in my direction.

"Remove eight sacks of grain from the barn and prop them up against the wall," the grain collector said.

I leaped with joy. The grain collector was leaving us with most of our grain. We would not go hungry over the winter, and we would even have some grain spare to trade at Brackford Market. Mum put her hand on my shoulder to calm me down.

Scour pointed his stick at Gannett, Stropper, and Taggle. The three lads hurried into the barn, bumping into each other in their haste to bring out the eight sacks so they could be loaded on to the cart, and the grain collector would be on his way before he had a change of heart.

"What will we buy at the market?" Meg whispered.

"Warm winter blankets," Mum murmured.

"Chivel's been talking about a new bull to replace His Lordship," Meg whispered. She sucked on her pipe, making the bowl glow orange.

"I think he's trying to give Scour a hint," Mum murmured.

Meg giggled and coughed. Puffs of smoke leaked from her mouth.

In no time at all eight full sacks of grain leaned against the wall of the barn.

The grain collector smiled. It was a thin-lipped and cruel smile that did not reach his eyes; my heart sank.

"Now remove all the other sacks of grain and load them onto the cart," he said.

We were being left with only eight sacks of grain to live on.

"Have mercy, sir," Scour pleaded, "We won't all survive the winter on so little."

"You should let the weakest among you die so the rest can eat their share," the grain collector said.

For a moment, I thought Scour would raise his stick at the grain collector; his knuckles were white as his hand clenched it. The bowmen notched arrows while the fat guard and the thin guard drew their cudgels.

We outnumbered them, but the moment passed. Scour sighed and ordered the men of the village to form a line from the barn to the cart. The sacks of grain were handed from man to man and tossed up on to the cart.

In a short while, the procession was ready to move off. The shaggy horse twitched its shoulders and the laden cart lurched forwards. We watched as our dreams of full stomachs and warm blankets retreated before our eyes.

The horse had left its own comment on the proceedings; a pile of steaming droppings. I scooped up a handful. The fat guard and the thin guard, walking behind the cart, were still in range. I hesitated. Which guard should I aim at? The fat one, I decided. He was a larger target. I drew back my arm, ready to throw.

My mum yanked my arm hard and the droppings fell from my hand. The fat guard turned to look back at us. Mum had her arm tight around my shoulder.

"Wave," she whispered.

We waved at him and the guard stared at us, shook his head, then turned, and walked away.

"You're an idiot sometimes, Keth," Mum said in a fierce whisper.

"Yeah, well, if everyone else is so smart, why are we all going hungry?" I whispered back.

I wasn't trying to be nasty but I was angry at the way we did nothing when we were being bullied. Someone takes away all the grain you've struggled all year to grow and you scarcely manage a murmur of complaint.

"We're all going to starve to death, sir."

"Well spotted, humble peasant. You're quite right."

"Very good, sir, I was just checking, sir."

Mum tugged at my sleeve, distracting me from my thoughts.

"Watch this," Mum whispered.

She gave a small twitch of her right arm and a leather strap slipped from her sleeve into her hand. She picked a pebble out of her pocket with her left hand and placed it on the leather strap.

"What are you up to?" I whispered. The guards were now out of throwing range.

Mum raised her right arm, whirled the leather strap

three times above her head then flicked her wrist.

The pebble zinged through the air and a moment later the fat guard gave a distant bellow of pain and held his bum. He stared at us, his face crinkled up with suspicion. The strap had disappeared back down Mum's sleeve and she had dropped her arm.

The thin guard said something and the fat guard shrugged. It couldn't have been us; we were out of range; it must have been a wasp. They plodded on after the cart with the fat guard rubbing his bum.

"Where did you learn to do that, Mum?" I said, grinning at her.

"My brothers taught me," she said with a gentle smile.

I remembered three huge laughing red-haired men who had visited us once when I was little and tossed me high into the air and caught me. All three of them had died fighting against Prince Dorian.

**

Just before dusk, everyone met in the village square.

Scour spoke first. "I don't see any point in us going to the market at Brackford," he said. "We have nothing to trade. Every other village will be in the same position. No one will have any joy to share. We're better off saving our energy for the long winter months ahead."

I gaped in disbelief at what I was hearing. Market day at Brackford was the most exciting day of the year. People from all the surrounding villages gathered together and there were games and stalls and a cattle auction and best of all, there was a troupe of strolling players putting on plays that were so exciting you forgot you were hungry. The more miserable things were here in Mottle, the more important it was that we went to Brackford

Market.

I was about to tell Scour to stop talking rot when my mum's elbow dug sharply into my ribs and took my breath away. Only adults were allowed to speak at the meeting, even if they talked nonsense.

"I think you're right, Scour," Chivel said, and his saggy face drooped down even further.

"But I wanted to have an ale at the Flaming Cockerel," Taggle said. He was the youngest adult and had only taken his place between the shafts of the cart two summers ago.

"The ale is so weak now you might as well drink water," Stropper said.

"And we have no coin," Gannett said, clinching the argument.

I was going to speak up and give Taggle a bit of support but Mum gave me a look that was as sharp as her elbows, and I shut up.

"How are your cousins doing, Meg, the ones from Bledger?" Mum asked Meg loudly.

"As well as can be expected. Mind, I've not spoken to them since last market day," Meg replied.

People started thinking about all the folk who lived in the other villages, and who they only ever saw once a year at Brackford Market.

"You can't go to a market with nothing to trade," Scour said.

"We're trading gossip," Meg said.

"Swapping misery more like," Scour said. "Where's the use in that?"

"If no one goes to the market then the market will die," Mum said.

"Maybe it's for the best," Scour said.

Mum looked sad and fell silent. Had Scour defeated

her? Was I going to have to sneak off to the market by myself?

No one spoke as the light began to fade and the midges buzzed about us.

Scour coughed, clearing his throat, ready to call the meeting closed.

"How long has the market being going?" Mum asked.

"My grandfather told me he went there as a child," Scour said, "and he said that his grandfather said that he had been but a baby when he was taken to the first market at Brackford."

I struggled to get my head around such a length of time.

"Long time," Mum said softly.

"Long time," Meg echoed.

"Your grandfather's grandfather was a baby," Taggle said to Scour and shook his head in amazement. "The market has been going on so long it doesn't seem right for us to be the ones to stop it."

Scour poked his stick into the dirt and worried at his upper lip with his two remaining stumps of teeth. I watched as, inside Scour's head, respect for ancient tradition battled with the need to snuff out any spark of joy from village life.

"We have to go," Scour said, and that was settled. Ancient tradition had won.

I grinned up at Mum. She was trying to keep her face respectful and composed but I saw the sly smile twitching at the corners of her lips.

3 BRACKFORD MARKET

Market day at Brackford fell five days after our visit from the grain collector. Mum woke me an hour before dawn. I dressed quickly, putting on my woolen breeches, a cloth shirt that had so many patches it was more patch than shirt and a sheepskin jerkin. Last of all, I put on my prized possession, a pair of battered leather boots that had belonged to Taggle and a dozen village kids before him. He had outgrown them. They were still too big for me, but I padded them with straw and that made them warm as well. Mum and I ate breakfast together. I had just enough porridge in my bowl to remind me how hungry I was.

We joined the other villagers and prepared to set off for Brackford. In previous years, we had dragged the village cart along with us, the young men taking it in turns to pull it. This year we left it behind as we had nothing to put in it and we'd be bringing nothing back.

We left our fields behind and followed the track into the woods. It was a fine morning, with the promise of sunshine later, but we marched in sullen silence. In previous years, we had sung songs but this year people lacked the enthusiasm, even for 'The Turnip Song.' I tried singing it but no one joined in and, worse, no one bothered to tell me to shut up.

At length we emerged from the woods. We were on top of a ridge, looking down on the stubble of the recently-harvested fields around Brackford. We followed the track sloping gently down to the river, which soon joined other tracks and widened. We saw other groups of people making their way to market, which cheered us up. We didn't feel so isolated.

We crossed the ford, the water coming to just below my knees. Green stuff floated on the surface, smelling of vegetable stew. It must have been poisonous or someone would have eaten it.

After the ford, we climbed up High Street. Brackford was a proper town with streets, more than one of them, and a cobbled market square at the center. The houses were crammed together side by side, with occasional gaps for alleys that led to other streets.

The stalls began on High Street before you reached Market Square. I started to doubt whether coming to market would cheer us up. In previous years, the stalls had been packed tightly together but this year gaps showed like missing teeth, and instead of the stalls being piled high with goods to tempt you, most stalls looked bare. An old, white-haired cobbler had no swanky new shoes for sale, and his display boasted just three pairs of scuffed old boots that he had repaired. The spice lady had set up her stall with the big wooden bowls of herbs and powders but this year, they had all been picked from the surrounding fields, and the exotic smells I loved were faint ghosts from previous years still clinging to the bowls.

Mum put her hand on my arm. "Keth, I know you're about to disappear off and do your own thing, but I want you to promise me to behave," she said.

I nodded my head and continued scanning the stalls.

Her grip tightened on my arm, and I gave her a bit more attention. "I'm serious, Keth," she said. "This is an unhappy time. If you go looking for trouble, you'll get more of it than you bargained for."

We made our way through the market. Something was missing, and it wasn't just the goods on the stalls; it was noise. It was stall owners shouting out their bargains. It was shoppers haggling and looking to get the cheapest price. Merchants had nothing to sell, and shoppers had nothing to buy it with.

Mum gave a shout of delight. It was so out of place among the misery that people stopped to look at her. She had spotted her friend Elsis, who had grown up in our village but then married a man from Bledger and now lived there. Mum and Elsis would have their annual chat, when they would cling to each other and talk and talk, and then one of them would say they must be getting on and they would talk about how they needed to get on, and then they would go on talking. I was glad Mum would be happy for a bit and wouldn't be worrying about me. I slipped away.

***

Arky, Gumber, and Jenna had also slipped away from their parents, and together we entered the market square.

Brackford liked stone. The more stone you had, the more important you were. The market square was cobbled with smooth gray stones fitted together, like a wall that had been laid flat in the ground. All the houses surrounding the market square were made of the same stone with gray slate roofs and stone chimneys to let out the smoke from their fires.

We decided we would do a circuit of the market square. We passed one of the town's inns, the Flaming Cockerel. The inn was quiet instead of being noisy. Peeping inside, we saw men drinking but they were silent with none of the loud laughter and back slapping of previous years.

We stopped by the town hall, the largest building in the town. You didn't just get an entrance door; you got steps and columns holding up a bit of roof above the door. All the windows had been boarded over and two guards stood in front of the door, a fat guard and a thin guard. I recognized them. They had been two of the party that had helped themselves to our grain.

"Nice door," I said to the guards. "Make sure no one steals it."

They scowled at me in unison. Arky dragged at my arm, wanting us to move on.

I made eye contact with the thin guard. His nose and lips twitched liked a rat sniffing the air.

"Doesn't it worry you, working with Fatty here?" I said. "Someday he's going to get hungry and eat you."

The fat guard's eyes narrowed. He took a step towards me but his thin mate put a hand on his arm. They'd get in trouble if they left their post. We could tease them all day if we liked.

I looked around to share this fun with the others. They had scarpered. I was alone.

"Wait until we get off duty," the fat guard said, punching his fist into the palm of his other hand, making a meaty, slapping sound.

"Have to catch me first," I said.

"We know where you live," the thin guard said. His voice was squeaky, the squeak of a rat; it matched his face.

I sauntered away, not feeling as calm as I tried to appear.

***

I spotted my friends watching a game of 'Toss the Horseshoe.' A playing area had been roped off and covered in straw to protect the cobbles. A lanky man, with a face like a worn leather boot, squatted at one end of the playing area, holding a horse shoe in one hand and sizing up the wooden stake at the opposite end.

I sneaked up behind Arky and clapped him on the shoulder. "You're under arrest," I boomed in a deep voice.

Arky yelped and jumped so high he could have seen over the roof of the town hall.

The lanky man jerked his throwing arm and the horse shoe flew wide off the stake. He glared at us.

"Just me," I said in my normal voice.

Arky swung round and threw a punch at me. I ducked. The pock marks on his face were pale white while the skin around them had turned bright red.

"Go away, you idiot," Arky said. "Just go away."

I stayed where I was. Arky turned and walked away. I grinned at Gumber and Jenna. Gumber's twisted lips puckered into a scowl. He and Jenna turned and followed Arky. I stopped grinning.

I walked after them. Jenna turned back to me. Her hair was drawn back even tighter than usual and her high forehead looked like a wall. "Just go somewhere else, Keth," she said.

Her voice was so sad and weary; I was starting to get alarmed. "What have I done?" I said.

"You're always being an idiot, and we all end up getting into trouble," she said, folding her arms across her chest, a bad sign, "My mum reckons I should avoid you."

I swallowed. Had I gone a bit too far, teasing the guards?

"You're almost a grownup anyway," Jenna said.

Ouch! I didn't want her to see how much that had hit home. "Enjoy the rest of your day, kid," I said. I gave her a grin then turned back to watch the horseshoe tossing. The lanky man with the worn boot face was scowling at me. I decided not to hang around.

***

I mooched over to the food stalls. The cauldrons of stew bubbled away but the stew was thin and watery and smelled rank, as though it had been scooped straight from the river.

A hand bell clanged. This was the sign that the cattle auction was due to start. In previous years, I had enjoyed watching folk, the worse for drink, staggering out of the inn and reeling into each other as they made their way to the auction ring. This year only a few men bothered to leave the inn when the bell rang, and they were sober and serious as they made their way to the ring. No one was drunk; perhaps the ale was as weak as the stew.

Only a few people were watching the auction and I was able to find a space right by the rail. The cattle were led on, one by one, and paraded around the ring. The bones jutted out beneath their skin. No one was bidding.

The man standing next to me was a townsman, judging by his suit of fine cloth. Looking closer, I saw it had been patched and the cuffs were frayed.

"Are you going to be bidding?" I asked.

"Why buy a cow when you can't afford to feed it over the winter, so it will have starved to death by the spring?" the townsman said.

He fell silent but I sensed he had some words building up inside of him. I waited.

"You know what really makes me furious is that all our grain is sitting right under our noses in our own town hall," he said. "If we had that grain, we could feed our hens and cattle, and we'd have milk and fresh eggs."

It now made sense why the windows of the town hall had been boarded up and guards put out the front.

"We should break down the door and take it back," I said.

The townsman edged away from me along the rail. Why was everyone so terrified of standing up to Prince Dorian? Well, he could have you tortured and executed, but wasn't this slow starvation a form of torture and execution?

Someone needed to strike a blow against Dorian. If I stole some of the grain from the town hall, it would make a point; it might inspire others to do something.

I had promised my mum to stay out of trouble but as long as I didn't get caught, I could keep my promise. Mum had also made it plain that stealing was wrong, but in this case, it was less stealing and more taking back what was ours.

I would check out the town hall. If I could not find a way in then that was fine. I didn't have to do anything wrong. There was no harm in just looking.

Dorian had taken our dances; he had taken our food; worst of all, he was taking our spirit. Well, I had a bit of spirit left, and I was going to show him.

***

An alley ran down one side of the town hall. I thought about sneaking into it without being seen by the guards on the door. The thing about sneaking is that it tends to draw attention to you. Everyone wonders why you are scuttling about and what it is you're doing that you don't want them to see.

I walked into the alley, as bold as you like, without looking at the guards. I stopped as soon as I was in the alley and listened for any cries of alarm or sounds of pursuit. All I heard was the anxious calling of the auctioneer from the cattle ring.

I explored further. The auctioneer's voice grew faint then disappeared. The cobbles had stopped and my feet stirred up plain old ordinary dust. The plain stone sides of the hall were a contrast to its grand front. The windows had all been boarded up with planks of wood. I breathed a little sigh of relief that I would not be able to break in.

At the back of the hall was an empty laneway. I noticed a plank of wood lying in the dirt. It had come from a gable window high up at the back of the hall. If I climbed up there and wrenched out the other planks then I might be able to squeeze in.

Stone walls are harder than trees to climb and I fell off a couple of times before I got the knack of it. With a branch you grasp it with your whole hand and you can fit your whole foot on it. An uneven wall has holds, but they will only take your finger tips or the edge of your foot.

Once I had a hand on the windowsill, I felt more secure. I was still just looking. I glanced up and down the lane. It was empty.

I tried the remaining planks. They were loose. I braced myself and gave them a hard yank. They splintered and gave way. My foothold slipped and I dangled from the window. I scrabbled with my feet, regained my hold, and peered in through the window. It was dark. The opening was small and my sticking my head in blocked out most of the light. It would be a tight squeeze but I reckoned I could worm my way in.

I hesitated. This was more than looking; this was breaking in. The sensible thing was to retreat, but that would mean Dorian had won, without him even having to raise a finger.

I grasped the sill and began to haul myself through the opening. I got my head and shoulders through with a strategic wriggle and I thought my body would follow easily. One of the few advantages of having so little to eat was that I was skinny enough to squeeze through narrow gaps.

Everything was going well until my hips caught. I was dangling half in and half out of the window. I struggled and flapped my arms and legs, but my hips were wedged solid. I wanted to cry out for help but I smothered the impulse. The sort of help I would get from the guards out the front did not bear thinking about.

A hand grasped one of my legs. I was captured. I thrashed my legs and the hand let go.

"Hold still, you idiot," a voice whispered, "or you'll knock me off the wall."

I stopped moving. The voice of guards making a capture is loud and triumphant. They bellow things like "Gotcha." This was the quiet voice of someone who did not want to be caught. I sympathized.

A hand grasped the cloth at the back of my jerkin. "Twist to your right," the voice whispered. "I'll help."

I did as I was told. I felt a grinding pain in my hips and I thought my body would snap then I rolled like a stick in a hole and slipped through the window, landing with a thump on the floor.

I listened. I did not hear cries of the alarm being raised. I stood up and looked out of the window.

My helper was a girl, about my age, clinging to the wall. She had a sharp face and silver hair under a black cap. She let go of the wall and dropped back down into the laneway, landing so lightly she did not raise any dust.

"Hurry up and grab a sack of grain," she said.

I liked her no-nonsense approach; food first, names and introductions later.

I had landed in an attic. Some furniture, a broken bench, and three chairs were stored here, but no bags of grain.

In the floor, I saw a trapdoor with a brass ring. I hauled it open to reveal a wooden ladder leading down. I climbed down it into the darkness. Chinks of light showed through the boarded up windows, but they just emphasized how black it was, inside.

When I reached the foot of the ladder, I stepped away from it and swept around with my arms. I touched nothing. I took another step, and this time when I reached out, my fingertips touched some rough material. I stepped in that direction and explored with my hands. Sacks had been stacked one on top of the other. They gave a little when I squeezed them. I had found the grain. I braced my knees and prepared to lift the top sack.

I heard a dull growl and the clink of a chain. Without thinking, I raised my arms in front of me, only just in time, as something heavy crashed into me, knocking me to the floor. A dog's heavy, panting body lay on top of me, pinning me down, and I smelled its sour meaty breath on my face. Its teeth thrust towards my neck. I got my hand beneath its jaw and fought to push it back.

I twisted sharply, and its weight slid off me. I struggled to my knees and lunged for the ladder; grabbing the rungs, I hauled myself up it. The dog's teeth sank into the seat of my breeches. For a moment, I clung to the ladder and the dog clung by its jaws to my clothing. The breeches ripped and the dog fell back. I shot through the opening on to the floor of the attic. Below me, the dog set up a ferocious barking.

I sprinted across the attic and dived out of the window. I got stuck half way through. I had forgotten to twist my hips. The girl, waiting in the lane below, rolled her eyes. I was relieved that she had not disappeared at the first sign of trouble. She took a run, jumped up, and grabbed my outstretched arms. I twisted at the same time, and her weight dragged me out of the window. We landed in a heap in the dirt of the laneway.

We heard people running down the alley by the side of the town hall. We scrambled to our feet and sprinted away. The girl was barefoot and wore a long black skirt. She seemed to glide over the dirt. I followed, arms pumping, struggling to keep up with her.

We dodged left down an alley way. I skidded in the dirt and almost fell. A hand brushed the back of my jerkin. The pursuit was about to catch us. I heard a man panting close behind me.

I dropped down, straight in front of him, curling myself up into a ball. He'd not expected this and he tripped over me. I recognized the thin guard as he flew over my head and landed with a thud. The fat guard was just behind him. He tried to stop and skidded in the dirt. He too tripped and flew over me, landing on top of the thin guard.

The girl had disappeared. I got to my feet and sprinted off, back in the direction I had come from.

***

I ran down the alley beside the town hall and emerged into the market square. I glanced at the entrance to the town hall. It was unguarded. Now would have been the ideal time for a robbery.

I slowed my pace to a brisk walk, forcing myself not to run. I weaved in and out of people. Many of them were giving me strange looks as I passed and I heard one or two of them snigger. I wondered if it was because I was covered in dirt; folk made an effort to be clean on market day.

If I failed to blend in with the crowd, the guards would soon capture me. I needed to find a place to hide. I was passing the Flaming Cockerel and I decided to slip in and see if I could find a place to hide in the yard out the back.

The inn was crowded with sour-faced men and smelled of sweat, tobacco smoke, and stale beer. I wormed my way in, slipping past men who looked down at me and scowled.

"Looking for my uncle," I muttered as I pushed past.

A ripple of laughter followed me that was out of place in the atmosphere of dank misery. I wondered why. I emerged into a parlor with a blazing wood fire and I turned round to get my bearings. A draft of warm air tickled my bum. A sick suspicion dawned on me about why I was being trailed by laughter. I reached behind me and felt where the dog had torn out the seat of my breeches. People were laughing because I was showing my bum to the world.

I ducked out of the parlor and entered a long passage that led to the rear of the inn.

"Will you stop that shoving," a man shouted from

near the front entrance of the inn.

"We're chasing a thief," a stern but breathless voice answered.

I bolted along the passage and out through a door, emerging into the inn yard. A horse stood between the shafts of a cart upon which was a large wicker hamper.

The gate to the inn yard was shut. I ran over and tugged it open a little way. I then ran back, climbed on to the cart and opened the lid of the hamper. It was filled with clothes. I jumped inside and shut the lid.

I was just in time. Through gaps in the wicker, I saw the two guards emerging into the inn yard. The thin guard spotted the gate open just wide enough for a lad to slip through. He sped over to it.

His fat comrade had had enough. He stopped, bent over, hands on his knees, gasping for breath.

"I'm all in, Scrape," he said to the thin guard.

"No sign of him, Podger," the thin guard, Scrape, replied.

"Unless he is hiding," Podger, the fat guard, said.

Podger looked around the inn yard and smiled. "Not too many places to hide here," he said and strolled over to the cart. "I reckon we should have a look in this hamper."

"I think you're right," Scrape said, coming over to join him.

I had an idea; well, less of an idea and more a last desperate gamble. "I am a magic hamper," I boomed in a deep voice.

"A magic hamper." Podger smiled and winked at Scrape.

"Let's just give him a good kicking and be done with it," Scrape said.

"And what do you do, magic hamper?" Podger asked.

"I foretell the future," I boomed.

"And what is our future, magic hamper?" Scrape said, making an effort to get into the spirit of the game.

"Really, really, bad," I boomed.

"But not nearly as bad as yours, magic hamper," Podger said, smacking his fist into his palm.

"Don't bet on it," I boomed. "I'm not the one who deserted his post, guarding the grain."

Podger and Scrape looked at each other in panic. They had been so caught up in the chase that they had forgotten they were meant to be guarding the grain.

"As if by magic, all Prince Dorian's grain has disappeared," I boomed.

Podger and Scrape fled back into the inn. I heard the bumps and curses as they pushed their way through, racing to get back to the town hall.

I wanted to get out of the hamper, but no sooner had Podger and Scrape disappeared than a huge, bald man emerged from the inn into the yard. He wore a sleeveless black leather jerkin, and his arms bulged with muscle as though they had been stuffed with giant turnips. He had a black beard, not on his cheeks but growing straight down from his chin; the hairs reached down to his chest. He strolled over to the cart.

"Good lad, Thespian," I heard him say and the horse neighed.

The next thing I heard was a scrape as the inn yard gate was opened. The cart lurched forwards. We were going somewhere. I planned to stay hidden and slip out of town.

4 THE TROUPE

Hidden in the hamper of clothes on the back of the cart, I wondered where I was going to end up, and when it would be safe for me to make my escape.

The cart left the inn yard and made a couple of sharp turns. The wheels clattered, and I was bounced by a series of small repetitive jolts. We were surrounded by a lot of voices, and I guessed we were making our way across the cobbles of the market square.

We stopped, and I opened the lid a fraction. We were in the center of the market square. I strained my eyes towards the town hall. Podger and Scrape stood in the entrance, talking to a hooded figure dressed in black; it was the grain collector. They were looking in my direction. I decided I was staying where I was.

"Alright my boys, set up our stage, and let's give everyone a rollicking show," a voice announced. It wasn't loud but it reached everywhere. It was an actor's voice.

The cart rattled as the huge, bald man in leathers jumped on the back of it. He shot back the metal bolts on the sides of the cart and they folded down to create a stage. I fought down my panic. I was hiding in the costume hamper of a troupe of strolling players, on stage, just as a performance was about to start. I lowered the lid and peered through the gaps in the wicker.

The troupe clattered on stage. Someone strummed a lyre, and they all sang about how entertaining the show was that they were about to perform. I imagined a large crowd, including my mum, forming around the stage while they sang.

After the song finished the actors went to the back of the stage, except for a ginger- haired woman with an enormous bosom, who was wearing a red polka dot dress, and a young boy about my age, dressed in rags.

The woman lamented that they were poor, very, very, poor, and her bosom heaved dramatically. Her young son was going to have to leave her and make his own way in the world. The only thing she had to give him was a magic cloak.

The woman made her way to the hamper. I was going to be discovered. The last thing I saw through the side of the hamper was an enormous polka dot bosom bearing down on me.

The lid was thrown open. I sprang up, holding a handful of clothing and began to sort through it.

"Waistcoat, no, bloomers, no, ah what about this, a lovely red cloak, red is your color, isn't it, Madam." I talked like a market trader. "Seeing as how it's yours, I'll sell it to you at half price."

This got a laugh from the audience. They knew about market traders.

The woman in the polka dot dress was a man; beneath layers of makeup, he was examining me with shrewd eyes and his mouth had twitched up into a half smile.

"You're probably wondering what I'm doing in your

basket," I said.

"It crossed my mind, dear," he said in his woman's voice.

"I was looking for some new breeches," I said and turned my bum towards the audience.

The audience screamed with laughter. The man dressed as a lady clapped his fingers to his eyes, opened them a gap and closed them shut with a groan of mock horror.

"And I was looking forwards to dumplings this evening," he said. "I can't face them now."

In a single movement, he bent down, plucked a smock from the basket, and plopped it down over my head. It reached down to my ankles. I struggled to find the arm holes. The audience laughed.

"This is my long lost son," the man said. "I haven't seen him since breakfast." He hugged me to his bosom. I pretended I was suffocating, which was close to the truth.

"I'm your Ma, dear, everyone calls me Ma," he said. "What do they call me?" he asked the audience.

"Ma," they shouted back. I bet it was the first time that day people had forgotten they were hungry.

He helped me out of the basket and led me over to the boy who, close up, was actually a girl, and not just any girl but the girl who had helped me break into the town hall.

"This is your brother," Ma said to me. "I forget his name, but I call him Stupid. Don't smirk, dear. I call you Idiot."

Ma faced the audience, with one arm around me and the other around the girl.

"The family reunited," Ma said.

"Stop right there," a voice bellowed from the crowd. It was Podger, who was shoving his way through the crowd, with Scrape following behind him, jabbing his boney elbows into anyone Podger had missed. "That boy is under arrest," Podger said.

"He tried to steal the grain," Scrape added.

Bad mistake that, the crowd hissed. They didn't like the two guards.

"Which one is your boyfriend, Ma?" I asked.

"They both are." Ma threw his hands open wide, knocking me and the girl flat on our backs. I think the girl was expecting it as she didn't grunt like me when we hit the stage. The audience laughed.

"Are my two handsome lover boys going to join their favorite little blossom on stage," Ma said in a gushing, girly voice.

I sat up. Podger was now as bright red as when he had been running. Scrape was even redder. They stood frozen in horror as around them the audience laughed.

Ma winked and beckoned them. They retreated, shoving their way back out of the crowd.

"Later then, my precious petals," Ma called after them.

***

Without any discussion, the players worked me into their play "The Troll Kings Lair."

The girl and I did this thing where Ma told the audience what loving brothers we were and behind his back we were silently squabbling and thumping each other; then, as soon as he turned round to look at us, we turned all sweet and innocent.

Ma gave us the magic cloak and we found out that what was magic about it was we could fly on it. It didn't really fly. We sat on the cloak on stage and the girl described the woods, lakes and mountains we were flying over. I said "What's a lake?" and that got a huge laugh.

Anyway, we flew so far we got lost, and we could not get home. The girl said we were feeling unhappy so I sang 'The Turnip Song' to cheer us up, and the audience joined in.

After that we met this handsome prince who was pretending not to be a prince, only he had wavy, blonde, shoulder-length hair and was so handsome and noble you knew he was going to be a prince.

Anyway, the prince had to save a princess who had been kidnapped by the troll king, who lived in the highest, coldest mountains and no one knew the secret road that led to his lair.

Well, of course, we didn't need a road, and we flew the prince up there on our magic cloak. We all sat on the cloak, swaying from side to side and saying how we had just missed hitting bits of mountain and cliff faces.

We didn't know where the princess was in the lair until she came out and sang a song. It was the woman who had played the lyre. She walked and talked like a young woman but close up you could see wrinkles around her eyes and her jet-black hair had flecks of gray at the roots.

The prince got separated from me and the girl as we searched for the troll king, played by the huge bald man with a beard who drove the cart, only now he wore a mask like a wild pig that had run into a stone wall.

He captured me and the girl and dangled us by our ankles, one of us in each hand. My smock fell over my head and this got a huge laugh because everyone could see my bum again. We were thrown in the dungeons.

The handsome prince had a big battle with the troll king all over the stage, and it looked like the prince would lose but at the last moment, the troll king got over confident and the prince killed him in the end.

The prince rescued me, the girl and the princess, and

we all flew back to Ma on the magic cloak. The prince married the princess and Ma was made a lady of the royal court, and we all lived happily ever after.

***

At the end of all this, we lined up on stage and once again sang 'The Turnip Song,' with the audience joining in. After the final chorus, we bowed and the audience applauded wildly. I looked among them but I did not see my mum.

The applause was so enthusiastic that Ma gestured that we should sing the song again. I slipped to the back of the cart as they began to sing. I would have loved to bask in the warm glow of audience appreciation but it was time for me to flee. I lowered myself down from the cart and prepared to run.

"And where do you think you're going?" I heard my mum yell out. She was striding towards me with all the fury of an approaching storm. She stopped in front of me, hands on her hips.

"I've got to go, Mum," I said.

I moved to step around her, but she blocked me. "You promised to stay out of trouble then you get into more trouble than even I could imagine you getting into," she shouted.

I looked over her shoulder. The fat guard and thin guard, Podger and Scrape, were approaching.

"We've got you now, lad," Podger said.

"You're under arrest," Scrape added.

They shoved past Mum and grabbed at me. This was too much for Mum. "Get your hands off my boy," she shrieked.

Mum went on the attack. She yanked Podger's helmet

down over his eyes and barged into Scrape, sending him stumbling backwards. "Run!" she commanded me.

I could have scarpered but it would have meant leaving Mum in the middle of a fight. She was now grappling with Scrape. Podger prized his helmet from over his eyes. I dived forwards and head-butted him in the stomach. He doubled over, gasping for breath.

"Stop that!" a voice commanded. Podger and I paused in mid-punch. I saw Scrape stop and drop his arms. Mum took her chance to biff him on the jaw, sending him sprawling before she too stopped.

Ma stood at the back of the stage, looking down at us. "Stand up!" Ma said.

We got to our feet. It was a struggle for Podger. He was still winded.

Ma climbed down to join us, taking care not to catch his dress on the side of the cart. He stood beside me, and Mum took up position on my other side.

"We're arresting this boy for attempted robbery, at the town hall, this afternoon," Podger gasped out between breaths.

"I blame his mother, and we're arresting her too," Scrape said, rubbing his jaw.

"Not this lad." Ma folded his arms across his bosom. "I worked him hard all afternoon. He was never out of my sight."

I was shocked. Ma had only just met me but he was telling huge and dangerous lies on my behalf.

"We know him," Podger said. "We saw him in one of the villages around here a couple of days ago."

"He's from this area," Ma said. "I gave him leave to visit his village for a few days. Boys get homesick."

"And how come, when we arrived, this woman was angry with him for getting into trouble," Scrape said, pointing to Mum.

"I was embarrassed," Mum said. "He'd been boasting to the whole village about what a great actor he was and I thought he would be the lead, but he's just being daft and showing everyone his bum. I'll never live it down."

I was shocked. I had never realized Mum was a champion liar. It made me wonder if she had slipped any other untruths past me over the years.

Podger tucked his fingers under his armpits and coughed to get our attention.

"Showing his bum, you said, Madam," he said. "I think that proves the case against him. The person who attempted to steal the grain had the seat of his breeches ripped out by a guard dog." He nodded at Scrape, who nodded back, and they looked smug.

"Coincidence," Ma said. "We always do the bum gag every time we perform, starts the show with a big laugh."

"You said he was never out of your sight," Podger said. "Where were you when he was the ring leader of a group of vicious young thugs giving us cheek while we were on guard duty in front of the town hall?"

"Watching him from a distance," Ma said. "He tried to skive off with his old village chums. Shortly after that, I gave him a clip around the ear, and he went back to work. Trust me, he didn't try to slip away again."

"We're still going to arrest him," Scrape said. "We're in charge, not you."

"As you wish," Ma said. "I will take the matter up with Master Twist when we return to the city."

At the mention of Master Twist, it was as though a cart load of fear had just been delivered to the faces of Podger and Scrape.

"As Prince Dorian's Master of Revels, Master Twist licenses all troupes of strolling players," Ma continued. "I would be obliged to inform him of your disruption and point out your incompetence."

"It's your word against ours," Scrape whined and his rat-like face twitched with alarm.

"And of course, he would need to torture you to make sure you were telling the truth," Ma said.

Podger and Scrape paused to think about this and winced.

"Thumbscrews are Master Twist's favorite device," Ma said.

Scrape hid his hands beneath his armpits.

"But these gentlemen answer to me and not Prince Dorian's fool." We were interrupted by the arrival of the grain collector. He stalked over to us. A raven sat on his shoulder and gave me a hard stare.

"This is the villain who broke into the town hall and attempted to steal the grain," Podger said, putting his hand on my arm.

Mum knocked his hand away.

"And this vicious mad woman assaulted us when we tried to perform our duty," Scrape said, pointing at my mum but keeping his distance from her.

"The boy is a member of my troupe," Ma said. "He's been in my sight all day."

"Are you wintering in Russett this year?" the grain collector said to Ma.

"That's where we're headed," Ma said.

"Excellent. I expect I will catch your performance at one of the inns there," the grain collector said.

"You're a patron of the performing arts?" Ma said.

"I'm something of a connoisseur," the grain collector said, with a small smug smile on his lips.

I had no idea what a connoisseur was but it seemed to mean that he was on our side. Podger and Scrape thought the same way and were looking at their master with despair and confusion.

"Your uniforms are filthy," the grain collector said.

"That's on account of chasing this villain, sir," Podger said.

"And being assaulted by mad women, sir," Scrape added.

"I'm not interested in your excuses," the grain collector said. "Clean yourselves up."

Podger and Scrape retreated with their shoulders slumped.

"I enjoyed your performance, boy," the grain collector said, looking at me. He cocked his head to his left side and so did his raven. "It was raw and spontaneous, just like at Mottle. People with special gifts should look after each other."

The grain collector turned and stalked away across the market square. It was mid-afternoon, and a group of people, perhaps an entire village setting off home, crossed his path. He hopped through them, forcing them to scatter. He was so like one of his ravens I wanted to run after him and offer him a worm.

"Thank you, sir," Mum said to Ma.

"A pleasure, dear lady." Ma bowed.

"I'm Ailsa and this is Keth," Mum said, butting in before I had a chance to make the introductions.

"I'm Ma," Ma said. "May I talk with you about Keth?"

He took Mum's arm natural as you please and led her away. I was going to follow, given they were talking about me but I was distracted by the arrival of my friends.

***

"Keth, you were amazing," Arky said.

He, Gumber and Jenna swarmed around me, clapping me on the shoulder and patting me on the back

"You were brilliant," Jenna said

"I know," I said.

"I laughed so hard, I wet myself," Gumber said.

Given that Gumber never lied, I was not sure I wanted to know this.

I would be the talk of the village for the next few days, no, for longer than that; I would be immortal. The story about the market day when Keth took the stage by storm would become a legend.

"Do that bit again, when you fell off the flying carpet," Arky said.

"And the bit where Ma chased you with a frying pan," Gumber said.

I acted out the funniest bits for them. We were all doubled up with laughter when Mum and Ma returned.

"I need a quiet word with Keth," Mum said, smiling at us.

"You were great, Keth," Arky said, and clapped me on the shoulder.

"Keth's the best," Jenna said to my mum.

My three friends waved to me and ran off. Mum looked serious. Maybe, I was going to be arrested after all.

"Ma has made us an offer, love," she said. "He wants to take you on as an apprentice, teach you the craft of being a fool on stage."

I was stunned. My mind turned a triple somersault and landed in a heap. "But they travel," I said.

"You'd travel with them," she said.

"But you need me," I said. "Who's going to help you look after the hut? We have to repair the thatch on our roof before this coming winter."

"I'll miss you but I will manage," she said. "Ma

reckons you belong on stage, and I think he's right. There's nothing for you in the village."

"I've never fitted in," I grumbled.

"Ma will feed you and teach you to read," she said.

"Don't need to read if you can plough," I said.

"Don't need to plough if you can read," she replied.

"Can't it wait for a year?" I said, trying to put off this sudden change.

"They may not come back this way," she said. "This Master Twist person decides the routes that the troupes take." Tears began to leak from Mum's eyes.

"Don't cry, Mum," I said.

"Why not? You are!" she said.

I touched my cheeks and they were damp.

"Give us your breeches, dear, and I'll patch them up," she said.

Mum always had a needle and thread on her. She sat, resting her back against a cartwheel, with my breeches in her lap, sewing briskly. I sank down beside her. I was still wearing the smock Ma had given me from the hamper. I wished Mum would take forever, so I could sit watching her and my world would stay unchanged.

"Finished," she said and handed me back my breeches.

"Can I keep the needle, Mum?" I asked. She handed it to me. It was shaped from bone and as long as my middle finger. I carefully pinned it inside my jerkin so I would not lose it.

Mum looked at the position of the sun in the sky. No one felt safe travelling in the woods after dark, and folk gave themselves plenty of time to get home. "Our village will be heading back soon, Keth," Mum said. "If we make a big fuss over this, someone like Scour will spoil it for you."

"But he hates me," I said. "He'd pay Ma to take me

away."

"He thinks you belong to the village," Mum said. "I'll tell everyone you're spending a few days with my friend Elsis in Bledger to learn carpentry from her husband. Scour will complain but he'll accept it because it's a practical skill."

We stood up. Mum hugged me and we whispered goodbye to each other. "I have to go now," Mum said, stifling a sob. "I won't look back but remember I'll always love you."

My vision blurred as I watched her set off across the market square, disappearing among the crowd. She kept her word and didn't look back.

***

I sat thinking about how I had planned to spend the winter boasting to Arky, Gumber, and Jenna about my exploits on stage. It wasn't going to happen. Arky would become the kids' leader. He would be sensible and responsible. For a little while, there would be an idiot-shaped gap where I used to be but I would soon be forgotten.

"Nice work on stage." The girl with silver hair jumped down from the back of the cart and landed lightly beside me.

"Thanks," I said. "I'm Keth."

"I'm Silva," she said. "Did you like it on stage?"

"All that applause and laughter, it was horrible." I grinned in spite of my tears. "I need to do it again to test if it was as bad as I thought it was."

We talked about the performance. I lost track of time as I relived my favorite moments. Silva watched me with her blue-gray eyes and listened to me without interrupting; I was not used to that. She had high cheek bones and a narrow chin, and a nose that was not large but sharp and definite.

The sun was low and sparkling on the cobbles when we finished discussing variations of the 'Turnip Song.'

"Can you give me a hand with the costumes?" Silva said.

We climbed back on to the cart and started folding the costumes and packing them into the hamper. I had never had a cloak to fold, so I watched how Silva did it. I winced when I saw my dirty hand prints on the cloak. I glanced at the costumes in the hamper, and they showed dirty marks where I had touched them.

"Sorry about the dirt," I said.

"It'll brush off or wash out," she said. "You picked it up in a good cause."

I slipped off the smock, folded it and put it in the hamper then scanned the market square. The crowds had thinned out. Most of the villagers had left for home. I saw no one from Mottle.

"You don't like Prince Dorian, do you?" Silva said.

No one had ever asked me that question before, not even my mum. Was the answer too obvious or maybe too dangerous?

How much was I prepared to trust Silva? We had shared in the attempted robbery at the town hall, and she had rescued me twice when I got stuck in the window. I wanted to trust her because I needed a guide to this strange new world I had stumbled into.

"Dorian killed my father," I said.

"He killed my brother," she said.

I lowered my voice. "Almost everyone at the market today had a reason to hate Prince Dorian but only us two tried to do anything about it."

"When we get to our winter quarters in the city, I can introduce you to a few more people who think like we do," she whispered. "We're going to overthrow Prince Dorian."

A warm glow lit up inside of me. It hurt like mad that I was leaving Mum and the village but the pain would be worth it if I avenged the death of my father.

5 THE NEW APPRENTICE

My first night as a member of the troupe was spent in
Brackford. We stayed at the house of a merchant who
was friendly with Ma. They gave us supper in the kitchen
and it was a thick stew containing chunks of carrot,
turnip, and potato served with hunks of fresh bread.

After supper, a servant showed us to a barn at the
back of the main house where we would be sleeping. It
was ten times bigger than the hut Mum and me shared
and full of fresh straw.

The troupe had introduced themselves to me during
supper. Ma looked totally different once he had taken off
his padded red polka dot dress, ginger wig, and makeup.
He had iron gray hair, cut short, and his body was thin
and wiry. Silva was Ma's daughter, although she didn't call
him Dad in front of the troupe. She did comic roles like
the idiot son or the prince's servant, always playing a boy
rather than a girl.

Grunter was the name of the huge bald man with the
beard. He specialized in ogres, trolls and giants, and he
took care of Thespian, the troupe's horse. He was

married to Elba, who played the lyre. She did two different roles on stage, being both the wicked witch and the beautiful princess. Her hair reached down to her waist and was jet black, except for the gray flecks at the roots.

Crag Storm, with his good looks and wavy blonde hair, played the prince and all the other heroes. He was in his early twenties and the way he strutted about, I knew he thought he was the best thing ever.

Ma handed me a blanket and we settled down to sleep. My new companions were all soon snoring but I lay awake, unable to sleep. At first I thought it was because I was not used to having a full stomach but after a while, I realized I was frightened. I had entered a strange new world and I had no idea how to fit in.

The barn door was not barred. I slunk across the straw-strewn floor and slipped outside. In the sky the splinter was visible and it gave me enough light to see the back of the house and the stone water trough in the yard. I could escape back to Mottle, where I would tell my mum and my friends about my amazing adventure and it would be a finished story rather than a scary one that I was living through moment by moment.

I reminded myself of my earlier conversation with Silva. This was my chance to help overthrow Prince Dorian and avenge the death of my father. If I ran back to Mottle, I would have let him down.

Having settled this, I crept back inside the barn. I thought I would fall asleep straight away but I remained awake. I'd loved being part of the play that afternoon, but how could I expect to be part of this troupe? They were beautiful, exotic, and talented. They belonged on stage. I was a peasant. I belonged in a muddy field.

In the cold light of dawn, Ma would realize he had made a mistake, and I would be sent back to Mottle. I relaxed. I saw how things would sort themselves out. I was soon asleep.

***

Just before dawn, Ma shook me awake and we all went to the kitchen, where they served us bowls of porridge and fresh bread. We returned to the barn with Grunter and Crag carrying wooden buckets filled with hot water.

Ma lathered his face, and Silva shaved him with a razor whose blade glinted in the dawn light. Elba shaved Grunter's cheeks and trimmed the edges of his beard. She then shaved the top of his head. Crag shaved himself. It was a long process. He had a small fragment of mirror, and he kept stopping to admire himself.

Elba took a small leather case from the back of the cart, opened it, and took out a small green glass flask with a wax stopper. She noticed me watching her.

"I buy this from the alchemist," she said with a smile. "It's the secret of eternal youth. It's called hair dye."

She and Silva disappeared around the back of the barn with a bucket of water. A little while later they came back, and Elba's hair was damp. The flecks of gray had gone from the roots of her hair, but the early morning sun still showed the wrinkles around her eyes.

"Fold the blankets, Keth," Ma said.

I got to work on that, happy to have something to do. Crag was now brushing his blonde hair, making sure that he put a wave in it. I carried the blankets out to Grunter, who was loading the cart.

So far no one had mentioned that I did not belong in the troupe. Perhaps they were embarrassed. How was Ma going to tell me that his enthusiasm from yesterday afternoon had worn off? I decided I had better help him out.

"This isn't going to work, is it?" I said. I had to strain to keep my voice from quivering.

"It only looks like chaos," Grunter said. "It's like this every morning."

"I think Keth means something different," Ma said, stepping forward.

Elba and Silva joined us and looked at me, puzzled. How was I going to explain this to them? Crag chose that moment to step out of the barn. He turned his face in profile to the morning sun, and its rays touched his skin and made it glow.

"I'm a peasant," I said. "I have a peasant face. Your faces are beautiful. People want to look at them."

"Beautiful?" Grunter grinned and mimed pouting into a mirror and brushing an imaginary wave of hair across his bald head.

"You're incredibly strong, Grunter," I said. "That's even better than being beautiful. You're all talented. I'm not."

"You made the audience laugh yesterday," Ma said.

"That's because I was showing my bum," I said.

"Only twice," Ma said. "You earned a lot more than two laughs."

"But I'm nothing special," I said.

"You have the traditional peasant face," Ma said.

"He means you have a face like a battered turnip," Crag said.

"I mean," Ma said, "that if you had been in the audience yesterday instead of on stage, you would not have stood out, except perhaps for your red hair, and that matched my ginger wig. The audience identified with you because you're one of them, and that made what you did ten times funnier."

"Being good on stage needs a little bit of talent and a lot of training," Elba said. "You've got the little bit of talent and we'll give you the training."

If you want to return to your village," Ma said, "I won't stop you, but you're good enough to be part of my troupe."

They looked at me, and I realized they were waiting for me to make a decision. I wished I could have some time to think about it and talk it over with my mum. Everything had happened so suddenly since yesterday afternoon.

"We're heading for our winter quarters in the city of Russett," Ma said. "We're taking a zigzag route to get there so we can perform in as many villages as possible on the way. Once the troupe leaves Brackford, you're committed to us."

I had to make my choice, now. I owed it to my father to help defeat Prince Dorian and besides, if I walked away from this adventure, I might never get the chance to have another one.

"I'm with you," I said.

"Good lad," Ma said, clapping me on the shoulder.

Grunter finished loading up the cart while Silva brought Thespian out of the barn. Thespian waited patiently between the shafts while Grunter fastened the harness on him. Grunter whispered in Thespian's ear and we set off. Thespian pulled the cart at a slow plod. He might have dreamed of gallops and canters but in his professional capacity, he kept a steady, measured step.

We left Brackford. I decided not to look back.

Silva fell into step beside me. "It's good to have you with us," she said.

***

In the middle of the morning, we stopped at a patch of waste ground. I inspected the brambles for berries – all eaten by birds – and saw the brambles were strangling wheat that was now growing wild. Beneath the brambles, I saw the outline of huts and a little way off was a stretch of broken wall where a dead garden had been.

"We played here many years ago," Ma said. "This was once the village of Weck."

No one asked what had happened. They had done something to upset Prince Dorian, and now the village only existed in memory. Ma led us a little way off the trail around the side of a small hill. We were no longer visible to passers-by, not that the trail had been busy.

Ma and the others formed a circle around me. For a moment I felt vulnerable until I saw everyone, except Crag, was smiling.

"We have a tradition that when an apprentice joins the troupe, he or she is welcomed with a dance." Ma said. "Now, Prince Dorian has said all dances are banned, and we no longer include dancing in our performance. But in private, out of sight, we keep up the old traditions, not to offend Prince Dorian or anyone else but for bigger reasons. Nothing lasts forever and that includes the prince. I don't say that to be rebellious. It is just the way nature is. If we preserve these traditions then when times change, they can be handed back to the people."

"I don't dance," Crag said. He stepped back from the circle. "If it's true that nothing lasts forever then that applies to traditions as well."

"Crag never dances," Silva said. "It's not personal."

"Actually it is," Crag said, looking at me. "You're an extra mouth to feed when we're on short rations, and the villages give us little for performing. Ma is the boss and I'll be professional about it but to be honest, you're not welcome." He stalked over to the cart.

"Ignore him," Ma said.

"Everyone else does," Silva added.

Elba had wooden clappers in her hands that made a clacking sound as fast as crickets chirping. The group circled around me, taking short small rapid steps in time to the rhythm. They circled first one way and then the other.

I realized that I had joined in without thinking and I was walking on the spot in time to the clacking. They expanded the circle a little, and a gap formed between Silva and Grunter. Taking small steps, I moved from the center into the gap. We completed three circuits in each direction and then Elba stopped the clacking.

"Welcome to the troupe," Ma said. "You're one of us now." They all shook hands with me, except Crag, who lounged against the cart. It had only been a short dance but it left me with a warm glow. I had been accepted as a member of the troupe.

***

During the rest of the day, we passed through several villages that still existed. At each one, we put on a play chosen by Ma. My role was to shadow Silva and work off her to make the audience laugh.

Every village tried to give us something to eat, a few husks of bread or some cabbage leaf soup. Everybody had suffered the same fate as Mottle, with the grain collector taking most of their grain for Prince Dorian.

It was mid-afternoon and we were part way between the villages of Hinge and Duffet when Ma called a rest stop. He sat on a rock by the roadside, and called me over. I squatted down beside him.

"Do you know where we come from, Keth?" Ma said.

"We had a bull and some cows in our village," I said, "and I've seen calves being born."

Grownups get embarrassed when they try to talk about stuff like this, so I wanted to head him off.

Ma's lips twitched into a smile. "I was thinking on a more mythic level," he said. "How was the world created? Why do people exist?"

I shrugged. I hadn't thought about stuff like this. I don't think anyone in Mottle did. Most of the time we were too busy wondering whether we would eat the next day.

"We don't know the answers," Ma said, "but we have a story."

He rested his hands on his knees and leaned forwards. I paid close attention so I could reproduce the tale if he chose to test me on it later.

"The land was woven from threads pulled from a star," Ma continued. "To stop the fragile cloth of the land being blown through space, they weighed it down with heavy mountains. They put the Lavatongue Mountains on one side and the Scuthering Peaks on the other.

"The weavers sewed water all through the world. Just as they finished, a great wind blew through space. The mountains of the land stood firm, but elsewhere the cloth of the land rippled. Water from one side of the land ran to the other side, leaving nothing but a choking red dust, the Red Desert, on one side, and the Emerald Ocean on the other. Not all the water made it to the ocean; some of it became trapped in a deep hollow in the middle of the land, and this became the Sea of Wrack. The weavers were worried that if the Sea of Wrack overflowed it would drown the land, so they made a great trench that would drain excess water from it into the Emerald Ocean.

"Having finished the land, many of the weavers left to build new lands but two groups chose to remain. One group lived here and they became the first people of the land. The second group lived in a world beyond the splinter, and if ever our land is damaged, they will crawl through the splinter and sew it back together again.

"What do you think of that, Keth?" Ma asked.

"It would be tricky to stage," I said, "and I don't know where you would put the comic bits."

"Stories are more than entertainment, Keth," Ma said. "My old master used to tell me that all stories were sacred because they were threads plucked from the land."

He picked up a stick lying close to where he was sitting and began drawing a picture in the dirt. "These are the Lavatongue Mountains," he said, drawing triangles with little curls coming out of the top of them. "They are volcanoes and they give off hot poisonous smoke."

He drew a circle below the triangles and put little zigzags inside the circle.

"This is the Sea of Wrack. If Twist permits it, we will sail across it next year."

He drew some more triangles, this time below the circle.

"These are the Scuthering Peaks. They are so tall that the tops of them are covered in snow all year round."

To the right of the circle, Ma drew a smaller circle with little lines coming out from its edge. I guessed it was the sun.

"That's the Red Desert," I said, "and on the left is the Emerald Sea."

Ma nodded and drew some zigzags on the left of the circle. He drew two parallel lines from the circle to where the first of these zigzags began.

"The Sea of Wrack drains into the Emerald Ocean

through the straits of Yaul," he said. "The story is telling you about your world."

A thought struck me. If this was a picture of the world then we were on it somewhere.

"Where's Mottle?" I said.

"Here," Ma said, drawing a little dot midway between the Sea of Wrack and the Scuthering Peaks. "And we're heading for Russett." He drew another dot, close to the edge of the circle but still on the Scuthering Peaks side of it.

I looked at the picture. It was more world than I had ever imagined, but instead of feeling free, I felt hemmed in.

"What lies beyond the mountains or across the desert or on the other side of the ocean?" I asked.

"Nobody knows," Ma said.

"You must have heard stories," I said. "Don't people go into the mountains?"

"They do," Ma said, "but they never come back."

I stared at the picture. No one had shown me my world before.

"We'd best get on to Duffett," Ma said, getting up from the rock and stretching. Crag walked over the picture, scuffing his feet in the dirt.

6 GRINDLE

Our last stop on my first day with the troupe was the village of Grindle. Like all the other villages we had passed through, it looked just like Mottle. It had the same cluster of huts around a village square. The sides of the square were occupied by a pen for animals, a walled-off dead garden, a stone barn, and the elder's hut, which was the largest hut in the village. Ma always made sure the first thing he did on arriving in a village was pay his respects to the elder.

In Grindle, the elder was a frail old man who looked even more ancient than Scour. Rather than a stick, he was supported by two daughters, one on either side. He welcomed Ma and the troupe to the village.

Since every village looked the same as Mottle, it was hard for me to feel homesick as my home seemed to be following me around, but I did wish my mum was with me. I kept thinking of all the amazing things I was going to tell her before we went off to sleep in our hut; then it would hit me that I was a long way from Mottle, and she was not here.

I helped Grunter unbolt the sides of the cart and set up the stage for our show. The sun was an orange ball slipping behind a range of distant hills when we came on stage, singing our song of welcome.

The play we were going to do was 'The Grumpy Giant.' Grunter was the giant of the title who made life hard for the villagers because of a misunderstanding provoked by Elba, playing the wicked witch. Crag was the handsome farmhand who set out to capture the giant, and Ma was his mother. Silva and I were the village idiots.

Silva and I bounded on stage to do a routine she had taught me during the day. The idea was that I'd lost my carrot and was trying to find it, but we lived in a village where everyone was named after vegetables.

"Have you seen my carrot?" I said.

"Old Carrot or young Carrot?" Silva said.

A beam of light hit my right eye and I blinked and flicked my hand across my face. Silva was looking at me, tight-lipped.

"It was fresh this morning," I gabbled out my line.

My timing was off and the only laughter came from a lad and a girl sitting together. The lad was handsome, like a younger version of Crag except he had dark curly hair. The girl had blonde hair and large front teeth that seemed to wedge her mouth open. They both looked a year or two older than me.

A circle of light played on Silva's cheek like a bug then jumped into her eye, making her duck her head.

The girl with the teeth gave a braying laugh and gazed adoringly at the handsome lad, who had a smug little smile on his lips. He was fingering a small, flat, shiny brass disc on a chain around his neck. The rat was using it to flash light into our eyes to distract us.

I made eye contact with the lad. He gave me a cocky

smirk.

"I'll give you my carrot for your bit of jewelry," I called out to him. "It would look nice on a girl." I took Silva's hand and gave her a simpering look.

"I'd sooner have your carrot," she said, and pulled her hand away.

"But I've lost my carrot," I said, turning to the audience in dismay.

The audience gave us a big laugh.

I glanced at the boy. He was giving me a cold hard stare. The jibe that jewelry was for girls had struck home.

Silva and I continued with our routine, getting far more laughs than the material deserved. I had a feeling that the villagers didn't like the boy and girl. We came off stage to a round of applause.

"That boy was using a piece of brass to blind us," I whispered to Silva.

"It's called a medallion," Silva said. "I saw him do it. Keep an eye on him and his idiot girlfriend. We might be able to get a bit of fun out of them later in the show."

As the show went on, the boy and girl continued to be annoying. They started yawning and pretending to fall asleep then they moved on to coughing loudly in the middle of scenes. Things got worse when the girl got bored with that and decided they should get all lovey-dovey instead. The boy was embarrassed at first then he noticed how distracting it was for us. They were so soppy it was sickening. What was strange was that the audience was annoyed by them too but tried to ignore them rather than stop them.

I noticed that the boy liked to toss his head so that his curls bounced up and down. He also had a habit of fondling his medallion. I wondered what his voice would sound like; bossy and arrogant, I decided.

We came to the climax of the show. The giant had been captured by the farmhand and was about to be executed. Silva and I had to do some comic business that would make the giant laugh. This would make the farmhand realize the giant was a good fellow, after all; they would become friends and kill the wicked witch instead.

Grunter, as the giant, was kneeling in front of Crag as the farmhand. Crag unsheathed his sword. This was the cue for Silva and I to come on stage.

"I demand the best seat for the execution," I said, strutting on stage, tossing my imaginary curls and polishing an imaginary medallion.

"And you'll let me sit on it, lovey wuvey," Silva said, clinging on to my arm. She stuck her front teeth over her bottom lip and brayed with laughter.

The audience applauded. They knew who we were sending up.

Silva and I squabbled over an imaginary seat and ended up collapsing together in a heap.

"You don't love your Bunny Wunnykins," I howled.

"I love my Bunny Wunnykins," Silva wailed.

"I fell on my botty wotty," I blubbed.

"Poor Bunny Wunnykins's botty wotty," Silva lamented.

"Please hurry up and execute me," Grunter said to Crag. "I can't stand any more of this."

The audience roared with laughter. This gave Crag the cue to realize the giant was not all bad, and soon after, Silva and I left the stage, arm in arm, blubbering pathetic endearments at each other.

I glanced over at the boy and girl. She was white with fury and chewing on her lower lip. The boy's face was empty of expression; I found that scary.

***

"Give Grunter a hand with the tents, Keth," Ma said, after the play had finished. "It is safer being among people than out on the open road, and the elder is happy for us to camp here."

I would have been happier putting some distance between us and the boy and girl that Silva and I had mocked, but I put the worry out of my mind.

I'd never seen a tent before never mind put one up, but I was anxious to help, and Grunter showed me what to do.

We found a flat piece of earth and I picked out any stones that I saw. Grunter laid a sheepskin blanket on the ground. He then took a collection of narrow wooden poles and bound them together with cord to make what looked like the frame of a small hut. We placed the frame over the blanket and put pegs in the earth to hold the frame in position. Finally, we took another sheepskin blanket, larger than the first one, and laid it over the frame, tying it into position with leather straps.

We had two of these tents and each fitted two people. The sleeping arrangements were that Ma and Silva shared one tent, and Elba and Grunter shared the other. Crag and I had blankets, and we slept under the cart.

As the light faded, we helped the villagers build a fire in the village square then we shared a communal meal with them. Ma was careful to add our own portion of rations to the pot. I got to eat just enough so that my belly reminded me I was still hungry, no different from living in Mottle.

The boy and girl were at the meal but they kept their distance from us.

After the meal, Elba played her lyre and everyone sat

around the fire, singing and telling tales. The stories were all about great heroes of old. No one told the story of how Prince Dorian trampled on our soldiers and left us scrabbling in the dirt; too recent, too painful.

After a final song, the elder wobbled to his feet, supported by his daughters, and thanked us for bringing joy. The villagers retreated to their huts.

"The villagers used to dance," Elba said as she gently wrapped the lyre in its goatskin cloth. "People whirled about the fire, kicking up their heels. That was real joy." She placed the lyre in its wooden case and closed the latches.

Ma, Silva, Elba and Grunter went off to their tents. Crag and I crawled beneath the cart.

"Tents are amazing," I said to him as I watched the red glow of the dying fire.

Crag grunted.

"They're like huts that you carry with you," I said. "And they're so easy to put up."

"Who knows," Crag said. "If you work hard over the next few years, you might even get to sleep in one."

I had a feeling that he was being sarcastic. "Goodnight," I said.

Crag ignored me.

"Sleep well," I said. I didn't like being ignored.

Crag turned away from me.

"Sweet dreams," I added.

"Goodnight and shut up, Keth," Crag said.

I lay on my back, wrapped in my blanket, and watched the fading light from the fire dance across the timbers on the underside of the cart.

As I drifted off to sleep, I heard Crag slip out from beneath the cart.

***

I was woken up by something pulling hard at my legs. I was yanked out from beneath the cart, and a wedge of material stuffed in my mouth. Before I could react, someone looped rope around my wrists and pulled it tight, burning my skin. In the dull red glow from the embers of the fire, I saw my assailants were the boy and girl. He flipped me on to my back and jumped astride my chest, knocking the breath out of me. She tied up my legs. I struggled, but it was no use.

He cupped my chin in his hands. They were soft. How could he live in a village and have soft hands?

"Not so funny now, is it?" the boy said, his eyes drilling into mine.

"Hit him, Dawyn," the girl said.

"Let's have a look at their cart," he said.

"Hit him first," the girl said.

"Shut up, Braida," Dawyn said to the girl. He left me and climbed onto the cart.

Braida looked at me, as if she was trying to decide whether to thump me or follow her boyfriend. True love won out, and she climbed onto the cart.

I worked on the knots. They had been tied in a hurry and were loose in places. Given time, I would get free of them.

I heard a soft thud, followed by a rustling from on top of the cart. I guessed they had opened up the costume hamper and were rummaging through the contents. I had almost slipped the rope from my wrists.

"Go on, put it on." Braida's whisper was carried to me on the breeze.

"I am king," Dawyn said in an intense whisper.

I heard a thump as something or someone fell over in

the cart then I saw something round fall from the cart and bounce beneath it. I thought it was a head. Braida screamed.

Her scream brought people rushing out of the huts and our tents. I untangled myself from the ropes and pulled out my gag just as they arrived.

Grunter wrapped his hands in cloth and pulled a burned branch from the fire. He whirled it a few times, and the end glowed orange. He moved over to the cart.

"It's Dawyn," Braida sobbed. "He's collapsed."

"His head," I said to Grunter, pointing beneath the cart.

Grunter thrust the branch under the cart.

"It's just a crown from the costume hamper," he said.

Ma and a man from the village lifted Dawyn down from the cart. He was conscious, but his eyes were wide and staring and a silver slither of drool hung down from his gaping mouth.

Elba and Silva helped Braida down from the cart. Braida's mother, a woman with even longer front teeth than her daughter's, took charge of her.

Crag and the village elder's two daughters appeared. Crag shot me a look of irritation, as though this disturbance was my fault. The daughters took charge of Dawyn and ordered him to be carried over to the elder's hut.

I crawled beneath the cart and picked up the crown. It was a shabby thing made of wood that had been painted silver and decorated with red glass beads. I ran my fingers over the spiky teeth at the top of the crown and thought about trying it on.

"Pass it here, Keth," Ma said. He was kneeling down, peering under the cart. I gave him the crown and crawled out.

The troupe clustered around the cart. After a while, one of the daughters emerged from the elder's hut and came over to us. "Dawyn has had a seizure," she said, "but he's going to be alright."

She sounded irritated rather than relieved, as though Dawyn was just a nuisance.

"Let's get back to sleep," Ma said. "We have an early start tomorrow."

We returned to our beds. Crag rejoined me under the cart.

***

We broke camp with the first light of dawn. I was stiff and cold. Grunter showed me a series of stretches he did every morning, and I copied him, enjoying the feeling of my body loosening up.

I fetched a bucket of water from the village well. The ash from the communal fire was cold so Silva collected sticks for a small fire. Silva shaved Ma, Elba shaved Grunter, and Crag shaved himself. I was entrusted with brewing the tea.

Breakfast was a hard biscuit and a mug of tea. I tried to bite through the biscuit and my teeth almost splintered. Silva laughed and showed me the skill of biscuit dunking to soften the biscuit.

Ma visited the elder's hut before we left. He reported that Dawyn was dazed but awake and had no recollection of the events of the previous evening. We sang a song of goodbye to the villagers, and left.

As we plodded along the track to the village of Stibble, our next stop, I fell into step beside Ma.

"Who is Dawyn?" I said.

"The youngest son of the elder," Ma said. "His mother

is dead. His older sisters are actually half-sisters."

"His hands are soft, like he has never done a day's work," I said.

"Now how would you know that?" Ma said.

That was an awkward one. "We shook hands after the show yesterday, to show we held no grudges," I said.

"Good lad," Ma said.

I was not sure if he was praising me for this behavior or the speed with which I made up stories. "So, why are his hands soft?" I persisted.

"Can you keep a secret?" Ma said.

I nodded.

"So can I," he said.

***

I was not going to get any more information from Ma, and after a while, I let him walk on ahead of me. I fell into step with Silva. We dawdled until we were a little way behind the cart.

The track we were following ran through woodland. The sun was up and fragments of light shone through the canopy of leaves and dappled the ground ahead of us.

Pieces of a brilliant idea had been forming in my mind since yesterday, and now I wanted to share it with her. "We go to all these villages," I said.

She nodded, and we trudged on.

"If we do shows in four or five villages every day, and we're on the road for most of the year then that is a lot of villages," I said.

She nodded and plucked a leaf to chew on.

"If in every village you performed a play to inspire people to stand up to Prince Dorian and fight back against him then in no time at all you would have a rebellion," I said.

"Why didn't I think of that?" she said and slapped her forehead.

"Well, sometimes an outsider can spot ..." I trailed off. She was being sarcastic.

"Ma won't let us put on those sorts of plays," she said. "His rule is that in performance we must be neutral to Prince Dorian."

"But he lied to save my skin, and he does dancing, when it's banned," I said.

"He sees that as being private stuff," she said. "On stage, we have to be neutral. He believes it is our duty to keep the show running so that when Prince Dorian falls, we won't have lost all our traditions."

"But we want to give Prince Dorian a shove and not just wait for him to fall of his own accord," I said.

"Yes," she shrugged, "but its Ma's troupe and Ma's rules. Wait 'til we get to Russett."

Rules are flexible, I thought. It might be wrong to do a whole play that was against Prince Dorian but that did not mean every single line had to be neutral. At some stage, I might be able to put into practice a small part of my brilliant idea.

7 DIVOT

We zigzagged through the countryside, visiting village after village, while the weather got colder and wetter and the days got shorter. As we travelled, different members of the troupe taught me different bits of their craft.

Elba worked on my singing with me. She said I hit all of the right notes but not in the right order. At first I didn't believe her, but she convinced me that 'The Turnip Song' had a tune, and you didn't just have to belt it out as loudly as possible.

Grunter taught me about movement and fighting on stage. If you're a troll or a giant, you don't have that many lines so you have to say things with your body. Also, when you fight on stage, you have to avoid hurting each other, especially if you're doing five shows a day. We practiced falling a lot so I could take a tumble without breaking any bones.

Ma taught me what all the different plays were. They had a lot of things that were the same but they all did the same things differently. I asked him why we needed to know so many plays when we could perform the same play in each village and our audience would never know. He said that we were stewards, and our job was to keep all the plays alive.

Silva taught me the comic routines. As soon as we had a rest stop, she would be drilling me on all the bits of funny business we could stick in a play. We didn't learn lines, instead we learned where a scene started and where it finished and which scene came next. Our job as fools was to get a scene from beginning to end, cramming in as many laughs as possible.

Crag was not an enthusiastic teacher although he did take pains to work with me on the hero-servant routines so that I did not mess up his performance.

I loved learning all these things and then putting them into practice on stage in the villages. Every time we performed, we got a different response, and while the laughs always came, they arrived in different spots.

***

Although I missed my mum and my village friends, I settled into the routine of life with the troupe. We had been on the road more days than I had fingers to count them on when something happened that reminded me I must take nothing for granted.

It was a crisp, autumn morning and we were breaking camp when Ma made an announcement. "We're performing in the village of Divot this evening," Ma said. "I think if we performed 'The Black-Eyed Witch,' it would go down well."

I didn't know the play, and I went on folding the blankets.

"That's a lot of doubling," Elba said, kicking dirt on our cooking fire to put it out.

"It would be if you played both the princess and the witch," Ma said, stowing away our pots and mugs.

"I always do," Elba said, pausing now to give Ma her full attention.

"What we'll do this time is get you to play the witch, and Silva will play the princess," Ma said.

"But I'm the servant," Silva said, dropping the folded-up tent skin she had been about to lift on to the cart.

"Keth is a fast learner, and we don't need two servants," Ma said.

I glowed with this praise. I looked around the group. Everyone else was scowling or looking miserable. I hid my grin behind the blanket I was folding.

***

That morning, we followed a track through grassy meadows beside a stream. At our morning rest stop, Ma led Crag and I a little way across a meadow to practice the hero-servant routines for 'The Black-Eyed Witch.' Elba and Silva stayed with the cart to work on princess stuff.

The rehearsal was going well until we got to the scene outside the witch's lair. I was carrying all the prince's weapons and I had to keep dropping them and picking them up and dropping them again because I was shaking in terror.

We did the scene once. Crag stood at the front of our imaginary stage, side on to let the imaginary audience admire his profile. He ignored me as I dropped and picked things up.

"This scene never works." He pouted.

"That's because you're not reacting to what I'm doing," I said.

Crag swung round sharply, tossing his wavy blonde

hair. "You don't tell me what to do," Crag sneered. "I'm an experienced actor. You're nothing but Ma's ... apprentice."

Crag had paused before saying the word apprentice and I assumed he had bitten back a different and ruder word. Arky and I had made a collection of all the rude words we knew that summer, and I was disappointed that I was not going to get to add another one to the list.

"Keth," Ma said, folding his arms, "I'm responsible for giving Crag direction."

I still thought I was right about what Crag needed to do to make the scene work. I wondered how Ma was going to feed him my suggestion.

"We'll move on to some hero work," Ma said. "I don't need you for this, Keth. Take a break."

I was cross, because I was being told off when I was trying to be helpful.

***

I made my way back through the meadow to the cart where Elba and Silva were rummaging about in the costume hamper.

"This isn't going to work," Silva said. "This is so stupid." Her jaw had tightened and that made her narrow chin even more pointed, like a dagger blade.

"Don't take it out on me, my girl," Elba said, with her hands on her hips. "Do you think I enjoy being told by my master that I'm an old hen, only fit for the pot?"

"But I can't be the princess," Silva wailed. "I haven't got a chest."

It began to make sense. They were searching the costume hamper for an important prop. Princesses had jewelry and fine clothes, so of course they would need a chest to keep them in. It might be a vital part of the story.

"Can I help?" I called up to them. "What does your chest look like?

They turned to me and scowled. I sensed I was not welcome, but I ploughed on.

"Do you know who had hold of it last?" I asked.

"You're so not funny," Silva snarled.

"Clear off, Keth," Elba snapped at me.

They turned back to the costume hamper. I slunk off.

***

I saw Grunter sitting cross-legged on a patch of grass beside the stream. Thespian stood near him, cropping the grass. I went over to join them.

As I got closer, I saw that Grunter had one of the tent skins stretched across his lap and a clay jar beside him. He put his fingers into it and they came out covered in white gunk, which he smeared on the skin.

"It's a mixture of tallow and bees wax," Grunter said to me as I sat down beside him. "It keeps the skins waterproof." He massaged the gunk into the skin with circular movements of his fingers.

"There's a problem with props," I said, "but Elba and Silva won't let me help."

"Don't fret, Keth, it might be woman thing," Grunter said.

I thought about this. "No," I said, "Silva was going on about not being able to perform tonight because she does not have a chest."

Grunter doubled over, and I thought he was choking. He straightened up, with tears rolling down his face.

"And what did you say, Keth?"

"I offered to help find it," I said.

He doubled over again. I got up ready to stalk away.

"Calm down, Keth," Grunter said. "Don't be so jumpy, lad."

I sat back down, and Grunter explained to me which chest was being referred to. My face turned red. He mimed, warming his hands from the heat coming from it. Everyone is a comic genius when you don't need them to be.

"Things are going to be a bit tense for a while," Grunter said. "That's why I'm here with Thespian. You never lose your temper, do you, lad?" Thespian looked up at us for a moment then went back to cropping the grass.

"Why is everyone so on edge?" I asked.

"Ma's casting for the 'Black-Eyed Witch' has brought up a few uncomfortable truths," Grunter said. "Elba does not want to grow old just yet, and Silva is not quite ready to grow up."

It sounded a bit like going between the shafts of the cart in Mottle.

I spent the rest of the break with Thespian and Grunter. I gave Grunter a hand with the waterproofing. It kept us out of trouble.

***

We reached the outskirts of Divot late in the afternoon. The sky had clouded over and a cold little breeze nipped at us. The troupe had played Divot on the circuit they had made the previous year, and the audience had loved them. We should have been in good humor but Ma's choice of play had put us all on edge.

As we approached the village, I became even more uneasy. The outlying fields were uncultivated and brambles were already struggling with wild grass for space. I wondered if we would find the village or just a place where the village used to be.

I was relieved when the track crested a small rise and we saw the stubble of fields that had been harvested and the huts of the village in the distance.

We sang our song 'Happy Days and Jolly Plays' loudly as we arrived in the village square but no one came out of the huts, and the village was quiet.

Ma walked over to the elder's hut; not only was it the biggest in the village but it had a wooden door rather than sacking across the entrance. He rapped on the door.

"The players are here to perform for your pleasure," he called out.

The silence was so solid you could chew on it. The hairs on the back of my neck prickled. I glanced sharply around the square. I thought I saw a piece of cloth twitch across a window.

"It might be plague," Grunter murmured. He too had spotted the movement. "We had best move on."

"Crag!" a young woman screamed and burst out of a hut, her ragged blonde hair dancing in the breeze.

I jumped out of my skin, and Crag stood, petrified. Grunter swiftly moved to Crag's shoulder.

"You were great last year," the woman burbled.

I thought she might be mad but Crag relaxed and began preening himself. Women, their arms tight around their children, emerged slowly from the huts; no men appeared.

The door of the elder's hut opened. A tall gray-haired woman stood framed in the doorway.

"Forgive our initial lack of welcome," she said. "We had hoped you would take the hint and pass through. We have no food and no joy to offer you. It is not too late to reach the next village by night fall."

"We bring our own food," Ma said. "We wish only to perform for you."

"You are welcome then," the elder said with sad formality. She beckoned Ma to come into the hut. Ma gestured we should start setting up the stage then he followed her.

The women and children clustered around our cart and made a fuss of Thespian, except for the women fussing over Crag instead.

We had almost completed setting up when Ma emerged from the hut and joined us. He told us that last spring, all the men had been taken from the village by soldiers of Prince Dorian. The men had danced the harvest dance the previous year. Spring had just arrived, and they were preparing to sow crops when the soldiers arrived, and all the men were arrested for dancing and taken away.

***

We began our performance of 'The Black-Eyed Witch.'

At one point during the play, I would be on stage all by myself, and I would get to do all the talking. The situation was that the prince and me, his servant, were going to journey into the great forest to find the lair of the black-eyed witch. The prince was brave and had no problems being heroic, but I was not a hero. As I packed my master's saddlebags for the journey, I told myself and the audience jokes to cheer myself up.

I had a plan for what I would do when I was alone on stage. Ma had a rule that the troupe be neutral to Prince Dorian, but you never knew the limits of a rule until you tested it. I understood that we would get into trouble if we did a whole play that mocked Dorian but it could not hurt if we included one or two lines that did.

Silva had taught me some jokes to use and they all followed the same pattern, so I had been working on some of my own involving Prince Dorian.

We approached the point in the play where I would be left on stage alone. I was nervous about what I planned to do. I was struggling to get my breath and my right leg started trembling.

"Don't tell the Dorian jokes this time," a little voice inside me suggested. "Wait and ask Ma if it's okay."

"But he'll say no," a different voice inside of me replied.

"Pack my bags, good servant," Crag said to me and left the stage, flashing me a sly grin.

Crag had seen me trembling and probably thought I was suffering stage fright at being on stage alone. I was furious that Crag thought that, and this gave me the burst of energy I needed to carry through my plan.

I did a couple of Silva's jokes to get things started, and the audience laughed a little. I took a deep breath then tried out a joke of my own. "Why is Prince Dorian like a plague of locusts?" I asked. "They both come and take all your harvest."

The audience laughed and in the little space after their laughter receded, the elder said, "At least the locusts leave your men folk behind."

The audience erupted in a storm of laughter. My body tingled with excitement as though I had climbed to the thinnest branch at the top of the tallest tree. I felt like the lightening in a storm, and I prepared to strike again.

Crag stumbled on stage. "All packed," he said. "Good work, servant. We're off to the forest."

My connection with the audience was broken, and the

play swept on.

**

As the play continued, I noticed Crag was slowing his scenes down. He seemed to have taken up residence at the front of the stage, and his speeches had long pauses when he would look brooding and handsome at the audience. The children were bored but the women were lapping it up. All their men had been taken away. He represented their lost son or missing husband. They drank him in.

I stood at the back of the stage, ignored as Crag milked the attention of the audience. I felt embarrassed and uncomfortable. I hated the way that Crag was playing on them. He was satisfying his own vanity and not doing it out of kindness.

Crag was taking so long the daylight was fading. In the dusk, a midge buzzed past my ear. I swatted at it. A girl in the audience tittered. I had missed the midge but it had given me an idea. I pretended to be beset by an imaginary midge. I'd swat at it, relax as I thought it had gone then flinch as it reappeared.

The children began to laugh. Crag was unsure what was happening. It was his turn to lose his connection with the audience.

I caught my imaginary midge. I opened my hand to check. It flew out. I panicked and flapped around. I caught it again. I smirked at my clenched hand. Another imaginary midge buzzed me. I caught it with my other hand. A third imaginary midge buzzed me then landed on my nose. I crossed my eyes to look at it. I unclenched my hands to get at this midge, and the other imaginary midges escaped and attacked me.

Everyone in the audience laughed. Crag stopped brooding and turned to stare at me. I ran up and down the back of the stage, flapping at the imaginary midges. The audience roared with laughter.

Crag strode up to me and grasped the front of my jerkin with one hand. His eyes glinted. I made my body go limp, expecting him to throw me. He slapped me hard in the face, three times. Slap! Slap! Slap! He held my jerkin tight so I could do nothing to lessen the impact.

"That's taken care of the flies," Crag said.

He let go of my jerkin and I collapsed in a heap, my cheeks burning and my ears ringing. The audience screamed with laughter. They thought this was the payoff.

I stumbled through the rest of the play, hearing only scraps of dialogue because of how much my ears were ringing.

***

After we took our bows, I helped Silva pack up the costumes. She wasn't saying much and I was in a state of shock but trying to pretend everything was normal.

Grunter tapped me on the shoulder. "Ma wants to have a word with you," he said.

The last light of dusk was trickling away as Ma took me by the arm and walked me a little way from the village square. His grip was firm, and I knew I was in trouble.

"I'm sorry about the midges business," I said. "Crag let me know on stage what he thought about it. I won't do it again."

Ma shook his head. "You made a joke about Prince Dorian," he said.

"They laughed," I said. "The elder topped me and got the biggest laugh of the show."

"You know my rule," Ma said. "On stage we are neutral to Prince Dorian."

"It was only one joke," I said.

"Only because I shoved Crag on stage to stop you," Ma said. "You were getting ready to unleash a bit of a routine, the sort of routine that gets the whole troupe banned." He put his hands on my shoulders and stared hard into my face. "If you make another joke like that, you're out of the troupe. Understand?"

"I promise I won't make any more jokes about Prince Dorian," I said.

I meant what I said. I was not going to lose my chance to travel to the city and join the rebellion that would overthrow the evil prince, just for the sake of poking fun at him.

That night we camped in Divot. Crag didn't sleep under the cart, which was a relief. I lay awake and huddled in my blanket, wanting to overthrow Dorian, while at the same time wishing I was back in my hut in Mottle, safe with my mum.

8 CROUCHERS HOLLOW

For the next few days after our performance in Divot, I was careful to keep my antics on stage under control. It made me less funny but it meant I didn't get into trouble.

We were eating breakfast one morning, having camped in the village of Bittock the night before. I was concentrating on softening my biscuit in the tea without letting it get so soggy that it fell apart. Ma coughed loudly, which meant either he wanted our attention or he had choked on a crumb.

"I expect some of you recognize the land we are heading into," Ma said.

I looked around the campfire. The land was new to me but the others were nodding their heads and looking solemn.

"In two nights' time, we're performing at Crouchers Hollow," Ma said.

Silva shivered and wrapped her cloak tightly around her. Ma put his hand on her shoulder. We finished breakfast and Crag offered to wash up the mugs. This was unheard of, but no one made a joke of it. Everyone was trying to find quiet ways to be kind to each other.

We sang a song of goodbye to the villagers of Bittock and took our leave. I dawdled behind the cart. Silva fell into step beside me. She had stopped walking with me since my performance at Divot so I took this to be a peace offering.

"What's so special about Crouchers Hollow?" I asked.

"It's where the battle with Prince Dorian took place," she said.

I gasped. I knew the battle must have taken place somewhere but I had never expected to visit the spot.

"Were you there?" I asked.

"I was in the village," she said. "The battle took place on the moor above. I saw what was left of our army stagger back down afterwards."

Her face had a distant look on it as though she was in a different, less happy, place than the track we walked on.

My dad would have been one of those men, I thought, wounded and fearful, struggling back to the village.

Silva shook herself. She put a hand on my arm. "You'll be upset, Keth," she said. "We'll all be upset. The thing you must not do is get angry and silly. Promise me you won't make any jokes about Prince Dorian."

"I promise," I said and I meant it.

***

We approached Crouchers Hollow in the middle of the next afternoon. We saw the side of the moor rising steeply from the fields from some distance away. The tops were capped in purple, which Silva said was the heather in flower. She told me the moor was so flat and windswept on top, only the heather was tough enough to cling on.

The village nestled in a fold at the foot of the moor, hidden from sight until the last moment when the track dipped down into it.

We made our way through the huts to the village square. Ma led us in singing our song 'Happy Days and Jolly Plays,' forcing it to sound cheerful and normal. I thought everyone might stay in their huts, like at Divot, but they came out and assembled in the square. They were silent and Ma raised his hand, a signal for us to stop our singing.

A woman emerged from the elder' hut. She wore a long, green, woolen dress. Her white hair was swept back and fell in long thick tresses to her waist, where she had wrapped it around herself like a girdle. She made no greeting but moved into the center of the square and squatted down in the dirt. The other villagers sat down around her.

I thought we would start setting up the stage but Ma gestured for us to sit down and be silent.

After a few minutes, I started to fidget. Silva who was sitting next to me, nudged me to be still. "What's happening?" I whispered.

"The village has its own atmosphere because of what happened here," she said. "Guests are given a period of silence to get comfortable with it."

The longer I sat, the less comfortable I felt. I kept thinking about how my dad had come to this village healthy, and left it dying from stinking wounds. He would have seen these huts when he arrived. He might have spoken to some of these people. They would have watched my dad go off to fight.

I didn't want to sit here, trapped with my thoughts. I edged back on my bottom. Silva gave me a worried glance. I held my knees tight together and grimaced, to give her the idea I was bursting for a wee. Once I was on the edge of the group, I stood up and slipped away.

I walked around the edge of the village and picked up the track, leaving the village on the opposite side to where we had entered. It climbed a short distance then split into two. One branch was well used and kept to the foot of the moor. The other branch was overgrown and zigzagged up to the top of the moor. This track was marked by a knee-high, rickety, white fence.

I walked up to examine the fence then stepped back in horror. It was made up of thigh bones, arm bones, leg bones, ribs, and spines. All of them were human. The way to the top of the moor was marked with bones.

***

I stood shaking for I don't know how long. I think I might have been crying because I tasted snot in my mouth.

"Keth!" It was Silva.

She approached cautiously, as though I might take flight like an animal. She put her hands on my shoulders and waited while my shaking subsided.

"This is Bone Road," she said. "It's marked out in bones all the way to the summit. No one takes it anymore; everyone goes the long way round." She pointed to the well-used track.

"Our soldiers?" I asked, shuddering as I looked at the bones.

She nodded. "Dorian wanted us to have a permanent reminder of our defeat. All the survivors were forced to drag the bodies from the battlefield. Dorian constructed giant vats, and the bodies were boiled in them. When all that was left was the bones, Dorian made us use them to build this fence."

"Did you help?"

"Yes. I was only three. I helped the women sort out the different bones. Madoc, the lady in green, made it a game for me."

"Is your brother here?"

"His bones are, but that's all they are, bones. He's gone."

"Why don't the villagers just pack up and leave?" I said. "This place has a bad feel to it."

"Prince Dorian passed a law; they must stay," she said.

I traced out the bone road climbing the side of the moor then disappearing over the top. From the corner of my eye, I saw tendrils of mist drifting up from the bones. I shivered.

"We're going to start the show, Keth," she said. "Ma sent me to look for you. If you need to be lost for a bit longer, I can say I didn't find you."

"No. I'm fine," I said, and I thought I was.

"And no Prince Dorian jokes," she said.

"I promised," I said. "Trust me."

***

When I returned to the village square, Ma came up to me and looked me in the eye. "We're performing 'The Black-Eyed Witch' again."

"Fine," I said. "I promise I won't make any Prince Dorian jokes." I was getting fed up with having to repeat my promise.

"I know you've promised," Ma said, "and I know you meant it, but I don't want you blurting something out before your brain has got a rein on your mouth. For this performance, you're a mute."

"What's a mute?"

"They can't say a word."

I was furious. No one believed I would be able to keep my promise.

***

The day was drawing to a close when we mounted the stage and the sun hung low over the top of the moor. The slope up to the top was in shadow but the white lines of the bone road, etched into it, were clearly visible. That's impossible, I thought. I put the idea out of my head; I needed to concentrate on my performance.

The play began. Ma was the palace housekeeper. He wore his red polka dot dress, but with a starched white apron around his waist and a white handkerchief knotted in his ginger wig. He had a pink feather duster, with which he kept tickling Grunter's Captain of the Guards. He introduced me as the prince's idiot servant who had never talked sense and now never talked at all, having been cursed by the black-eyed witch.

We reached the point in the play where I was on stage alone, telling jokes to cheer myself up only now I had to do it in silence. I saw Crag grinning at me from the side of the stage. I knew he was going to delay his return entrance while I struggled to keep the audience entertained. I tried to remember everything that Grunter had taught me about movement because now I had no words.

I had an idea. As I tried to pack the prince's saddlebags, I would be assailed by imaginary midges. They had got me into trouble before, now they could help get me out of it.

As I picked up the prince's cloak, I ducked and

twisted, as the first imaginary midge buzzed me. From the corner of my eye, I saw mist in the window of the elder's hut form into a gaping wounded face. I dropped the cloak, and the audience laughed a little because they thought it was a result of the midge buzzing me. I looked at the window; the mist drifted out of it, as the face dissolved. I saw tendrils of mist rising from the mud of the village square.

Concentrate, I told myself. I picked up the cloak, ducked the midge, and dropped it again. My timing was better and the audience laughed louder.

I looked out at the audience. A figure of mist was kneeling behind Madoc. Its head had been cut off sharp, just above the nose. Madoc seemed unaware of its presence. Wounded men, made of mist, rose from the dirt and crawled among the audience, who did not see them. I remembered my mum telling me, last harvest time, that my ability to see the wraiths was a special family gift.

I wanted to dance the harvest dance. My feet itched. I danced the first steps of it. The wraiths turned to watch me, and the half-headed one behind Madoc leaned forwards, its smile a gaping hole.

I moved my feet: kick, step, cross and stamp; kick, step, cross and stamp. The mist edges of the wraiths fluttered, vibrating to my rhythm, and floated towards me. I saw them, and they knew I was there. I danced.

Suddenly, I was plucked into the air. For a moment, I thought the wraiths had taken me, and I was flying then I became aware of hands holding my legs, and my head bumping against Grunter's back. He had scooped me up and thrown me over his shoulder.

I heard the creak and thud of the lid of the costume hamper being thrown open. Grunter marched over to it.

He slung me into the hamper, my landing softened by the costumes. The lid slammed shut. I pushed up hard, but it would not budge. I saw, through the gaps in the wicker, two large thick legs. Grunter was sitting on the hamper. I was trapped.

The play continued without me. Ma said I had contracted a brain fever. He told the prince he had decided to be his servant, and he would tickle the witch to death with his feather duster. The audience was nervous, but they laughed.

Stuck in the basket, I curled up into a ball and held my legs tight, squirming with frustration. I was in so much trouble. I had kept my promise not to make jokes about Prince Dorian; instead, I had done much worse and broken his ban on dancing. I dreaded what Ma was going to say to me.

What had possessed me to dance? I had seen the wraiths and without thinking about it, I had danced the harvest dance, perhaps because that was when I had last seen them. I wasn't being a rebel. It had just happened. How would I explain that to Ma?

***

The show finished. Grunter had spent the remainder of the play sitting on the basket. He did not even stand up to take a bow and he went on sitting there after the applause had finished. They were waiting for the audience to disperse a little before they dealt with me. I felt sick in my guts.

After a while, I heard footsteps approaching the basket and Grunter stood up and stretched.

The lid was opened. Ma looked down at me. He had taken off his wig but not his makeup, and his short iron-gray hair looked out of place with his lipstick and rouge. His face was hard, like it had been carved out of stone.

"What possessed you to do that, boy?" he rasped. His voice was thick and choked. "You promised not to tell any jokes so you decided to play the rebel by doing a dance instead."

"It wasn't like that," I stammered. "Sometimes when a mist comes up, I catch a glimpse of wraiths. I've never seen them as clear as I saw them today. I was scared. I didn't think about dancing, I just did it. It's what I do on harvest day."

"There was no mist, lad," Ma said. "Did anyone see a mist?"

I heard murmurs of 'no'. The troupe was gathered on stage. I only saw Ma, as the sides of the hamper limited my vision.

"I can't let you go on stage again, Keth," Ma said. "It's too dangerous. You could get us all executed."

"I wasn't being a rebel," I pleaded. I tensed the muscles in my face, trying hard not to cry.

"We'll take you to the city," Ma said, "make sure you don't starve over the winter, and you can return to your village next spring."

Grunter helped me out of the hamper. We cleared up the stage in the normal way. I helped Silva fold up the costumes and pack them in the hamper. I didn't speak to anyone, and no one spoke to me.

***

That night I lay under the cart, unable to sleep. I was by myself. Crag, as usual, had disappeared. I felt alone now that I was no longer part of the troupe. I had left my village behind and I had now lost my role in this new world. I was nothing. The thought of having to travel with the troupe but not being one of them was more pain than I wanted to bear.

I crawled out from under the cart. The air was damp and chill. Heavy clouds had arrived during the evening and they now blocked the splinterlight. In the light from the embers of the campfire, I saw the outline of the village huts and our tents, except it was no longer 'our tents' because I was an outsider. I turned my back on them.

I walked, stumbling in the dark. I felt a little better for doing something rather than just lying still with my hurt. I picked up the track and used the ridges made by cartwheels to guide my feet. Without thinking, I had gone beyond the edge of the village and come to the fork in the track where Bone Road began.

An idea took hold of me. I could follow Bone Road onto the moor and let the wraiths take me. This was where my father had been mortally wounded, and it would be the right place to meet my end. Why carry my shame any further? I waited for a moment to see if anything inside me tugged me back, but nothing did. I had no other place to go. I stumbled up Bone Road.

***

The road was steep. With each step, I pushed my energy and frustration into the ground and stomped upwards. Soon I was out of breath and my chest hurt, but I refused to slow down. My feet followed ancient ruts made in the track, and a faint luminous mist rose from the bones in the fence, keeping me on course. The wraiths were preparing to take me.

As I reached the top of the moor, I was no longer

sheltered from the wind and a sudden blustering gust knocked me off my feet. Sharp droplets of freezing rain stung my face. I curled up tight against the cold and dug my hands deep inside my jerkin. I pricked my thumb on my mum's needle, still pinned there.

The sharp pain brought me to my senses, as though I had woken from a dream. If I remained out on the moor then either the wraiths would kill me or I would freeze to death; and however ashamed I might be, I wanted to live. I wanted to see my mum again.

I stood up and prepared to walk back to the village. The wind buffeted me then suddenly it dropped for a moment. My heart froze. I heard the heavy slapping footsteps of something climbing the bone road from the village. It made a high-pitched sobbing noise. I recognized words. It was singing a battle song. I had heard my father and the other men of the village sing it before they left to fight and die. Then the wind picked up and whipped the sound away.

Was this what a wraith sounded like, perhaps the one with the top half of its head missing, or was it a ghoul? I did not want to wait and find out. I turned and ran across the moor following Bone Road. The rain now fell in wind-driven flurries of fat drops, like over-ripe berries. I skidded along the path marked out by ribbons of luminous mist.

I slipped and fell over. I lay flat on my face, with my heart thumping in my chest. I looked back. A single yellow eye floated above the bone road. The creature was pursuing me. I scrambled to my feet and fled on.

I reached a crossroads, in the center of which was a pyramid of mist as tall as my head. Lightning struck. The whole area was lit up bright yellow for an instant. I saw the pyramid of mist was a cairn of human skulls, glistening as the rain ran down them. Everything went dark, followed by a huge crack of thunder that wanted to pound me into the earth. My ears rang. As they returned to normal, the wind dropped, and I heard the battle song and the slapping step of the creature pursuing me. I scrambled behind the cairn and hid.

***

The lightning flashed and the hammer blows of thunder followed. I huddled with my head in my hands. The creature approached the cairn. I heard a hollow chinking. It was tapping the skulls.

"Where are you, son? Which one is yours, Rul?" The creature spoke, and I recognized the voice. It was Ma, but his voice was high and strained, empty of authority and filled with despair.

I crawled out from behind the cairn. A flash of lightening lit us up. Ma's eyes were wide and staring. In his left hand, he held a lantern, the floating eye that I had seen earlier. The rain washed over the skulls in torrents, and split into rivulets where the fingers of his right hand caressed the eye sockets of a skull. Thunder shook the air.

"Is that you, Rul?" Ma said, pointing the lantern in my direction, dazzling me.

"It's me, Keth," I said, shading my eyes from the glare of the lantern. "I think we should go back to the village."

"I want to be with my son," Ma said. The lightning flashed. I saw Ma's face, mad with a grief that was echoed in the faces of the wraiths forming from the luminous mist around the edges of the crossroads.

I was scared. Ma was so full of grief, it had squeezed out his entire world and left him nothing else. "I should never have let Rul out of my sight," he said.

"I'm cold, wet, and scared," I said. "We should go."

The wraiths crept in from the edges of the crossroads. Ma balanced the lantern on the top of the cairn of skulls. He directed the beam so that the light spilled on to him.

"We were here in Crouchers Hollow, the night before the great battle," he said.

As he spoke, the wind picked up the lantern and sent it clattering down the cairn of skulls. The glass shattered, and the candle inside went out with a hiss. The only light now came from the pale glow of the mist that made up the wraiths' bodies, and I doubted Ma saw them.

He ignored the loss of light and continued talking. He was in some other place made of memories.

"We were entertaining our soldiers," he said, "making them laugh, making them forget they were frightened. Rul was Keth's age, and just as much of a stupid hothead."

"I'm Keth," I said. "I'm here."

Ma kept talking as though I was not there. "At dawn the next day, we sang for our soldiers as they marched on to the moor." He sang a few bars of the battle song in a cracked voice. "I told Rul he was too young to fight but he slipped away and joined them. We should have won. Prince Dorian only had a small army. We outnumbered him. The moor was flat and wide. We thought he was a fool to fight us here. We would encircle him and crush him."

The wraiths in the shape of wounded soldiers, bleeding threads of mist, crawled over to Ma and clustered around his feet. They looked up at him with confused, scared, screaming faces. The wraiths and I were Ma's audience.

"We heard the sounds of battle, as we waited in Crouchers Hollow," Ma said. "First we heard the distant clash of weapons then we heard the screaming. The first of our soldiers staggered down off the moor, wounded and gibbering. We tried to get them to speak but their words were garbled. As far as we could tell, our soldiers had encircled Dorian's army then charged. The attack had failed; our men broke ranks and fled.

"I lost myself among the wounded. I was treating a man with his stomach torn open, his face clenched in terror, not pain. I knew he was dying, so I started to sing him to his rest. For a moment, his face relaxed then a terrible look, worse than fear, crossed it. 'I've run away and left my friend,' he told me. The next moment he was dead. I think he died from shame.

"The next thing I knew little Silva was tugging at my arm. My first thought was to stop her seeing the dead man I had been tending. I picked her up. 'Where's Rul?' she screamed at me. I looked around and felt a heavy stone of fear lodge in my stomach. The color drained from the world. Rul was nowhere to be found.

"I saw his body later when it was carried from the battlefield. Dorian's soldiers would not let me take it. Rul's bones are part of Bone Road, and his skull sits in this cairn. I don't know which it is. I was his father, but I lost sight of him.

"I've grown so old and he's forever young and foolish. I'll take my rest and sleep beneath him."

Ma lay down at the foot of the cairn. The wraiths drifted over to him and settled on him like the thinnest of blankets.

The rain was freezing. I knelt down, crawled over to Ma, and curled up beside him. My body chilled when it touched the wraiths. I pressed my face into the dirt and listened to the water gurgling through the cairn of skulls.

***

I shivered as the wraiths settled on me and seeped into my bones. As the lightning struck, I seemed to float above my body, looking down at the cairn of skulls and our two huddled bodies then the crack of thunder spread me flat over the crossroads, and I felt as though I could ripple out over the moor and disappear. I had no need to return to my body ever again.

I thought of my father and how strong and proud he looked as he set off to fight Prince Dorian. He had fought and lost. At least he had given it a go. The sense of floating snapped and I thudded back into my body. Doing nothing meant letting Dorian win. He would win anyway but even so, you had to fight him.

I struggled to my knees, shaking with cold. I tried to stand up but I slumped over in the mud. I slapped my hands in the dirt and my palms stung; each blow sent a tingle of warmth through them. I kicked my feet as though I was trying to swim through the dirt. Pins and needles shot through me. I sat up and rubbed my feet and calves hard. At first my feet were lifeless stones but gradually feeling returned.

I stood up, wobbling in the rain. The wind pummeled me as though it wanted to sweep me off the moor. What had brought me here? I had danced a dance. Which dance? It was the harvest dance.

I thought of my mum and my friends, and how last harvest we had danced together in the ruins of the manor house. I remembered the cattle I had placed between myself and the path from the village, and I laughed.

I began to dance. I slipped and almost fell; staying on my feet became part of the game. As I danced, I started to warm up.

I saw the outline of Ma's huddled body, covered in wraiths. The wraiths slowly detached themselves from him and drifted around me, watching me dance.

I danced over to Ma, knelt down, and shook him. He groaned. I put my mouth to his ear. "Dance!" I screamed.

His body twitched. I pummeled his legs and feet, trying to put life in his muscles and get him moving. He struggled to his knees. "Dance?" He sounded bewildered.

"Dance!" I yelled.

"For the dead?" he asked.

"For the living," I shouted.

Putting my hands under his armpits, I tried to lift up his thin, wiry body. For a moment, I thought I would collapse under his weight but then he got his feet beneath him, and he stood.

I moved to his side and reaching up, put my arm around his shoulder. His arm flopped over my shoulder. I braced my knees and steadied us, keeping us both upright.

"Harvest dance!" I shouted in his ear. I counted us in, then began.

I danced us away from the cairn of skulls as I dragged Ma. His feet had no life and he stumbled against me. We toppled over into the mud. The wraiths swept around us, looking angry.

"Help me," I shouted at Ma. I struggled to my feet then levered him upright. The muscles in my arms ached from lifting him. Once again, I got my arm around his shoulder, and his arm fell loose and heavy across my shoulder.

I counted us in for the harvest dance, but this time I did not try to move us; instead, we danced it on the spot. Slowly Ma's feet began to respond, as though the dance was a distant memory that was gradually returning to him.

I began to edge us towards the bone road leading back to the village. Ma shuffled now rather than stumbled, and he was keeping time with me.

The ribbons of luminous mist marked Bone Road leading off the moor. I directed our steps along the path. The wraiths circled around us, imitating our dance as much as their wounded soldier bodies allowed. I concentrated on my steps and keeping Ma upright. The wind buffeted us, and sheets of rain drenched us.

The road abruptly began its descent from the moor. The slope took me by surprise; we skidded, lost our balance and fell over, landing in a tangle of limbs. I attempted to lift myself up but it was as though heavy bars had been placed across my arms and legs. I could not summon up the energy to move them.

I looked at the fence and saw tendrils of mist, like deformed fingers, beckoning me. The wraiths peered at me through eyes that were no more than holes in their mist bodies. They had won but they looked disappointed. Once more, I floated out of my body.

A bark of laughter in my ear snapped me back. "Move your left leg, Keth, and I can free my right leg," Ma said.

At first, I thought my body was a single solid lump. I concentrated and focused my thoughts on my left leg. It tingled. I slid it slowly to one side. Ma's leg brushed past it. Step by step, like solving a puzzle, we untangled our limbs.

This time it was Ma who hauled me upright. He counted us in and we danced, shoulder to shoulder, skidding and sliding down Bone Road. He provided the energy and I gave us direction, so that we would not crash into the bone fence.

My body began to feel connected with my feet and I was dancing with all of me. We moved in unison. Our steps became more vigorous as we fed off each other's energy. We laughed and sang and spun on our heels as we danced.

The wraiths picked up our energy and they swirled about us, no longer taking on the bodies of wounded soldiers.

Bone Road ended; ahead of us, sitting in the darkness, was the village. We wheeled around and I saw the outline of Bone Road tracing its way up on to the moor. We wheeled back and I saw lights bobbing towards us. We danced towards them.

The rest of the troupe and the villagers, carrying burning torches, met us as we reached the outskirts of the village.

"We heard you singing on the moor," Madoc said, her voice tight with fear.

As one, Ma and I sank to our knees, shoulder to shoulder, arms still linked. The wraiths backed away from us then faded into the night. The dance was over. We collapsed.

***

I must have slept. The next morning, I awoke from being jolted about. A pale autumn sun was high overhead. I was seeing sky rather than the underside of the cart. It's late, and I've been left behind, I thought with alarm.

I tried to get up but I was wrapped tightly in blankets. I turned my head and saw planks of wood on either side of me. It dawned on me that I was in the back of the cart and we were on the move, which explained the jolting. Satisfied, I went back to sleep.

When I next awoke, we had stopped. Ma was sitting beside me. "Thank you for last night," Ma said. "I'm reinstating you in the troupe."

Relief washed over me. It was as though I'd been

handed back my identity. I raised my head. In the distance, I saw the purple-colored tops of the moor, which we were skirting around. Last night, on the moor, I had encountered something beyond my understanding. I was happy to be heading away from it but I knew the wraiths would come to me again. I shivered.

"You've got a chill," Ma said. He sneezed into his hand. "And I'm not much better. Now remember, I'm watching you. I can't let you out of my sight."

He smiled then climbed down from the cart.

I was still part of the troupe. I lay back and drifted off to sleep.

9 AUTUMN

The nighttime adventure at Crouchers Hollow had left me with a bad cold. For two days, I travelled on the back of the cart wrapped in blankets, and I did not perform.

On the third day, I was able to go on stage although my performance was subdued. Crag said it was wonderful but Silva told me to ignore him. Between performances, I trudged behind the cart. I was tired and fell behind. Silva kept me company.

"Who is Master Twist?" I asked as we walked. I had remembered how the guards, Podger and Scrape, had reacted with fear when Ma mentioned his name.

"Master Twist is Prince Dorian's Master of Revels," Silva said. "No one is allowed to perform without his license."

I saw that her upper lip had turned up with disgust. She hated him.

"What happens if he won't give you a license?" I asked.

"You find a new job or starve," she said.

"Is Twist fair?" I asked.

Silva laughed. It was a loud cackle, an explosion of shock at the idea. "Twist is a vicious, sour-faced little squirt, whose only joy is hurting people," she said. "He is never fair. He is also Dorian's most powerful advisor. Folk reckon Bone Road was his idea."

"When we overthrow Prince Dorian, he will be out of a job," I said.

"If we want to get rid of Dorian, we have to get rid of Twist," she said.

***

In a few days, I had recovered but Silva and I had gotten into the habit of lagging behind the cart so that we had a chance to talk together. We took it in turns to tell each other our stories. I told her about my life in Mottle and the adventures that I had had with Arky, Gumber, and Jenna, while she told me about all the different places the troupe had performed in over the years.

Her best stories were about how they had travelled by boat across the Sea of Wrack to perform in other lands. Even now, it still made my head spin, thinking about a world that was so much bigger than just Mottle and Brackford Market. She had just finished telling me about a city that had been created by people burrowing into the face of the cliff, and how the troupe had performed there in a huge cavern, when I was struck by a brilliant idea.

"Why don't we persuade all these different people to send us an army to help us overthrow Prince Dorian?" I said. "We could pay them with our grain instead of handing it over to him."

"Dorian controls all those other places as well," Silva said. "He sells some of the grain that he takes from your people to the other lands at a low price. If they rebel against him, they run the risk of going hungry."

I was disappointed. For a moment, I had imagined a world beyond the Prince's grasp. My brilliant idea shriveled up and died.

***

Soon autumn had taken a firm hold and was shaking the leaves from the trees. One wet morning, we were trudging through a wood along a track carpeted with damp brown leaves. Our cart was ahead of us and its cartwheels had left us two identical silvery snail trails of crushed soggy leaves to follow.

I had just told Silva the story of how I wound up heading the grain collector's procession into Mottle, and she had laughed at my describing Scour's reaction.

A thought struck me. "My life must seem dull compared to yours," I said.

"Why's that?" she said.

"Well, you've been to all these amazing places and met all these different people," I said. "I've lived in the same village and seen the same people every day of my life, until I joined Ma's troupe."

"I'm envious," she said. She ran a hand through her silver hair and gave me a wan smile.

"Why?" I said. I struggled to find one attractive thing in Mottle that would make her jealous.

"You've had friends," she said. "The troupe is always travelling. We meet lots of people, but we move on before we ever get to know them."

I had not thought of that. It also hit me that I was now in the same position. I had all these fantastic stories to tell Arky, Gumber, and Jenna, and I imagined them hanging on to my every word, but when was that going to happen?

"Ma said you winter in Russett most years," I said. "Do you have friends there?"

"When we're not performing, I'm working with the rebels," she said.

"Any rebel friends?" I said.

"We don't get to know each other," she said. "That way, if we're captured, we can't betray anyone else."

"Well, we're friends," I said. As soon as I'd said it, I thought, I'm going to feel bad if she turns round and says 'No we're not.'

"Guess I'm stuck with you," she said. She was grinning, so that was all right.

We walked in silence for a bit. I watched the way Silva glided over the leaves on the track in the same way she had glided over the dirt when we had fled Podger and Scrape at Brackford Market.

"You're not doing it right," I said. "I'll show you."

I kicked my feet deep into the fallen leaves as I walked and the leaves rose up and fell either side of me, like they were bits of earth and I was the blade of a plough.

Silva joined in, laughing, and we became a pair of leaf ploughs, spraying the leaves from our path.

***

We rounded a bend in the track, ploughing through the leaves, and almost walked into the back of our cart.

"Oh look, it's the Woodcutter's Babes," Crag said, sneering. "Good of you to join us."

The cart was bogged down. The wheels had sunk down almost to their axles in the mud. Grunter had joined Thespian between the shafts of the cart, while Ma and Elba stood on either side. Crag was wedging thin strips of tree bark in front of each wheel.

Crag moved to the back of the cart, and Silva and I joined him there. Crag's blonde hair was streaked with dirt. He'd need to rinse it before he played the hero in our next performance.

"On the count of three," Ma said. "One, two, three."

I pushed with all my might. The cart lurched forwards, and the cartwheels crunched over the tree bark.

"Keep going," Ma called.

I kept pushing, my feet slipping and sliding in the mud.

"We're clear," Grunter called out.

I stopped pushing and sank to my knees, gasping for breath.

"Good work, everyone," Ma said. "I thought we might be stuck for good there."

"What a relief," Crag spat. "We don't want to miss out on performing in the villages of Rotting Cabbage, Stinking Hovel, and Dead Sheep."

"Is there a problem, Crag?" Ma said. He had a half smile on his lips but his thin wiry body was taut and he had his arms folded.

"Why don't we cut out all these hopeless little villages stuck at the end of muddy tracks?" Crag said. "It's not as if they can pay us for performing. We should head straight for Russett."

"We have a duty to perform for these people," Ma said, "regardless of whether they can give us anything in return."

"Is anyone else here fed up with working for nothing?" Crag said. "Why are we following this idiotic route?"

"Master Twist sets our route at the beginning of the season," Ma announced in ringing tones. "I'm sorry you think Master Twist is an idiot, Crag."

The words boomed out through the wood, sending birds flapping into the air.

"I never said that," Crag said, turning pale and darting hunted glances around him as though the trees were spies. Ma raised an eyebrow. "Master Twist is a wise and noble fellow," Crag said, treating hedgehogs, dung beetles and any birds still resident in the wood to the full power of his vocal projection. "His choice of route is inspired."

"I'm glad you've recovered your enthusiasm, Crag," Ma said. "Let's press on."

The cart rolled forwards. As Silva and I fell into step behind it, I wondered who was right, Crag or Ma. The people in the villages loved us, and it made me feel great to think we were one of the happiest things that had happened to them all year, but how long could we keep going if we never got paid?

"What are you thinking?" Silva said.

"Nothing," I said. I didn't want her to know that I doubted her father.

***

It was late autumn when we finally saw signs that we were getting close to the city of Russett. We were trudging through a wood where only a few withered brown leaves still clung to the trees. We emerged from it, and in front of us was a wide river. Our track led down to a well-made road that ran beside it.

"That's the river Brack," Silva said. "We follow it for a couple of days until we reach Russett."

"Is that Brack like in Brackford?" I said.

"It's the same river," she said.

I thought of the river dawdling through Brackford, so

slow it had time to get covered in slime, and now here it was, far wider and flowing briskly.

The road was busy but the river was busier. Men with poles were steering rafts laden with sacks and boxes through the water. Everyone was heading in the direction of Russett. Winter was fast approaching; bits of it were arriving with each cold flurry of rain, and people who moved about the country during the rest of the year were now looking for a place to shelter together.

I was excited because I had never seen a city before. So far our route had taken us through villages and small towns that were no bigger than Brackford.

***

At midday of the next day, a fine clear day with just a trace of warmth from a pale late-autumn sun, we arrived at Fledge, the last village before Russett. We performed there and they fed us bowls of fish soup. I was excited that we were now so close to the city.

Soon after we left Fledge, Ma brought our cart to a halt beside the road. "Let's take our first view of Russett," he said.

"Seen it," Crag said. "I'll stay and watch the cart."

The rest of us climbed to the summit of a small grassy hill. As we reached the top, we caught a breeze coming from the direction of the city. Grunter was a little way ahead of me. He sniffed the air and turned to me with a contented smile on his face.

"The Russett Welcoming Committee," he announced.

I took a deep breath. My eyes watered. My throat constricted and I gagged for breath. I was scared. Sweat broke out on my forehead. My hands trembled. The smell was vile but I had no idea why it frightened me.

"The glorious smell of rotting animals, stewed in their own poo and mixed with putrid vegetables," Elba said with a happy sigh, putting her arm around Grunter's waist. "It's how they tan the animal skins."

"Russett is famous for its skins and dyes," Ma said.

"And its pong," Silva added. "Are you alright, Keth?" She had noticed my reaction.

"Foul smell," I said, shivering and putting my sleeve across my nose and mouth.

"You'll get used to it," Silva said. "When we leave in spring, you'll miss it."

"Fresh air has no taste to it," Grunter said.

"This is the taste of home," Elba said.

From the top of the hill, I had my first view of Russet, once I'd blinked the tears from my eyes. It was built on several small hills with the river making a loop around their base. The summit of the tallest hill was crowned by a golden palace that gleamed behind high white stone walls. It commanded a view of the city, the river and all the surrounding countryside.

A gray stone wall dotted with guard towers surrounded the city. Behind the wall, houses were crammed together. Silva had explained to me what a lake was. The city was like a lake of houses and the city wall was a dam that prevented them from flowing out and spreading across the fields.

From where we stood, the red and gray rooftops seemed to form a lid over the city except for one hill on the opposite side of the city to the palace, which was topped with green.

"What's the green bit?" I asked Silva.

"The dead garden," she said.

The road we were on was on the opposite side of the river to the city. I traced its path, winding beside the river until it crossed over on a magnificent stone bridge and entered the city through a large gate tower. I counted the bridge arches, nine in total.

Some distance beyond the bridge, boats were moored in the middle of the river and at a stone quayside. Smaller boats darted about the river like flies skating on top of a pond. These smaller boats had a man standing on the back of them, holding a long oar in the water.

"Where's the sea?" I asked Silva.

"Two hour's walk beyond the city takes you to Brackmouth," she said, "where the Brack meets the sea."

The others wondered back down the hill. I stayed looking at the river that led to the sea and beyond that to strange kingdoms. The thought made me giddy, and I sucked in a deep breath. Big mistake. I was hit with the full force of the vile stink. It filled me up with fear and left me spluttering and coughing.

Silva turned back to look at me and raised her left eyebrow. I stumbled down the hill to join her.

Why was I so afraid of a smell? Perhaps I was nervous because I was coming close to my enemy Prince Dorian.

***

The cart rolled forwards but I did not follow the others straight away. I was shaken by my reaction to the smell and I wanted a moment to calm down. They disappeared around a bend in the road and I was surprised to find that it was Crag, rather than Silva, who remained with me.

"The stench of Russett is the stench of opportunity," Crag said. "Ma is a fool, performing for people who can't pay him. This is where the rich folk live. It's our chance to get noticed by them."

"Ma keeps us fed," I said. I resented Crag's disloyalty.

"How many rings does Ma have on his fingers?" Crag said.

I thought about it. "Two. One on the left, one on the right."

"He had three last season," Crag said, "and he'll be down to one soon. The troupe won't survive much longer."

"Why are you telling me this?" I said.

"You've done a nice job of getting your feet under the table," Crag said.

"What?" I gave Crag a puzzled look.

"Playing the part of Ma's dead son," Crag said, "and chumming up with his daughter. It's clever but it won't do you any good when Ma goes broke. If the two of us worked together, we could make it big in Russett."

The way Crag's mind worked was sickening. I was furious and I threw a punch at him. He dodged back and the blow missed.

"Damage my face and I'll slit your throat," Crag hissed with alarm. He broke off and strode away from me.

I gave him a head start then followed him.

"What happened between you and Crag?" Silva whispered to me, when I rejoined the troupe.

"Nothing," I said. "We were just getting to know each other better."

***

The road to Russett took us beside the river and passed harvested fields, now muddy and waiting to be sown with seed in spring. We approached the bridge and turned onto it, joining a queue of carts waiting to get into the city. The gate tower at the far end of the bridge loomed over us. It had a stone archway through which the carts were passing.

I ran to the side of the bridge nearest the sea. I was disappointed to find that the boats and the stone quay were hidden by a bend in the river. The opposite side of the river to the city had no buildings, and the land was used for grazing. The muddy riverbank sloped up to lush grassy fields dotted with cows.

I looked down at the water. It was flowing briskly beneath the bridge and churning up against the stone arches.

"Tide's coming in," Silva said as she joined me.

"What's a tide?" I said.

"The sea goes in and comes out twice a day," Silva said. "When it comes in, it pushes water up the river, and when it goes out, it sucks it back down again."

I was impressed. This sea was something to be reckoned with.

***

As each cart entered or left the city, it was searched by guards. We edged our way forwards in the queue, moving out of the sunlight into the shadow cast by the gate tower, where the air became chill. At last, we reached the archway and two guards jumped on to the back of our cart and began poking at our belongings. One guard stank of stale sweat and he had damp yellow rings under the armpits of his uniform. He was searching our costume hamper, thrusting his hands deep inside.

"What do you reckon to this?" He pulled out the silver crown made of painted wood, decorated with red glass beads. I recognized it from our stop in Grindle, when I had just joined the troupe. It was the crown Dawyn had been trying on when he collapsed.

"Reckon it would suit you," the other guard said, looking up from where he had been rummaging in our blankets. He had a lazy eye so it was hard to tell where he was looking. "Try it on."

"I am king," the sweaty guard announced, holding the crown high above his head.

"Careful," Ma said in a stage whisper and put a finger to his lips. "Only licensed players and Prince Dorian are allowed to say that and wear a crown. Anyone else gets executed for treason."

The sweaty guard quickly tossed the crown back into the hamper and shut the lid. He and his mate jumped off the cart and waved us through.

10 THE NIGHTMARE CROWN

We entered Russett through the gate in the wall and were immediately surrounded by houses. They were crammed together with no space between them, except for wormy little alleyways. The fronts of the houses reared up and jutted out over the street, cutting out the sunlight and leaving us in cold shadow.

"You two get on the back of the cart and keep an eye on our possessions," Ma said to Silva and me.

We climbed up. It was extra weight for Thespian to haul but the street was cobbled and we were moving slowly because of all the other carts ahead of us. Grunter walked at the front of the cart with Elba while Ma and Crag brought up the rear.

Gutters filled with stinking rubbish ran down both sides of the street. Ahead of us, a three-legged dog hobbled over to the gutter and nosed at the filth. It squatted and pooped. A small boy dressed in rags gave a cry of delight and darted between the carts in the direction of the dog, who limped away in alarm. The boy scooped up the droppings and placed them in a canvas sack hanging from his shoulder.

"That's disgusting," I said.

"The tanners pay good money for dog poop," Silva said. "They use it to tan the animal skins."

"No wonder this city smells like it does," I said.

"The boy earns a loaf of bread for a full sack," Silva said.

"I hope he washes his hands before he eats it," I said.

"Look sharp," Ma shouted at us.

We swung round. A woman was leaning out of an upstairs window and dangling a little boy, no more than three years old, by his ankles above our cart. He had raised the lid of our costume hamper with one pudgy little hand and with the other, he had pulled out the shabby silver crown that the guard at the gate had been fooling with.

The woman yanked the little boy back through the window and ducked out of sight. I bounded across the cart, planted my foot on the cart rail, and launched myself at the window. I thumped against the window sill, knocking the breath out of me. I gasped for air then pulled myself through the window into the building.

I landed on the floor of an empty room that stank of pee. The door was open and I heard footsteps inside the building. I scrambled up and dashed after them. I emerged onto a landing smeared with dirt and covered with bits of plaster that had fallen from the walls. A rickety staircase led up to the next floor. I saw the skirts of the woman disappearing from sight as she climbed it.

I sprinted for the stairs. I put my hand on the banister and the rotten wood splintered in my grasp. I stumbled, regained my balance, and bounded up the stairs. I emerged onto another landing. The woman was at the far end in front of an open window. She was going to climb out of it.

"Stop," I yelled.

She turned to me. The skin was drawn tight over the bones of her face and her arms were thin as twigs. She clutched the little boy in one hand and the crown in the other. She needed both hands to climb out of the window. She put the crown on her head, and her body sagged. They were going to fall out of the window. The little boy screamed, kicked out his legs, and pushed against the window frame. The woman fell back onto the landing. The crown rolled off her head, down the landing and stopped half way between me and them.

The little boy bit his lower lip and stared at the crown. He was thinking. Did he stay with the woman or make a grab for it?

He looked at me then lowered his gaze to the woman. He nudged her with his foot. She groaned. He smiled.

I walked forwards and picked up the crown. A small, flat, shiny brass disc on a chain around the woman's neck had slipped from beneath her thin brown dress. It reminded me of the one owned by the obnoxious Dawyn whom I had teased at Grindle.

"Keth, are you alright?" Ma was shouting from the foot of the stairs. He must have climbed in after me.

The woman pulled herself into a sitting position and rested her back against the wall. The little boy placed himself in front of her and growled at me. I wished I had a slice of bread or something to give them.

"Keth." Ma's voice was urgent.

"I'm fine," I called back.

I retreated to the top of the stairs. The woman stroked the little boy's hair with a thin hand, showing streaks of pale white skin beneath the dirt. With a flick of her other hand, she popped her medallion back under her dress.

I descended the stairs. Ma was waiting at the bottom. He held out his hand and I gave him the crown. I wasn't going to try it on. I had seen its effects twice now, and I wanted answers from Ma.

"What is special about this crown?" I whispered. "People collapse when they put it on."

"We're blocking traffic," Ma said and walked back to the room overlooking the street.

"We never use it in our shows," I said.

"Don't want Crag collapsing when he puts it on," Ma said.

We were by the window overlooking the street. Grunter was standing at the back of the cart with his arms folded. A long queue of carts with angry, red-faced carters had backed up behind us.

Ma and I lowered ourselves down from the window into the cart. Ma replaced the crown in the costume hamper, burying it deep down.

"Sorry about that, Ma," Silva said. "We got distracted."

"You and Keth walk behind; Crag and I will take your place," Ma said.

Silva and I got down from the cart. She was bright red in the face, making a sharp contrast with her silver hair. Grunter went back to the front of the cart, and we set off again.

I was shocked by the dirt and dishonesty of the city. In the country we had nothing, but we kept that nothing clean, and we didn't try and steal anyone else's bit of nothing. Then again, if I was as desperate as that woman and her little boy, perhaps I would be thieving as well.

***

Silva and I trudged behind the cart, not speaking. After

a short time, we emerged into a square. "This is now called Dorian's Square," Silva said.

In the center of the square was a statue of a handsome man wearing a crown and a flowing cloak, and resting his hands on the hilt of a huge sword. The statue was twice as high as an adult man and made of a white stone that glowed in the sunlight.

A bald man with a droopy moustache was standing on a rickety ladder that was propped up against the chest of the statue. He was polishing the stone with a cloth and picking off the bits of bird poop from the edges of the crown.

Three young boys were crouched at the foot of the statue. They were thin and their faces were gaunt. The middle one had a shock of white hair. They sat listlessly and made no eye contact with each other or anyone else. I guessed they were starving and had no energy to move.

"That marble statue is Prince Dorian welcoming visitors to his city," Silva said. She scowled at it.

"Shame he forgot to feed his welcome committee," I whispered, looking at the boys. I was so angry my voice came out like a hiss of steam. How dare this wicked man dress up in fine clothes and reduce the rest of us to starvation. I hated the smug stone smirk of the statue, and I hated Prince Dorian.

I eyed the rubbish and filth in the gutters that ran along the sides of the square. Ammunition. I could give the statue cleaner a bit more work to do.

"Calm down, Keth," Silva said, reading my mind and squeezing my arm tightly. "Let's think this one through. Keth throws dirt at the statue. Prince Dorian is mildly irritated. Keth is executed. The kids continue to starve to death. Who wins? Prince Dorian, and possibly the statue cleaner if he gets paid overtime but I doubt it."

Reluctantly, I had to agree with her but I was seething inside. I took a deep breath and tried to calm down. Prince Dorian would pay for this, but not today.

***

We left the square and moved along a street filled with shops full of women's clothing. The clothes were hung on straw dummies so that you saw how a person would look in them. Three shops specialized in hats, and one shop sold nothing but gloves. The next street had similar shops but this time filled with clothing for men. I had never seen so much clothing for sale.

After the clothing shops, we walked down a street with shops that had empty metal hooks in the window.

"Are these hook-sellers?" I asked Silva.

She jutted her narrow chin out at me and widened her eyes, which was her 'are you trying to make a joke, Keth?' expression.

I continued to look puzzled, and she relented.

"These are butcher's shops, Keth," she said. "They hang the animal carcasses on the hooks. It's a bad sign when they have no meat to sell."

We turned into a street where the shop windows revealed wooden shelves filled with empty trays.

"I'm guessing these aren't tray shops," I said.

"These are bakers," she said. "The bread probably sold out first thing this morning."

"This is a strange city," I said. "Plenty of fancy clothes and no food."

"Dorian lets the guild masters and the merchants keep some of their wealth," she said. "They buy the clothes."

I shivered as I caught a putrid whiff from the tanneries.

"You don't like that smell, do you?" she said.

"At least the rich and the poor get to share it," I said.

"Not quite," she said. "The richer you are, the higher up the hill you live, because you're more likely to catch a fresh breeze and avoid the stench."

I grinned at this because the last couple of streets we had taken had been climbing upwards.

"Don't smile too soon," she said, reading my mind. "We turn downhill shortly. We're heading for Crib Street, where all the actors stay."

"Everyone who does the same thing lives in the same street," I said. "It's like the city is a lot of villages sewn together, with a village of butchers, a village of bakers, and a village of actors."

Silva shrugged.

"And a village of rebels?" I said.

"Not if people blab out loud about it," she said.

As Silva had predicted, we turned into a street that ran downhill. I put my sleeve across my nose as the tannery stink grew stronger.

***

Ma called us to a halt at a street corner, opposite a ramshackle inn with faded green paint peeling from its rotten wood.

"It's called the Green Room Inn," Silva said to me. "Crib Street is the street off to our right."

"Positions everyone," Ma said, climbing down from the cart. "Silva, at the front with me; you as well, Keth."

Ma, Silva, and I moved to the front of our group, followed by Elba and Grunter leading Thespian. Crag remained on the back of the cart.

"Ma likes to make an entrance," Silva whispered to

me.

"When I give the count, we sing 'Happy Days and Jolly Plays'," Ma said.

We turned into Crib Street, Ma counted us in, and we sang our song. People came out of doors to greet us. Ma and Silva walked at the front of the cart, shaking hands with everyone and introducing me as the troupe's new fool.

A tall man with a blotchy red nose and a mane of gray hair emerged from a house, took off his wide-brimmed, black felt hat with three blue feathers, and made us a sweeping bow.

"Charmed to see you and your splendid troupe, good sir," the man said to Ma.

"This is Master Garrick, the renowned tragedian," Ma said. "Master Garrick, this is Keth, our new fool."

"The wisdom of the fool is the delight of the wise man," Garrick said.

I wondered what a tragedian did but we were already moving on.

"Craggy, yoo-hoo, Craggy," a woman's voice trilled.

I looked back and saw a pretty, blonde lady about Crag's age leaning out of an upstairs window. Crag balanced on the rail of the cart and kissed her on the lips. He looked smug as the crowd applauded his balance and gallantry, and even I had to admit he was impressive.

Crag's moment of glory lasted only until the wooden shutters of the next window along flew open and smacked him in the face. He fell back into the cart.

"Craggy, where are you, Craggy?" A pretty, black-haired lady of Crag's age leaned out of the window. "Oh whoops," she added when she saw what she had done.

Everyone roared with laughter. Silva was laughing so hard, her silver hair flew up and down as her head shook.

"Oh whoops," I whispered to Silva with a girly lisp, and she cracked up even more.

We continued our progress. With every step, Elba embraced a different woman friend. Several of them had kids with them. The older kids fussed over Thespian while the younger kids hung off Grunter's arms and squealed with delight as he bounced them up and down.

Thespian plodded on. He had seen it all before.

The troupe was popular and I was proud to be accepted as part of it. I belonged. It was a wonderful feeling.

We stopped outside number 37, a narrow wooden house with a polished black door. Ma knocked on the door. We waited. The door opened and a fat lady filled the entrance. She had a pear-shaped face, topped with pale violet curls piled up high on her head. She wore a black dress and a bright red woolen shawl; the dress was long and got wider the closer to the ground it got, so it looked as though she was peering out from the top of a tent.

"My dear Madam Patwig, do you have rooms available for my troupe?" Ma said.

"My dear sir, by great good fortune, we have," the lady replied.

Silva grinned. I guessed this was a ritual they played out every year.

"This is our new fool, Keth," Ma said.

Madame Patwig hugged me to her bosom, almost suffocating me. I now knew where Ma had picked up that gag from.

Grunter led Thespian and our cart around to a lane that ran by the back of the house, while the rest of us were ushered through the front door.

***

After the noise of our welcome to Crib Street, the silence in the hallway of Madame Patwig's lodging house was a contrast.

"Would you give Keth a tour of the house, Silva dear," Madame Patwig said.

"With pleasure," Silva said. "Come on, Keth, we'll start with a peep in the parlor."

Silva swished down the hall in her long, black skirt, doing her impersonation of lady-like. She opened a door and the scent of dried flowers wafted out. I didn't mind; it was better than the tannery stink.

The parlor was the room at the front of the house. It was cluttered with ornaments in glass-fronted cupboards and on little tables covered with lace doilies. China horses vied for space with blank-faced porcelain dolls. Odd shaped vases were filled with dead grass and bowls decorated with bright swirling colors were filled with pink petals. Plates stood on their rims, displaying pictures of ducks, flowers, and fat little girls with milk pails.

Two stuffed armchairs stood in front of a fireplace filled with logs, unlit. Above the fireplace, and now looking sooty, was a painting of a man with a ferocious moustache. He was dressed in a red uniform and held a gold saber above his head.

"This is where Ma entertains visitors," Silva said.

I wondered how they managed to move around the cluttered room without knocking things over. "Who is the soldier?" I asked, pointing to the painting.

"My late husband, Colonel Patwig," Madame Patwig said from the hallway.

"Was he at Crouchers Hollow?" I asked.

"No dear, he fell into the river drunk, and drowned

twenty years ago," she said.

Silva led me on to the next room, heading towards the back of the house. This room had polished wooden floorboards and was empty. "Madame Patwig keeps it like that just for us," Silva said. "It's our rehearsal space."

At the back of the house was the kitchen. It was warm and smelled of freshly baked bread. "My favorite room," Silva said.

"Mine too." I nodded and grinned at her.

The kitchen contained a wooden table with six chairs. A large iron stove sat close to one wall with a wicker basket filled with logs set beside it. Pots and pans were hung from hooks in the whitewashed walls. Stacked on shelves were mugs and plain plates, with no paintings of ducks or flowers. The floor was laid with stone flags.

Between the rehearsal room and the kitchen, a narrow, wooden staircase ascended to the upstairs rooms.

"Madame Patwig has her lodgings on the first floor," Silva said. "Ma and I have one of the rooms on the second floor, and Elba and Grunter have the other. Crag sleeps in the attic.

I noticed that Keth was missing from the list of names of those sleeping upstairs.

"I'll sleep on the kitchen floor," I offered.

"Ragamuffin, my cat, would fight you over that," Madame Patwig said, entering the kitchen together with Ma.

A deep-throated purr came from beneath the kitchen table and Ragamuffin sauntered out. He was a large black cat with white socks and several old battle scars across his face. He looked at me, unsheathed his claws, and scraped them over the stone flags. I might not fight you now, he seemed to say, but in the middle of the night when you're sound asleep, that's another story, laddie.

"He's such a big old softie," Madame Patwig said.

"I've put you in the stable, Keth," Ma said. "It has a loft filled with hay and it's warm and comfortable."

"Is that okay, Keth?" Madame Patwig said.

She looked anxious, and I didn't want to upset her. "The stable is fine," I said. "I've been sleeping under a cart since last harvest, so this is a step up in the world for me." And I'll be able to slip out at night and help the rebels, I thought to myself.

"We'll complete our tour," Silva said. A back door opened from the kitchen into a long narrow back yard containing two rickety-looking wooden buildings. "The stable is the building by the back gate and the wash house is the building nearest us," Silva said.

The back gate opened and Grunter appeared, leading Thespian, who was no longer attached to the cart.

"Can we give you a hand?" Silva called.

"You could help with the cart," Grunter said, putting Thespian in the stable.

***

The cart was out in the lane. We began unloading our things and bringing them into the lodging house. This would make the cart lighter and easier to maneuver into the yard. Ma and Elba joined us.

"Where's Crag?" Ma said.

"He's busy peering into his mirror," Elba said. "He's terrified that he's scarred for life because of that crack from the window shutter. I tried to reassure him it will heal without a mark but he won't listen."

"Oh whoops, poor Craggy," I whispered to Silva.

She sniggered and snorted through her nose.

"Stop that, both of you," Ma said, but he was having

trouble keeping his face straight. "Carry the costume hamper inside."

Together Silva and I lifted the costume hamper down from the cart and carried it into the lodging house, leaving it in the rehearsal room. Once we got everything off the cart, we hauled it through the gate into the yard. This involved lots of sweating and getting cross with each other as it was a tight squeeze.

Having done that, the others went upstairs to unpack their things and settle into their new quarters. My unpacking was a short and undemanding task. I put my blanket in the stable loft. I had a good supply of straw to keep me warm and comfortable at night. Below me, Thespian did his bit to warm up the stable with some vigorous farting.

I mooched back into the lodging house; nothing edible was on display in the kitchen. I thought I would have another glance at the parlor. As I walked through the rehearsal room, I was drawn to the costume hamper.

No one was about. I lifted the lid of the hamper. Ma had buried the crown deep down when he had replaced it in the hamper so I rummaged for it. At first, I did not find it but eventually I touched one of its sharp points and dragged it out.

Close up, the crown was a sorry-looking thing. The silver paint was flaking off the wood, and in the dingy light of the rehearsal room, the red glass beads looked dull and sad. On the two occasions I had seen people put on the crown, they had collapsed but they were otherwise unhurt. The closer I was to the floor, the less painful would be any fall. I sat cross-legged with the crown in my lap and my back resting against the hamper.

A little voice inside me told me that what I was doing was stupid. I ignored it and put the crown on my head.

I sat cross-legged, resting my back against a stone on the summit of a grass-covered hill. Dotted around the hill were sheep, munching away on the grass. A track led down from the summit in the direction of some stone buildings with thatched roofs at the foot of the hill

The air was warm and the sky was blue, without a single cloud in it. It must have been midday as the sun was directly overhead.

I set off down the track. A fold in the land soon took the track into a gully with steep, grass-covered sides that blocked my view. As I strolled along, I became aware of a dull drumming sound. It was rapidly getting louder and coming from behind me. I heard a terrified bleat, like the blaring of a horn.

I looked back. A wall of stampeding sheep was heading towards me. I started to climb the sides of the gully. Sheep launched themselves from the top of the gully, tumbling down the steep sides. One struck me, knocking the breath from me and leaving me lying flat on my back on the track. The stampeding sheep were almost upon me. I leaped to my feet and fled down the track. I skidded around a bend and hit a net.

The net stretched from one side of the gully to the other. The strands of the net were like ropes coated with glue. I thrashed my arms and legs but they were stuck. The roar of the stampeding sheep filled my ears. I braced myself as they shot around the corner and slammed into me and the net.

The net stretched and bulged but it held firm. More and more sheep piled into the back of those already trapped. A great crush formed. I struggled to breathe because of the weight of the sheep pressing against me.

I craned my head around and looked at the heaving white mass trapped in the net. A giant black spider the size of a cow watched us from the top of the gully. Eight round yellow circles of different sizes sat above its massive jaws. They were eyes, and they were looking at me. I had no air in my lungs to scream with.

The spider tensed its legs then sprang high into the air, landing in the middle of the struggling mass of sheep. It ripped at sheep with its jaws, hurling them to the sides, while stomping at the ones behind it with its hairy legs, pushing them backwards. It was trying to reach me.

Two men in brown smocks came running along the track from the direction of the buildings. They each carried a long wooden pole with burning rags on the end.

The pressure from the sheep on my chest lifted enough for me to swallow a thin trickle of air. The spider was almost upon me. It raised its two front legs and reared up, ready to plunge its jaws into me.

One man thrust his pole through the web at the spider. The burning rags stank of tar; my skin was scorched as they passed me. The spider rocked back then lunged at me. The other man fended it off with his burning pole. The strands of the web smoldered, giving off a sweet sickly smell.

The men were twins. They had identical smooth faces with clear blue eyes that showed no signs of panic or fear in fighting the spider.

The spider lunged again. One man stuck his pole in the biggest of its eyes. The eye exploded and the burning rags were doused with yellow liquid, extinguishing them with a hiss.

The air was full of the sickly smell of the burning web. Flames now danced along its strands and burned my arms, legs, and chest. I screamed in pain.

"You idiot, Keth," Ma snapped. His face floated above me.

My eyes focused. I was in the rehearsal room, slumped against the costume hamper. Ma stood in front of me, holding the crown in one hand. We heard footsteps. Ma tossed the crown into the hamper a moment before Madame Patwig entered the room.

"What was that scream?" Madame Patwig said.

"Keth fell asleep and had a nightmare," Ma said.

I felt my skin; it was unburned. I smelled the air and only caught a faint whiff of dried flowers from Madame Patwig. The other troupe members hurried in.

"It's alright," Ma said, helping me up. I was groggy and he had to put his arm under my shoulder to support me. "The excitement of seeing a city for the first time got to him."

I was too dazed to say anything to contradict him. By the time Ma had guided me out to the stables and helped me up into the loft, my wits had returned. "What's that crown?" I said.

"It's a crown of nightmares," Ma said.

"Can you die in a nightmare?" I said.

"Would you like to put it on and try again?" Ma hissed. "You don't have the brains you were born with."

I had not seen Ma so furious since I'd danced on stage at Crouchers Hollow. A purple vein like a stiff cord throbbed in his forehead. He wasn't the only one who was angry.

"If this crown is so dangerous it makes people drop dead from nightmares, what are you doing carrying it in our costume hamper?" I said. "In the 'who has no brains at all' contest, I'm only an apprentice, you're the master."

This was a bad thing to say but the words had left my mouth before I'd had a chance to think about them.

Ma's lips twitched with the ghost of a smile. "You push your luck, Keth," he said, shaking his head.

"Why are you carrying the crown?" I persisted.

"I'm looking after it for an old friend," Ma said then frowned. "It's meant to stay hidden. I'd better find a safer place to keep it."

"What happens when I next go to sleep?" I said. I had visions of returning to being caught in a giant spider's burning web.

"Nothing," Ma said, "unless you're wearing the crown."

I wanted to ask some more questions but Ma put a finger to his lips. We heard a faint rustle. There was a knock on the stable door and Madame Patwig poked her head in.

"I thought Keth might appreciate a warm drink," she said.

She entered, carrying a mug filled with a hot liquid that smelled of hay. I drank it and soon afterwards, I fell asleep. Silva came out and woke me when it was time to go in for the evening meal. If I dreamed, I forgot them.

11 INVITATION TO THE PALACE

That evening we ate our meal together in the kitchen. Crag joined us, sporting a large plaster just above his right eye. It was our normal trail rations, which I thought was disappointing but no one commented on it.

After the plates were cleared away, Ma said that he had to go out.

"Remember to be back before curfew," Madame Patwig said.

"What's curfew?" I said.

"It's a bell that rings at eleven o'clock," Silva said.

"What is eleven o'clock?" I said.

Crag burst out laughing and looked smug.

"I'm from a little village near Brackford," I said. "We don't have one o'clock, never mind eleven of them."

"I wish you were this funny on stage," Crag said.

"That's enough," Ma told him. "The curfew bell is rung at the same time every night. After that, everyone is supposed to stay off the streets. Guards patrol the streets and if they catch anyone out of doors, they flog them. Just before dawn the curfew bell rings again and you're allowed to be out in the streets once more."

I went to bed soon after that. I was not tired but I was a bit hurt that my ignorance had been shown up and I wanted to be alone. Thespian farted as I entered the stables, but I took that as a sign of welcome.

I wrapped myself in my blanket and curled up in the hay, my head filled with images of the giant spider. I tried to get rid of them by thinking about all the new things that I'd seen in the city. I imagined I was back with my mum in our hut in Mottle, and I was describing it all to her. A dull ache settled in my stomach. I wished she was here to experience them with me.

Eventually, I fell asleep.

***

Next morning, we gathered in the kitchen for a breakfast that consisted of hot milk, porridge, eggs, and fresh bread. This is more like it, I thought. As Ma reached out for his mug, I noticed that the ring on his right hand had disappeared. He must have sold it the previous evening, I realized. I glanced at Crag, and he winked at me. The food didn't taste so good after that.

It was a fine day, and after breakfast, Silva tied a rope between posts in the backyard. I helped her carry out the costume hamper and we attached all our costumes to the rope with wooden pegs. She called this airing them.

I checked the costume hamper. The nightmare crown had disappeared.

Silva moved from costume to costume, examining each of them and making a note, with chalk on a piece of slate, about what needed repairing.

138

"Is that reading?" I said. I wanted to know what this reading was all about. I thought being able to do it might make me look smarter. I was still a little sore about all the 'o'clock' stuff from the previous evening.

"I'll show you reading when we've finished," she said. "Ma wants me to give you a lesson every morning." Once she had checked all the costumes, we went into the kitchen. She got some ash from the stove and spread it on the stone flag in front of it.

"Won't Madame Patwig be cross?" I said.

"I've promised her I'll sweep it up afterwards," Silva said, pointing to a dustpan and brush hanging up behind the basket of logs. "And I told her you'd clean the stove from top to bottom once it has cooled down enough."

She drew some marks in the ash. "That's your name. Keth," she said.

She got me to repeat the marks she had made, holding my hand to guide me. The stove was still hot and this was the warmest place in the house. I decided learning to read wasn't too bad.

I got her to write her own name and she was part way through helping me write it when we were interrupted by shouts coming from the street. "Twist is coming! Twist is coming!"

I leaped up, excited. I was going to see one of my enemies in the flesh. "Let's go!" I said.

"Calm down, Keth," Silva said, putting a hand on my shoulder. "Twist is dangerous. If you're strong, he'll break you just to show you he can. If you're weak, he'll take pleasure in hurting you."

"How should I behave then?" I asked. "You're not giving me many choices."

"Be yourself, except think before you do anything," she said.

***

We joined the rest of our troupe outside the front door. Grunter and Elba stood shoulder to shoulder, holding hands. Crag lounged against the wall; he had removed his plaster, and his skin showed a slight bruise. Ma stood, feet spread, hands on hips. He indicated Silva and I should stand either side of him. That's in case he needs to defend us, I thought. A sharp sense of unease ran through me.

I looked along the street and saw that actors were busy stretching and loosening up their bodies. I heard Garrick gabbling tongue twisters to loosen up his tongue. The two pretty ladies responsible for Crag's downfall on the previous day had taken out small leather cases and were briskly applying color to each other's faces.

"Why is everyone so excited?" I asked. I didn't believe they were all rebels greeting an enemy.

"He might be offering work," Crag said.

"Or coming to arrest someone," Silva added.

This was just like when the grain collector came to our village every year. All the actors had come out of actor village to meet their master and be judged. All the power rests with Twist, I thought, and we are just waiting for him like flies or sheep stuck in a spider's web.

Silence fell when Twist appeared at the end of the street. He was small and alone. I thought he would have arrived with a fanfare and an entourage, including several meaty guards of the 'thump first ask questions later' variety.

He was dressed in a tight-fitting yellow-and-black checked costume that covered his body, arms, legs, and head. His face was thin, sour, and rat-like. Three floppy yellow and black horns dangled from the head of his costume. The horns had bells on, and he had bells around his ankles and wrists so he jingled as he walked. He carried a short stick with what looked like an animal head on top.

"Twist always appears in that costume," Ma whispered. "It's called motley."

"And he always carries his stupid stick," Silva added.

"I'm looking for talented actors to perform at the palace tonight," Twist announced. "I've come to the wrong street." He did not shout but his words filled up the space and everyone on the street heard them clearly. Many of the actors dutifully tittered. Our troupe remained silent. Crag looked as though, with the exception of himself, he thought Twist was right.

Twist stalked down the street, jingling as he went. Once I saw him standing next to other people, I realized just how small he was. He would have only come up to my chest, and that was giving him the benefit of his horns.

The animal head on the end of Twist's stick turned and tilted, opening and closing bulging eyes. It was a toad's head. Every now and then, he would tap an actor with the stick and say, "Palace tonight."

Garrick was chosen and Twist moved on to the two ladies who had been putting on makeup. The toad head leered at them.

"Palace tonight," Twist said and the ladies shuddered as the toad stick tapped them.

Twist moved on to our little group.

"Greetings, Master Twist," Crag said, stepping forwards and making a low bow.

Twist waited until Crag had reached the lowest point of his bow then raised his foot, placed it on top of Crag's head and pushed Crag over into the dirt. Normally I would have enjoyed seeing Crag wallowing in the mud, but now it chilled me. Crag was too frightened to be angry. He stayed on his knees with a forced smile stretched across his mud-stained face.

"Come now, Master Twist, if you don't want the goods, don't maul them," Ma said.

Twist glared at Ma then fastened his bloodshot eyes on me. "What's that, Toadie?" Twist said. He held the toad head on the end of its stick to his ear. "You've never seen a turnip on legs before. It must be a novelty act." He shoved the toad head close to my face. Its eyes bulged and goggled. "What are you on stage, Turnip?" Twist asked.

"A fool," I said. I was pleased that my voice sounded normal.

"An unfunny one," Twist sneered. "The only way you could make me laugh would be to hurt yourself badly."

A pink tongue shot out of the mouth of the toad head and struck me in the eye. I yelped in pain and surprise. I wanted to wrench Twist's stick from his hand and jump up and down on it, and then I would jump up and down on Twist as well. I took a deep breath and fought to stay calm.

"Are you planning to resurrect your tedious 'Ma and her Little Lad routine' with Turnip here?" Twist asked Ma.

"It's very popular with everyone but you, Master Twist," Ma said.

"So is stupidity," Twist spat. "You and Turnip come to the palace tonight."

He tapped Ma on the shoulder with his toad stick. As the toad head came towards me to tap me, its tongue shot out again and hit me in my other eye. I yelped again. I kept calm but made a mental note that Twist would pay for that.

Twist moved on down the street. My eyes stung.

At the end of the street, Twist turned, looked back, and shook his head in disgust before walking out of sight.

***

"We've not finished your reading lesson, Keth," Silva said, and she walked back into the lodging house. I was excited and I skipped down the hall, following Silva back into the kitchen.

"I've never seen inside a palace, let alone performed in one," I said. "My mum would be proud of me. Only a little while ago, I was nobody from a nowhere village, and look at me now."

"You're a nobody who is performing at the palace," Silva said, kneeling in front of the stove.

"I can spell 'amazing comic talent'," I said.

I knelt down beside her and started to spell my name, Keth, in the ash. The joke stalled because I got as far as writing 'Ke' then forgot what the next letter was.

Silva unhooked the brush from behind the basket of logs and held it to her ear. "What's that, Toadie? Keth isn't as smart as he thinks he is," she mimicked Twist's voice and his silly toad stick.

"Are you jealous?" I teased.

"Yes," she said.

I was surprised. I had expected her to deny it.

She leaned forwards and whispered to me, "When you are at the palace, keep your eyes and ears open; observe everything. The rebels struggle to get information from inside the palace."

I had not thought of that.

"You've just remembered whose side you are on," she

grinned.

I went bright red. I would always be a rebel; I had just let success distract me for a moment.

We were interrupted by a delicate cough. Elba was standing by the kitchen door. "Ma wants to see you in the parlor, Keth," she said.

Silva began sweeping the ashes from in front of the stove into the dust pan. "When Ma's finished with you, Keth, don't forget to practice your hilarious 'Keth cleans the stove' routine." Silva smiled sweetly at me.

"I'll polish it so well, I'll be able to see my face in it," I said.

"Only if we get a bigger stove, your head's grown so big," Silva said.

Given a moment, I would have come up with a funny retort, but Elba interrupted us with a less delicate cough. "Ma wants to see you now, Keth," Elba said.

I headed for the parlor.

***

I pushed open the parlor door and entered. Ma stood by the window. The shutters were open but a gauze curtain had been drawn across the opening. I saw the shapes of people passing by in the street.

"The tradition is to knock on the door before entering," Ma said.

"Back in Mottle, we don't have doors," I said. "Except for the barn," I added, "that's got two, side by side. We have a gate for going in and out of the dead garden, but that's just for show. The walls are only waist high."

"Thank you, Keth," Ma said, looking hard at me. He sighed and motioned me to sit in one of the armchairs in front of the fire.

I gingerly navigated my way between the tables clogged with ornaments. I paused because a cabinet of stuffed birds had caught my eye. A jet-black raven with its beak set in a sneer was positioned between a pair of owls and a duck. Try stealing folk's grain from in there, I thought at the raven.

"In your own time, Keth," Ma said.

I jumped then hurried forwards, almost overturning a small table holding a china horses straining at a plough. I reached the safety of an armchair and sat down. Whoever had made it had put in a hard lump just where it would be most uncomfortable. I prodded at the lump with my fingers. "There's an awkward lump in this chair," I said.

"And he's called Keth," Ma replied.

Some days it was a real pain having a master who was a comic.

"Part of my job as your master, Keth, is to educate you," Ma said. He stood over me and rested his hands on his hips so I knew I was in for a lecture. "You have grown up in a little village, and now I am introducing you to a wider world. I have to explain it to you."

"Door shut, knock before entry, got it," I said.

"Try this one," Ma said. "Dorian powerful; soldiers armed; Keth behaves."

He leaned over me, his body tense, and his hands gripping the arms of the chair, gouging the material with his fingers. His thin wiry body and iron-gray hair made me think of a piece of tough old rope.

"I get the message," I said.

"Keth fools around; troupe banned; Keth executed," Ma said. He released the arms of the chair and stood up straight. "Do you give me your word to behave tonight?"

I thought about it. Silva had said that my only job was to keep my eyes and ears open to pick up information for the rebels. I was hardly going to get myself into trouble just doing that.

"I promise," I said.

"I don't know whether to be angry or reassured that you took so long making your mind up," Ma said. "We'll spend some time today going through the 'Ma and her Little Lad' routines."

***

Ma and I spent the rest of the day rehearsing, with two short breaks; one for lunch, and one to help Silva bring the costumes in off the line when rain arrived in the middle of the afternoon.

We brought the costume hamper back into the rehearsal room and Ma kitted me out in a costume he called 'the little sailor boy,' which had a white jacket and blue leggings. According to Ma, all the spoiled little rich boys in the city were dressed like this. The clever thing about the jacket was that it was red on the inside, and if you turned the jacket inside out, you became 'the little drummer boy.' Ma was going to wear his usual red polka dot dress and ginger wig.

At sunset, we put on our costumes and left the house. Ma had arranged to meet the rest of the actors going to the palace outside the Green Room Inn at the end of Crib Street. The rain had stopped and the sun, low in the sky, gave a golden sheen to the puddles of water in the street.

Two of our party were already waiting for us. They were identical twins, young men with slicked back black hair and pointy little waxed moustaches. They were dressed in blue vests and tights.

"We're Jim and Jam." They introduced themselves in unison. "We're acrobats."

They each turned a somersault, again in unison. I applauded. I did somersaults on stage, but only if I had a run up or Grunter tossed me in the air.

A short fat man and a tall thin man hurried along Crib Street to join us.

"These two gentlemen are Mutton and Chop." Ma introduced me to them as they arrived.

"What is it you do?" I asked them.

"We hit each other," Mutton, the short fat one, said in a deep, solemn voice.

"And people laugh at us," Chop, the tall thin one, said. His voice was quiet and serious.

"They are the masters of their art," Ma said, and Chop gave him a gentle, sad smile.

Garrick emerged from the inn, minus his hat. Clutching his arm was a fat lady with a beard, wearing a pink dress.

"I'm Lady Velda," the bearded lady introduced herself.

"Have you forgotten your hat?" I asked Garrick.

"I never wear a hat when I perform, young sir," Garrick said. "The brim casts shadows on my eyes, the windows to my soul."

"We're just waiting on Holly and Molly to make their entrance," Lady Velda said, looking around the group.

As if this was their cue, the two young ladies Twist had singled out earlier emerged into Crib Street and made their way to join us.

"These two ladies are Holly and Molly," Ma said, introducing me to them.

"What a cute little sailor boy." Holly giggled and shook my hand. She was the blonde one. I studied her eyes. They were as sharp as a Brackford Market trader. She only played dumb.

"I used to have a cat with fur the same red as your

hair," Molly said to me. She was the black-haired one. Her eyes were as empty as a beggar's food bowl. She was either genuinely dumb or an even better actor than Holly.

As our party set off for the palace, the sun went down and the temperature fell. It was twilight so we did not need lanterns, but the color was running out of the sky and the buildings looked gray.

Sheltering in doorways were figures dressed in rags. In one doorway, a group of three kids was huddled beneath a single thin blanket. Two of the kids seemed asleep, but the middle one was watching me. He had a long pale face, a shock of white hair and white eyebrows. He seemed familiar somehow.

"Hello," I said.

His eyes went wide, and the two thin bodies, either side of him, stirred beneath the blanket. I wished I had some food with me.

"Come on, Keth." Ma put his arm around my shoulder and bundled me down the street. The rest of our party was already a little way ahead. "You'll get used to sights like that," Ma said. "Soon you won't even notice them. I'm not saying that's right, but it's just how it is."

I wondered if I would be happier if I stopped being aware of starving children.

12 ROYAL PERFORMANCE

As our group of performers climbed towards the palace, the road became steeper, the air fresher, and the shop fronts wider.

The slope eased and we entered a cobbled square. On three sides of the square were tall houses, each a different shade of gray in the last of the twilight. On the fourth side, opposite us, was a high white stone wall, in the center of which were two stone towers with a gate between them, the entrance to the palace.

In the center of the square was a large wooden stage.

"Are we going to perform there?" I asked Ma.

"I hope not." He laughed. "That's where they hold executions."

We crossed the square and made for the gate, which was made of thick oak planks studded with iron nails.

Garrick rapped on the gate, wincing as he bruised his knuckles.

"We are humble actors who are performing at the feast tonight," he announced in ringing tones that everyone in the whole square, if not the whole city, heard.

A bolt was drawn back and a small door built into the gate creaked open. We shuffled into a dark space. I could just make out another gate opposite us. The door shut behind us with a bang. We were lit up and blinded by a lamp lowered through a trap door in the ceiling.

"Let them through," a voice from above us said.

A small door in the second gate creaked open, and we passed through into a large courtyard. A guard shone a lantern into our faces then spat on the ground.

"Follow me," he said.

In the last of the twilight, I saw the outline of the palace building. It was immense. It was at least five storeys high, judging by the shuttered windows, and it was as wide as Crib Street was long. It had a sloping tiled roof and you could have fit all of Mottle in the attic, with room to graze His Lordship and the cows left over.

The guard tramped across the courtyard. Ahead of us, a set of white stone steps flanked by gold railings led up to a pair of huge bronze doors illuminated by the arc of seven flaming torches set above them. Two meaty-looking guards, dressed in polished silver armor, stood to attention in front of the doors.

"Your entrance is around the back," our guard said.

He led us around the back of the palace and we were shown in through a small wooden door.

"This is the entertainment," our guard said, in a tone that suggested he doubted it. He was speaking to a new guard who had appeared at the door.

The new guard wore clean, pale blue livery underneath a polished silver breastplate and he had a silver helmet on his head with a blue plume that matched his livery. He looked as though he was for show, except he was armed with a short sword and a cudgel.

"We'll just check our makeup." Holly giggled.

She and Molly crouched in front of the guard and studied their reflections in his breastplate. The guard didn't crack a smile.

"This way, please," he said, picking up a lantern.

It was good manners that he had put a 'please' on the end but we all knew it was a command.

He marched us along a series of unlit stone passageways until we emerged into a large room, empty of furniture, with flagstones on the floor and white walls. It was dimly lit by a single oil lamp that hung from the ceiling. A guard in the same pale blue livery with a fierce bristling moustache and an even shinier breastplate stood in front of a door in the opposite wall.

We were left in the company of this new guard. "Sit down and stay silent!" the new guard bellowed before we had a chance to speak.

"Chairs would be nice," Garrick said.

"Silence," the guard bellowed, putting his hand on his sword.

I wondered if the guard ever spoke in anything softer than a bellow. We hurried over to the side of the room and sat in the shadows with our backs against the wall.

***

We sat and waited. I examined the walls. They had used thick creamy paint rather than a thin layer of whitewash. I scratched it with my thumbnail and made a little silvery crack in the surface.

We continued to wait. Ma seemed to be dozing. I thought my bum would go numb but it didn't. I touched the flagstones, and they were warm.

We did some more waiting. I wished I'd brought some ash with me so that Ma could give me a reading lesson. I scanned the room looking for a fireplace, warm flagstones but no fire. I thought about asking the guard if I might nip out and find some ash. I looked up at him, and he scowled in my direction. Why put him to the trouble of bellowing 'no'?

Stuck for something to do, Keth? What about a bit more waiting? Bored with waiting? Well, wait a bit longer and watch as nothing happens.

I knew how to write my name and Silva had told me it was important to practice. On the wall, close to the floor, I scratched out the marks that made up my name with my thumbnail.

The guard suddenly stood to attention and Ma woke from his doze. I brushed at my name etched in the wall but, of course, it would not come off. The guard opened his door and Twist walked in, dressed in the same yellow and black costume he had worn that afternoon, and carrying his toad stick.

We all got to our feet. Twist surveyed us with a sour look and the toad head on the end of its stick curled its lip. "You pathetic, untalented vermin," Twist said. "I have tried to come up with an entertainment low enough to match your lack of ability. You will perform a food fight for Prince Dorian and his guests."

Twist stared at each of us in turn, and so did the toad head.

"Should any of you decide that the entertainment would be enhanced by spattering any of the guests or the Prince or even me with food then you will all be flayed alive and buried in salt," Twist said. "What's that, Toadie?" Twist put the toad head to his ear. "It would be funnier if we forgot the food fight and just did that instead. I quite agree. You will be summoned when we are ready," he said, giving us one final look filled with contempt before leaving the room.

"What's a food fight?" I whispered to Ma.

"You throw food at each other," he said.

"Food?" I hissed.

"Yes, usually pies, anything with a soft sloshy filling. Generally, you aim for the face."

"Why is that funny?" I asked. Ma shrugged. "Kids are starving and we're throwing food."

I must have raised my voice, because the guard gave me a hard look, and his moustache bristled. I was shocked. Food, the one thing there was never enough of, was going to be thrown around and wasted. And that was supposed to be funny; an audience was going to watch it and laugh.

I imagined what life would be like in Mottle at the moment; Arky, Gumber and Jenna trying to sleep with empty stomachs, my mum's face changing as the flesh fell away from it and her cheekbones stood out, only her eyes and smile the same.

My body trembled with anger. "I won't do it," I whispered to Ma.

"Then they'll throw you into a tanners pit and laugh as you dissolve," Ma whispered back.

"How do we make it funny?" I asked.

"Pretend its mud," he said. "Our lives depend on it."

We had another long wait but I was too fired up with fury to feel bored. Eventually, the guard opened his door again, and Twist reappeared. "You're on," Twist said. "Begin when I jingle my bells and stop when Toadie whistles."

"Stay close to me," Ma whispered. He squeezed my arm and stood up.

I ran my hand along the wall, and touched where I had carved my name. What we were going to do was wrong. I would have to go through with it but I would remember who I was, and I would remember my anger.

I got to my feet and stood beside Ma.

***

We followed Twist down a wood-paneled passage. A whisper passed among us that Garrick would start the fight, helped by Mutton and Chop. We passed through a set of oak double doors into the banqueting chamber. It was a vast room that smelled of smoke and roast meat. The chamber was lit by lamps in holders around the walls and a glass candelabrum, filled with candles, hanging from the ceiling. On the walls were tapestries of hunting scenes with men on horses, dogs baying and stags, which were getting the worst of it.

Stationed around the wall at regular intervals were guards in pale blue livery. They held crossbows that looked practical rather than ornamental.

A long table stood at the end of the room with two wings extending down either side of the room. Seated at the table were guests dressed in fine clothing with lots of fur trim and jewelry. They lolled in their chairs with plates of half-eaten food in front of them.

Our view of the long table was partially blocked by a shorter table that had been placed in front of it and stacked high with pies. This was where Twist was leading us. We walked around this table and stood in front of the long table.

In the center of the long table, sprawling on an enormous oak throne with a purple silk canopy, was Prince Dorian. He had a handsome face with smooth skin and clear blue eyes framed with wavy blonde hair. He was broad shouldered with no trace of fat.

In front of Dorian were piles of empty dishes. One silver platter still held the remnants of a roast pig. Dorian hacked off a remaining hank of fatty meat from its rump with a carving knife and stuffed the meat into his mouth with his hand. A servant with a napkin leaned forwards and mopped away the grease running down his chin as he chewed once then swallowed.

This man had killed my father. He was a glutton who stuffed his mouth while his own people starved. He was only a few steps and the width of the table away from me. I saw the carving knife, its ivory handle pointing towards me, resting on the silver platter. I could grab the knife, lunge across the table, and stab the wicked prince through the heart.

I steeled myself to do it although my insides felt watery then I remembered the guards with their crossbows. I would be shot before I reached Dorian. I should wait until we were half way through the performance. Everyone would be distracted by the food fight. The air would be full of flying food, reducing visibility. I could make my initial steps part of my act, sliding towards the table.

"Do we have an entertainment for tonight, Master of Revels?" Dorian asked Twist. His voice was rich and flowed like a river. It carried to all parts of the huge chamber without an effort.

"Hey nonny, nonny and tinkle my bells, we have merriment-a-plenty," Twist said, in a voice that dripped with sarcasm. He danced a jig that made his bells ring as he skipped off to one side.

Garrick stepped forwards. "Noble Prince Dorian, ladies and gentlemen, this is a great honor." Mutton and Chop had picked up pies from the table and moved to either side of Garrick. Garrick continued as though unaware of them. "I will present to you the great and inordinately long monologue of King Olwyn the Tedious before the battle of Pomposia."

Garrick took a deep breath and just as he was about to speak, Mutton and Chop hit him in the face with the pies.

The other performers dashed for the table. Ma placed a hand on my arm. He pulled a disdainful face, as though to say we are above this, and turned away. I made as though I wanted to join in the fight. Ma raised a stern finger. We were better than that. A pie exploded against Ma's padded bottom. We slowly turned to look at the fight behind us. As soon as we did, we were struck by a volley of food. I had never tasted anything so rich and creamy. I gasped as it trickled into my mouth.

Ma lunged for the table to join in. I took a moment to clear my eyes.

Garrick had gone head first into a soup tureen and only his backside was visible. Jim and Jam were turning somersaults as they slipped and slid around the table, chasing Holly and Molly. Lady Velda was wringing custard out of her beard. Mutton and Chop stood toe to toe and belted each other with pies. The air was thick with flying food like a swarm of insects.

I glanced at our audience. Prince Dorian was helpless with laughter, his whole body shook, and tears ran down his face. All those around him were enjoying the performance. Now was my chance to pretend to fall, slide along the messy floor and launch myself over the table. I relaxed my body, the way Grunter had taught me, ready to drop.

"Where's my little lad?" Ma blundered towards me, blinded by pastry. He slipped, grabbed my shoulders, and fell on top of me; his weight knocked me off my feet.

"Where did my little lad go?" Ma wailed. "I can't see

him." Ma's padded breasts covered my head. He tried to get up.

"What are you doing under there?" he cried to me as he levered himself up.

I wriggled and tried to slide out from under him so I could make my lunge at Dorian.

"Whoops!" Ma cried as he slipped and fell back on top of me, this time winding me.

"Allow me to assist you in these chaotic times, dear lady," Garrick said. I twisted my head to look at him. He was wearing the soup tureen on his head like a helmet.

I saw him offer his hand to Ma. Ma reached up and took it. Ma's weight lifted off me. I braced myself. I knew what was coming next. Ma slipped and fell back on top me, and a moment later, Garrick landed on top of Ma.

The knife, although still only a few steps away, was out of my reach. I wondered if things could get any worse.

"Allow me to help you up, sir," Lady Velda said to Garrick.

Perhaps the audience saw my look of despair because they hooted with laughter. They roared when Ma fell back on top of me, followed by Garrick, followed by Lady Velda. We all said "Oof" loudly when she landed on top of us, although I saw how she placed her hands to help support her own weight.

We heard a high-pitched shriek of a whistle. It was Twist's toad head, telling us the show was over.

We struggled to our feet. Ma helped me up, keeping tight hold of my wrist. We formed a line, holding hands to bow. Mutton on the end slipped over backwards and one by one, we all keeled over. The audience loved this. I let my body go limp, so that we got a laugh when Ma hoisted me back up by my collar.

All of us performers were coated in food, but the mess

remained around the table. We had not spattered any of the guests. I was too winded to even think of attacking Prince Dorian any more.

Twist led us back to the chamber we had come from and then left us.

***

Garrick was licking his fingers. "Delicious food," he said. "I made sure I went head first into the turtle soup."

"They always do very well for themselves at the palace," Molly, or Holly, said. It was hard to tell under all the food. She was sucking the custard out of the cuffs in her dress.

I had an idea. If I gave my food-coated costume to the kids who were starving in the doorway then Prince Dorian would be helping to feed his citizens whether he wanted to or not.

"You don't have the room to build up to any of the jokes," Ma was saying to Mutton and Chop.

"True," Mutton agreed. "And no structure to top them, and no proper climax, just Twist's whistle."

"We could have got twice the laughs with a tenth of the food," Chop said, taking a piece of pastry from his hair and chewing on it.

"It's best to eat what you can now, dear," Lady Velda said to me. "We get sluiced down at the gatehouse, so you can't take it with you."

How typical of Prince Dorian was that. He would make sure that the food got wasted, flushed down the drain, and presented to the rats.

How could I stop it? I came up with a plan.

I made sure I was at the back when the guard came to lead us out of the palace. Ma was busy discussing the missed comic opportunities with Mutton and Chop. Jim and Jam and Holly and Molly only had eyes for each other. Garrick and Lady Velda were discussing meals that they had eaten with the famous, and Garrick was saying how he would now boast of having dined with Prince Dorian at the palace.

As we walked, I dropped back a pace or two and turned my jacket inside out so all the food was now on the inside.

**

At the palace back door, we were handed over to our original guard, who marched us back to the gatehouse. We entered the pen created between its inner and outer gates. Slots rattled open in the ceiling and ice cold water cascaded down on us.

"This is freezing, sirs," Garrick protested.

"Be grateful it's not boiling oil," a voice above us laughed.

I moved in close to Ma and sheltered beneath the bosom of his costume. He thought I was upset and put a hand on my shoulder. No one seemed to notice that I was now the little drummer boy rather than the little sailor boy.

The outer door creaked open and we left the palace. We moved off as a group, heading back to Crib Street. It was a clear, freezing night and we had just been doused with cold water so we did not linger. We had splinterlight to see by, which was good, as none of us had brought a lantern.

I stayed quiet and moved to the rear of our party. Every now and then, Ma would glance back and make sure I was all right, but he was still engrossed in discussions of comic theory with Mutton and Chop.

We passed the doorway where I had seen the starving children on our way to the palace. In the splinterlight, I saw the lump they made beneath their blanket. I stopped walking and allowed our group to disappear into the distance. I slipped off my jacket and stood in the doorway. "Wake up," I hissed. "I've got food."

I saw the outline of three heads emerge from beneath the blanket as though they were a single creature. They sniffed the air and looked in the direction of my jacket.

Three pairs of hands emerged from beneath the blanket. I passed them the jacket. They didn't snatch at it but took it carefully. The three heads bent close together and methodically set about licking, sucking and scouring the jacket clean of food.

"You'll need to wash that jacket, Keth." It was Ma. He joined me in the doorway. The three boys clung tight to the jacket. "Finish your meal, lads," Ma said.

The three boys returned to eating.

"The others were worried you had got lost, but I told them I reckoned I knew where to find you," Ma said.

We stood in silence while the boys finished licking my jacket.

"Thanks, mister." The middle boy handed my jacket back to me. "I never tasted anything so good." The other two boys nodded.

I was going to slip my jacket back on. A freezing cold wind blew through me as soon as I stepped from the shelter of the doorway. Ma took my jacket from me. He turned from me and fiddled with his costume then turned back and slipped something heavy and warm around my shoulders. It was his false bosom. We walked together through the dark streets, his hand on my shoulder guiding me home.

"Comedy is all in the timing, Keth," he said. "My falling on you when I did kept things funny. Those palace guards are too well trained to get distracted by a food fight. You would never have got close to Dorian."

I expected Ma to be furious but he sounded tired and sad.

"I knew you'd want to try something," Ma said. "You're as daft as my son was." He sighed. "This time, I'm keeping my eye on you."

We walked on in silence. I was uncomfortable that Ma had compared me to his dead son; it reminded me of what Crag had said just before we arrived in Russett. I felt as though Ma was giving me a difficult role to play.

13 REBELS

After breakfast the next morning, Silva spread ash in front of the kitchen stove and we kneeled down, ready to continue my reading lessons. We were alone except for Ragamuffin, who was sleeping under the kitchen table.

"I almost killed Prince Dorian last night," I whispered.

"Start the lesson then you can tell me," Silva said. "Write your name, Keth."

I wrote 'Keth' without hesitating. I'd practiced on the palace wall the previous night. After a couple of goes, I was able to write Silva's name too.

"Writing is like a code," Silva said, "a series of symbols that you string together to say something. What I'll show you next is the alphabet."

Silva went through the alphabet, writing the letters in the ash one at a time and getting me to copy them. I was getting impatient to tell her about my adventures of the previous night.

Eventually, she raised her head and looked around the kitchen, checking we were alone.

"Alright Keth, tell me what happened last night," she

whispered.

"I would have stabbed Dorian but Ma fell on top of me." I said. "I saw a carving knife on the banqueting table and I was going to lunge for it."

"Start at the beginning," she said.

"I was born to simple peasant folk in the humble farming village of Mottle," I said, deliberately misinterpreting what she meant.

"From when you arrived at the palace," Silva said, jutting out her narrow chin and rolling her eyes, which was her 'Keth, stop being an idiot' look.

"We entered through the gatehouse," I said. "We were stopped between the outer gate and the inner gate and someone examined us through a trapdoor in the ceiling."

"How big was the trapdoor?" she asked.

"Hard to say." I paused for thought. "I was dazzled by the lantern. Once they let us through the inner gate, a guard led us around the back of the palace to an entrance, and then another guard led us through some passages to an empty chamber where we had to wait."

"How many guards did you see inside the palace?" she asked.

"Two or three," I said. "Well, actually about twenty or thirty if you count the ones in the banqueting chamber."

"Can you describe the route you took through the palace to get to the banqueting chamber?"

I thought about it. "It was passages mostly, and then there was the room we waited in, and then another passage."

Silva rolled her eyes. I had the feeling she was unimpressed by my powers of observation. However, we had now reached the important part of my story where I almost stabbed Prince Dorian.

"Sit at the table and pretend to be the prince," I said to

her. I was going for the full dramatic re-enactment.

"Good idea, Keth, and we can invite the others in to watch," she said.

"They could pretend to be feast goers," I said. "I'll arrange the chairs."

Silva raised her left eyebrow. She often used her eyebrows to communicate when words failed her. This particular level of raised eyebrow indicated she was being sarcastic.

"A performance would be a bit too noisy," I said.

She nodded.

I had an idea and drew in the ash a diagram of the banqueting chamber, showing where we performed, the arrangement of the tables, where Prince Dorian was seated, and where the guards with crossbows were. This seemed to get her approval.

"I saw a carving knife in front of Dorian," I said, "and I was going to grab it and lunge at him during the performance, but Ma fell on top of me before I could put my plan in to action; otherwise I would have brought about the revolution single-handed."

This was not strictly true given that the guards would have shot me before I got near Prince Dorian, but I did not want to spoil a good story.

"Who was sitting to the left and right of Prince Dorian?" she asked.

I struggled to remember. In my mind, the guests were a vague mass of expensive clothes, fur, and jewelry. I had been so focused on Prince Dorian that I had not looked at them. "I saw a servant behind him to mop his mouth clean," I said. "Does it matter? We're only interested in Dorian."

"You have to learn to observe, Keth." Silva pursed her lips. "Being a rebel is more about watching than doing. If we know who is close to Dorian then we can use those people to get at him."

By this stage, I was feeling cross. Silva was clogging up my dramatic story with unimportant detail; worse still, it was unimportant detail that I had not noticed.

"And how did they escort you from the palace?" she asked.

"On foot," I said. "Same guards, same passages. They dumped buckets of water on us at the gate house."

I wondered whether to tell her about the three starving boys and my food-covered jacket, but she seemed to have lost interest now that my tale had left the palace, so I decided to leave that bit out. "When are you taking me to join the rebels?" I said. "The sooner we overthrow Prince Dorian, the better."

Silva was silent. She frowned.

"I could meet them tonight and report what happened at the palace," I said.

"No," she said. "They will decide if and when they want to meet you."

She said this so firmly, it was clear she was not going to listen to any of my arguments. I pretended to accept her answer although I was already making other plans. We continued with my learning the alphabet.

***

In the afternoon, I practiced "The Unsuitable Suitor" routine with Grunter and Ma in the rehearsal room. The idea was Grunter was Ma's suitor, only he just wanted to steal her belongings. I was Ma's little lad and I knew what Grunter was up to. As Grunter pinched things, I would pinch them back, and put them back. We went over and over the bit with the spoons.

That evening I went to bed early, saying I was tired after the previous night's trip to the palace. This was true but I forced myself to stay awake. I sat peering through a crack in the stable door, watching the house.

Soon after the curfew bell had tolled, a shadowy figure climbed down into the yard from an upstairs window. It was Silva. She crouched low and flitted across the backyard before slipping out of the back gate.

I followed her and cautiously stuck my head out of the gate.

"Going somewhere, Keth?" Silva whispered. I could just make out her outline. She was leaning against the fence.

"I was having trouble sleeping," I whispered. "I thought a late night stroll would help clear my head."

"So you were not planning to follow me?"

"It never crossed my mind," I said, trying to look innocent even though it was dark.

"That's good," she whispered. "Because if the rebels saw you tailing me, they would kill you first and ask me about it later."

"Please take me with you," I pleaded, in what I hoped was my most winning voice.

"Not until they invite you," she whispered.

I decided I was not going to win this one. "Have a fun time," I whispered, and shut the gate, with me on the lodging house side of it.

Disappointed, I returned to my bed in the stable loft. I wanted to stay awake and feel sorry for myself but I was so tired I soon fell asleep.

***

The next morning, Silva and I were kneeling in front

of the kitchen stove, ready to begin my reading lesson. She glanced at me, and I looked away. I knew she would be expecting me to ask about the rebels but I had decided to give her the silent treatment, to let her know I was annoyed by how she had behaved last night.

She spread the ashes in front of us and began drawing the letters of the alphabet in them.

It occurred to me that when it came to dishing out the silent treatment, she might well be a master while I was an apprentice. No one in Mottle had ever accused me of being too quiet.

I held out until she had reached 'p' then I broke. "What did the rebels say about me?" I asked.

"A senior rebel wants to meet you tonight, Keth," she said. "I'll collect you after the curfew bell."

"Yes!" I shouted and leaped to my feet, punching the air with excitement.

"Is everything alright?" Madame Patwig put her head around the kitchen door.

"Sorry," I said. "I'm a bit excited. I've just spelt my name correctly." I knelt back down. I glanced at Silva. She was grinning at me, so that was all right.

During the rest of the day, I found it difficult to concentrate, and when we rehearsed the 'Unsuitable Suitor' routine, I kept dropping the spoons. At one point, I got my hand stuck in Grunter's pocket, and we spent ages trying to work out how to build that into the routine. Ma was anxious that we should be perfect because he wanted one of the inns to hire us to perform there.

***

When night came, I was too excited to fall asleep. I waited for Silva to appear. It was a damp night with a smear of drizzle falling and clouds covering the splinter. It was too dark to see the back of the house from the stable door. I heard the curfew bell toll then a little while later, I heard the faint sounds of Silva padding across the yard.

She plucked my sleeve and I followed her. We slipped out of the backyard gate into the lane, where she lit a lantern that gave out a narrow beam of light. We made our way through the back streets towards the river. We slipped through a gap in a fence, and suddenly I was hit full blast by the foul stink of the tannery, as though two dead rats covered in their own poop had been shoved up my nostrils. I was trembling with fear. I banged into the fence as I tried to get back out into the street.

Silva grabbed my arm. "Are you trying to get us caught?" she hissed. Her face was white with fury.

We froze as we heard footsteps approaching down the street. Silva killed the light in her lantern. We pressed back against the fence. Someone paused in front of the gap in the fence, and the beam of a lantern shone through. Beads of sweat formed on my forehead and chilled there.

An arm holding the lantern poked through the gap. This was followed by a man's head. He had a crumpled face and a limp moustache. He held a small cylinder between his teeth. That's a whistle, I thought. One blow and he would summon help.

The light from the lantern shone on the upright timbers of the tannery vats. It fell just short of where Silva and I crouched against the fence, but if the man swung his lantern a little, it would reveal us.

"Rats," the man whispered through his teeth, and his whistle gave the ghost of a peep. "It was rats I heard."

This man is as scared as I am, I realized. He is hoping

he does not find anything. The man pulled his head and his lantern back through the gap. We heard his footsteps retreat down the street.

I gently released the breath I'd been holding. "Sorry Silva," I whispered. "It's the smell. I thought I'd got used to it."

"Go home if you're scared," she whispered, relighting her lantern.

I wanted to do just that but I knew if I did, it would be the last I would ever hear about the rebels. I put my sleeve across my nose and mouth and nodded to Silva to let her know we should go on.

We crept through the tannery yard, passed stinking vats filled with rotting skins until, at last, we slipped out through another gap in the fence. We walked down a narrow street that smelled only a little less foul than the tannery. We heard a baby screaming and the scuttling of rats. We ascended a set of stone stairs and passed through a wooden gate.

We were in some sort of park. We no longer had the feeling of houses pressing in on us from all sides. We followed a gravel path, walking on the grass beside it so that our feet did not make scrunching noises. The path was climbing. It led us through a gap in a hedge and we found ourselves in a circular garden, walled by the hedge. The lantern beam reflected on a pond in the center of the garden; arranged around the pond were white stone benches.

"Sit on the bench," Silva said. "A rebel will come and question you. I'll return later."

I did as I was told. I watched the progress of her bobbing lantern as she left the garden.

***

It was silent. I waited. Back in Mottle, we played a game where you slipped out at dead of night and sat in the dead garden while the other kids pretended to be ghosts to try and scare you. I was never scared. It was one of the places where I felt most at peace.

"Greetings," a voice rasped in my ear, and I jumped. I heard someone sit next to me on the bench, but it was too dark to see him. "Silva tells us that you want to be a rebel."

I tilted my head down in the direction of the voice, so I guessed that the speaker might be smaller than me. "Yes," I said.

"Why do you want to join our group?" the rebel asked.

"I hate Prince Dorian," I said. "He killed my dad."

"What skills do you …" The rebel broke off with a coughing fit.

"Are you alright?" I said.

The coughing continued. It sounded like he was trying to bring something up, his lungs perhaps.

"I'll get you some water," I said, thinking about the nearby pond.

The rebel spat. Something thick and heavy splattered on the ground. "Don't bother," the rebel said. "What skills do you have?"

"I'm an actor," I said. "I got to perform in front of Dorian two nights ago, and I would have stabbed him but my master fell on top of me."

"How many fireplaces did you see in the palace?" the rebel said.

I struggled to remember. "I wasn't looking," I admitted. He's going to ask me who was sitting next to Prince Dorian, I thought. I decided I would make something up.

The rebel spat and another chunk of something thick

and gooey hit the ground. "So to sum up," the rebel said, "you have loads of enthusiasm but no real skills, and if we need an untrained assassin, you'll volunteer."

I had a feeling the interview was not going well. I wished I had paid more attention inside the palace. I should have at least noticed the fireplaces. A thought struck me. "The rooms we went into didn't have fireplaces, but they were still warm," I said. "In one room we sat on the flagstones for a long time, and my bum didn't go numb."

"Underfloor heating," the rebel said. "We'll be in touch."

I didn't hear him move away but a change in the air told me he had gone. I sat quietly on the bench. After a while, I was picked out by the beam of the lantern and Silva approached me.

"He's not sure about you, but he'll give you a chance," she said.

***

For the next few days, I pestered Silva about when my career as a rebel would begin. She kept telling me to be patient. I had almost given up hope when one morning, as we settled down to my reading lesson, Silva leaned in close to me and whispered, "We're going to a rebel meeting this evening. They contacted me in the cloth market yesterday afternoon, and I was told to bring you."

I had visions of us plotting the downfall of Prince Dorian. Silva must have read my mind. "It's a bit boring, Keth," she said. "Usually Ash just gathers reports from everyone."

"Who's Ash?" I said.

"You met him a few nights ago."

"The boy with the nasty cough?"

"He was a chimneysweep's boy," she said. "They die young, and they die badly. He doesn't expect to live too much longer."

"All the more reason to do something now," I said.

Silva bit her lip and looked worried. "Keth, don't get carried away at the meeting," she said. "Don't speak unless you're asked to. We all sit in the dark and take it in turns to report, pooling our knowledge."

"I understand," I said, although I was confused. If you are rebels, why not attack Prince Dorian rather than sitting around talking?

I was so excited about the rebel meeting, I was buzzing all day. I put my energy into the rehearsals, and Ma was pleased with the results.

**

That evening, waiting for the curfew bell to toll, I found it hard to sit still. At last it rang. It was a dark wet night and the patter of rain covered the sound of Silva creeping across the yard, so that her tug on my sleeve was a surprise even though I was expecting it.

We jogged through the back streets. Initially, we took the same route as we had a few nights before but I was relieved that instead of entering the tannery yard, we continued down towards the river until we reached the city wall.

Silva shone her lantern on the wall and pointed out where someone had chipped holds in the stone. She killed the light in her lantern, attached it to the back of her belt and swarmed up the wall, on top of which was a walkway that guards patrolled.

We were easy to spot so we did not linger but climbed

swiftly down the other side. I missed my hold and fell a short way but landed on dirt and did not hurt myself. It reminded me of when we tried to steal grain from the town hall in Brackford.

"Do you remember how we first met?" I whispered to Silva.

"This isn't a date, Keth," she hissed back.

I was glad it was dark because I knew my face had turned bright red.

"It's too dangerous to use the lantern; just walk straight ahead," Silva said. We walked down a shallow slope through what felt like knee-high grass until our feet clicked on wooden planks. Silva hooted like an owl; from somewhere close by, an owl hooted back. "This is a landing stage," Silva whispered. She took my hand and placed it on her belt. "Follow me."

We edged across the wooden planks; water lapped against the underside of them. "We are at the edge of the landing stage," Silva said. "The river is on your left, a lighter is moored beside us. Kneel down and climb into it."

I guessed a lighter was a kind of boat and did as instructed. The lighter rocked in the water. I heard the breathing of someone else already in the boat.

We pulled away from the wharf. The only sounds were the patter of rain on the water and the occasional gentle splash of an oar. "Don't we need the lantern?" I whispered.

"I know where we are by the current," the oarsman whispered back. He had a boy's voice.

Our oarsman directed us close to the bank and then we entered a narrow canal. I knew this because of the sound the water made, lapping against the walls on either side of us. After a short distance, the canal entered somewhere undercover and the rain stopped beating down on us. The canal widened out and I guessed we were in some sort of basin, perhaps inside a warehouse. The place had the sour, musty smell of animal skins. Our oarsman moored up against the side.

I started to get out but Silva restrained me with her arm. We sat in silence. I heard people coughing and fidgeting, which suggested several other boats had already moored here. We heard two more boats arrive and moor up. Being a rebel seemed to involve a lot of sitting in the dark, saying nothing.

Eventually, the silence was broken by someone hacking up a wad of phlegm, followed by a splash as they spat it into the water. Ash was ready to begin the meeting.

***

"Welcome to this meeting of the rebels of Russett," Ash said. "Our first report is from Harness."

"I was working in the leather room of my master's workshop when Prince Dorian's Master of Horse ordered three new saddles," a boy with a thin piping voice said. "He did not say what he wanted them for."

My guess would have been to put on the backs of horses, but I kept quiet.

"Our next report is from Pin," Ash said.

"My mistress took measurements for a fine suit of cloth for Prince Dorian," a girl with a self-important voice announced.

This was more like it. A garment full of hidden poison pins could be delivered to the wicked prince and after he pricked himself, he would die instantly, or perhaps after several long seconds of dreadful suffering.

"Did you or your mistress visit the palace?" Ash asked.

"No. The Prince's Master of the Robe gave us the measurements," the girl said. "When he collected the garment from us, he said it was most excellent work." She sounded smug.

Another missed opportunity, I thought. The rebels didn't seem to have grasped the idea that overthrowing Prince Dorian would require them to do something more than just keeping an eye on his shopping list.

"Our next report is from Nut," Ash said.

"I was in Palace Square roasting chestnuts all the time, except for curfew," a boy with a wheezy voice said. "I didn't see Prince Dorian leave the palace."

"Our next report is from Pot," Ash said.

"I was waiting on the tables at the inn where I work." Pot had a thin nervous voice. "No one mentioned Prince Dorian."

Several more kids made similar reports to Nut and Pot. They had seen nothing of Dorian and done nothing to bring about his downfall. I was feeling fed up with this band of rebels, which didn't seem to be making any visible efforts to stage a rebellion.

"Our next report is from Urchin," Ash said.

"I didn't see anything of Dorian," Urchin said, "but something unusual did happen. Early one evening we were keeping watch from a doorway on Garter Street. This group of ten people walk past, heading towards the palace; one of them, the only lad in the group, stops, looks at us and says 'hello' before a fat woman with a man's voice tells him to keep going."

I realized Urchin was the middle one of the three kids I had given my food-stained jacket to.

"Just before the curfew bell rings," Urchin continued, "this same group walks past, heading back from the palace. This lad hangs back by our doorway, takes off his jacket and the inside is covered with food. He hands it over to us, and the food tastes …" Here Urchin made a dreamy sigh.

"That was me," I called out. "I'd just been performing at the palace. I almost stabbed Prince Dorian."

The rebels in the other boats gasped. I knew I had my audience hooked.

"We had been summoned to the palace by Twist, Prince Dorian's Master of Revels," I continued in my best dramatic voice. Silva jabbed her elbow under my ribs, and I was suddenly left breathless.

"Be quiet!" Ash hissed and broke into a spasm of coughing. I sensed my audience tense up. I had lost my hold on them. "We report one at a time," Ash snapped. He coughed some more then continued. "We do not interrupt. We only speak when asked to."

I noticed the 'we' did not include Ash, when it came to interrupting.

"Continue, Urchin," Ash said.

"Well that was pretty much it," Urchin said. "The fat woman with the man's voice came to collect the lad with the jacket."

"That was Ma," I said.

Once more, Silva jabbed her elbow hard at my ribs but I was expecting it so I blocked her with my arm.

"She was kind," Urchin said. "She let us finish eating. That food was …" Once again Urchin gave a happy sigh. "Thanks for the jacket, friend," Urchin said in my direction.

"My pleasure," I said. "Call me Keth. I'll see you around."

I heard Silva slap her forehead. I was only being polite. I was sure it did not count as an interruption.

"Our next report is from Silver Fox," Ash said.

176

Silva began speaking and I realized Silver Fox was the group's name for her. I wondered if all the other names had been made up ones. My saying I was called Keth might have been a mistake.

Silva began to tell my story. "As mentioned just now, my associate, Turnip, was summoned to perform in front of Prince Dorian."

"That's right," I said, preparing to pick up the story and choosing to ignore the fact she'd called me Turnip.

"And he will shut up while I speak or I'll tip him out of the boat and he can swim home," Silva said.

The audience sniggered but she grasped my jerkin and slipped one of her legs beneath mine so I knew she was serious. The water would be freezing. I was furious with her but I held my tongue.

Silva told my story but she ruined it. She put in all the facts but left out all the drama. I was disappointed. We had an audience in the palm of our hands and we wasted the opportunity.

When she finished, I was expecting questions, and I hoped I might be allowed to say a word or two without my supposed best friend threatening to drown me

"Our next report is from Punt," Ash said, moving on without a pause.

With an effort of will, I kept my mouth shut. Silva released her hold on me and patted me on the shoulder.

Punt turned out to be the name of our oarsman. "Since the harvest, large amounts of grain have been brought down river on rafts and stored in Dorian's granary," Punt said. "Large sea-going ships have anchored mid-river, and we've been ferrying the grain from the granary out to these ships. The grain is going overseas."

"Our next report is from Bead," Ash said.

"All of the larger grain ships have now departed,"

Bead said. She had a quiet but clear voice. "The ships still moored mid-river carry skins. Several smaller grain ships have moored at Stone Wharf. The last few of these will sail in the next day or so, before the winter storms make the sea voyage too dangerous."

I turned over in my mind how we were going to steal back the remainder of the grain.

"All reports have been received, and the meeting will close," Ash announced.

"Hang on," I said, shocked. "Aren't we going to plan how we're going to steal the grain back?"

A murmur of agreement came from people in the other boats. It was a quiet murmur, but it was real.

"The meeting is closed," Ash said.

Silva tried to renew her grip on my jerkin, ready to tip me out the boat, but I was ready for her and blocked her. "I think this meeting is just getting started," I said, appealing to my fellow rebels. "We're not letting Dorian sell off our grain when our people are starving."

The murmurs of agreement grew louder.

"There's no point just reporting what happened," I said. "We have to take action." I raised my voice. "Are you with me?"

The rebels gave a mighty cheer. They were on my side.

"Could you shout that a bit louder?" Ash said. "Prince Dorian might not have heard you."

Everyone fell silent. We were out after curfew. We had just made a loud noise; worse, that noise had been a cheer, a sound that was unusual in Russett these days. My audience was terrified. I had lost them once again.

"Leave quickly and quietly," Ash said. "The meeting is closed."

The water in the basin stirred as lighters were maneuvered into position. The departure was brisk and orderly, the oarsmen taking it in turns to slide their lighters out into the night.

***

The lighters took different routes and soon we were alone out on the open water, heading back to our landing stage. The splashes from Punt's oar were louder and so was his breathing. I guessed he was working harder. It must be the current. Going to the meeting we had been with the tide, but now we were travelling against it.

One thing I had noticed about the rebels was that they were all children. No adult voices had been heard at the meeting. Perhaps with Nanny Ash in charge, spitting gunk on any suggestion of doing anything rebellious, they didn't need a grownup to tell them not to do things.

"What is your report, rebel?"

"I cowered under the table with a bucket on my head, and guess what? I didn't see Prince Dorian."

"Excellent report, but try and do less in future."

We nudged the landing stage, and the little bump interrupted my thoughts. Silva and I climbed out of the lighter. "You were brilliant, Keth," Punt whispered. "You really gave it to Ash. I'm sick of just watching and doing nothing."

"Thanks, Punt," I said.

I was pleased because of his support, and he had called me Keth rather than Turnip.

***

Silva and I made our way back to Crib Street in silence. We were concentrating on not getting caught.

We slipped into the backyard of our lodging house. I

wondered if Silva was still upset about the way I had behaved. I put my hand on her arm to steer her towards the stable so we could have a talk. She slapped my hand away with venom and flitted across the backyard. I didn't pursue her. I thought I had better give her the rest of the night to cool down. I saw her outline as she climbed the back wall of the lodging house and swung in through a window.

I entered the stable and climbed up to the loft. I was tired but I found it hard to sleep. I kept going over the details of the rebel meeting. Someone needed to goad them into action, but perhaps I was wrong to have tried to do it on my first visit.

14 CONTACTS

The morning after the rebel meeting, I awoke, having not slept well. I had let my frustration with the rebels get the better of me, and I had upset Silva. I needed to clear the air with her.

After breakfast, I kept quiet until Silva had spread out the ash in front of the stove, ready to begin my reading lesson. "Did I talk too much at the meeting last night?" I said. "I think I might have got a little carried away."

Silva said nothing. She spelled out a word in the ash 'F-A-T-H-E-A-D'.

"What does that say?" I said.

"Make the sounds of the letters," she said.

"Fa – fa - is it father?" I guessed.

She shook her head.

"What about farted?" I said.

She didn't even crack a smile.

I tried again, and after several more goes, I got the word 'fathead'.

The rest of the lesson consisted of her spelling out four more words for me to read: idiot, stupid, moron, and blabbermouth.

I was getting fed up with this, and it was a relief when she brought the lesson to a close. "Thanks, Silva," I said. "I get the message you're unhappy with me about last night."

"You don't understand do you, Keth?" Silva said, shaking her head. "I'm not the only one who is unhappy."

She got up and stalked out of the kitchen, leaving me to sweep up the ash.

***

In the afternoon, Ma sent Silva out on shopping errands while Elba took me out in the backyard to practice singing harmonies with her. Ragamuffin joined in when I tried to reach the high notes, which was a bad sign.

When Silva came back from her trip, I tried to get a chance to talk to her alone but I got the feeling she was avoiding me. The more I played over in my mind what had happened at the rebel meeting the previous evening, the more I felt guilty that I had let her down. As soon as I got the chance, I needed to apologize to her.

That night, I stayed awake and kept watch on the back of the house. The curfew bell rang. I waited. Silva did not appear, and I fell asleep by the stable door. Thespian nudged me awake just before dawn. I was stiff and frozen.

***

I was impatient for my next reading lesson when I would have another chance to talk to Silva alone. During breakfast, Silva looked serious. Afterwards, she spread out the ash in front of the stove with a certain solemn formality, the same way that old Scour would sprinkle the ashes of the dead in the dead garden back in Mottle.

"Keth, I've got something to tell you, and I need you to be quiet and listen," she said.

"Can I say something first," I said. "I'm sorry about how I behaved at the rebel meeting. I let you down."

"It doesn't matter." She shrugged and looked sad.

I was thrown by this response, but I ploughed on. "It matters to me," I said. "You're my best friend, even if you did try to tip me out the boat, and I should have respected your instructions instead of ignoring them."

"So you've learned your lesson, Keth." She put a hand on my arm. "Now, promise me to hold your tongue while I speak."

I was worried by how serious this was all getting. "I promise," I said.

"I got word from the rebels yesterday afternoon," she said. "You're being dropped from the group."

I felt like I'd been kicked in the stomach. "That filthy coward Ash," I muttered.

"You promised," Silva said.

"Promised what?" I snapped.

"To hold your tongue and listen," she snapped back.

I choked back my words. They jammed up inside of me, and I thought my head would explode.

"Ash thinks you're too dangerous to have around," Silva said. "You're a hothead who will act without thinking about the consequences, and you'll get everyone else arrested."

"I just wanted the rebels to do something," I spluttered, "instead of sitting on their backsides watching and taking notes on what a bad fellow Dorian is."

I got up and stalked about the kitchen. I was so angry

I wanted to thump something, to break it or bruise my knuckles. Ragamuffin took one look at my face and fled outside.

"You can't let off steam here, Keth," Silva said. "You'll give us away. Come with me. I know a quiet spot."

***

We left the lodging house and Silva led the way through the city while I clumped along behind her, stamping on rubbish in the gutter, pretending it was Ash.

We climbed a short steep street that ended in an iron fence with a gate in it. Silva worked the latch to open the gate, and we passed through. We were in a park with green lawns and empty flowerbeds.

To our left, the park sloped down in the direction of the river, while to our right it climbed to the summit of a hill.

"This is the park you brought me to, a few nights ago, to meet Ash," I said.

"We entered further down the hill that night," she said.

Ahead of us a ridge ran up to the summit of the hill. Stone plinths were positioned along the ridge. On top of each one was what looked like long thin metal basket made from iron strips.

"What are they?" I pointed to them.

"That's where the bodies are burned," she said. "This is the dead garden. They burn the bodies at dawn."

We crunched along a gravel path that swept across the lawn to our right. Although it was a fine day, once we were away from the houses, we were exposed to a chill wind. I hunched my body and shivered.

The path curved around the side of the hill. We entered a circular garden sheltered from the wind by hedges. It had stone benches arranged around a pond. I had met Ash here. The rain had washed away any traces of his phlegm.

Silva sat on a bench. I sat beside her. I had begun to calm down. "Why is Ash kicking me out after one meeting?" I said. "Is that fair?"

"You challenged his authority," she said. "He believes we need to watch and learn about Dorian, so that we can find his weak point before we attack. You want to attack Dorian straight away."

"And how does Ash expect to find Dorian's weak points without attacking him?" I said. "Was he expecting Dorian to make a public announcement of them in the Palace Square?"

"It's a clash of ideas," she said. "Ash has his strategy, and you have yours. If no one had liked your suggestions, Ash might have given you a second chance, but a lot of the rebels think the same way as you do. If he let you stay, you would be a threat to his leadership."

"I bet Dorian pays Ash to be the rebel leader," I said. "That way Dorian knows there will never be a revolution. Ash is too gutless to organize one."

"That's unfair," she said.

"Let's start our own rebel band," I said. "You and I would be the leaders. We'd make things happen, and others would join us."

"Too dangerous," she said.

Something was puzzling me about Silva. Her attitude seemed to have changed since I had first met her. I needed to get to the bottom of this. "Do you remember attempting to steal grain from Brackford town hall?" I said.

"Being chased by the guards." She smiled at the memory and nodded.

"You were happy to take risks, then," I said. "Why are you being cautious now?"

She looked at her hands and began to pick at her fingernails. I left the question hanging in the air between us. Eventually, she heaved a sigh and looked me in the eye. "Ma is getting suspicious of me," she said. "He's keeping a closer eye on me than he did in previous years. I had to slip a sleeping potion into his cocoa before I snuck off to the rebel meeting."

"So I have to do this on my own," I said.

"Can't you let it drop, Keth?" she said. "Splitting the rebel band in two is playing into Dorian's hands. We have to stay united to succeed."

"I'm a rebel," I said, folding my arms. "If I'm not allowed to be part of Ash's group then I have to be part of my own group."

"I'll talk to Ash," Silva said. "He will have cooled down in a few days. He'll realize that it's safer to have you in the group than outside of it."

I fell silent. I had a plan forming in my mind.

After a while, Silva broke the silence. "We should get back to the lodging house," she said.

"You go," I said. "I need some time alone to think about all this."

She patted me on the arm and left the garden.

I had no intention of doing nothing until Ash decided I was forgiven. Many of the rebels at the meeting had responded with cheers to my call for action. If I could get in touch with them then we could strike a blow against Prince Dorian. Once the rebels had developed a taste for successful action, they would insist on more of it. Ash would be forced to change his strategy.

It upset me that I would not have Silva's help and support, but if I told her of my plans, she would try and talk me out of it or perhaps even try to sabotage me. According to Bead, the last of the grain ships would be leaving Russett in the next day or so. If we were going to steal grain from one of them, it would have to be done tonight.

***

Apart from Silva, the only rebel I knew by sight was Urchin. If I was going to put my plan of stealing grain from one of the ships into practice, then I would have to find him. I decided that the first place I would look was Garter Street, where I had met him and two other boys in a doorway on the night I performed at the palace.

I left the circular garden and walked to the summit of the hill from where I looked out across the city. It was a crisp, clear day, and the palace stood out on top of its hill. I knew if I headed in that direction, I would, at some point, cross Garter Street. Confident of where I was heading, I left the garden and plunged into the bustling laneways of the city.

I was soon lost. Streets twisted and turned before becoming alleys then doubling back or ending in stonewalls. I would have enjoyed exploring the city but I had a robbery to organize and I was wasting time.

Eventually, having asked directions from a fishwife, a carter, a baker's boy, a drunk, the drunk's friend, a pot seller, a man who cleaned up after horses, a woman sweeping her doorstep and her neighbor who just happened to put her head out the window, I made it to Garter Street.

I walked up and down the street, peering into

doorways. Many of them had people in but not Urchin. "I'm looking for a kid with sticking up white hair and white eyebrows," I asked a man dressed in rags and huddled in a doorway.

"I know who you mean," the man said. He narrowed his eyes and scraped his fingers over his scabby chin. "He hangs out with two other kids."

"That's him," I said. "Where can I find him?"

"What's it worth?" the man said and he smiled, showing three black stumps of teeth.

I realized that I had no money or food on me. I was after information but I had nothing to trade for it. "My master will be grateful," I said.

"Who's your master, boy?" the man said, leaning forwards.

"It doesn't matter," I said and I turned and walked away from him.

My asking after Urchin was a piece of information that the man might use to trade for money or food, and I did not want to draw attention to myself.

Tired and frustrated, I sat in an empty doorway. It was then that I remembered where else I had seen Urchin before. He was one of the three boys I had seen in Dorian's Square sitting beneath the statue of Prince Dorian when we had first entered the city. It was worth having a look.

***

A well-dressed gentleman gave me directions to the street with all the shops with men's clothes, and from there I retraced the route the troupe had taken when we first arrived in Russett until I emerged into Dorian's Square.

Huddled together at the foot of the statue of Prince Dorian were three kids, wrapped in a thin blanket. The middle kid had a long pale face, a shock of white hair and white eyebrows. It was Urchin.

Now that I had found him, I wavered about approaching him. I would have to trust him with my plans, and if he wanted to be part of them then he would need to trust me. It was one thing to have an idea in my head, where it was safe and hidden, but the moment I spoke it out loud then the risks increased. It might be sensible to slip away and forget about my plan but then I would be no better than Ash and his 'do-nothing' strategy. I had to go through with this.

I wasn't sure what the rules were for starting a conversation with fellow rebels. The only rule was probably that Ash had banned it. I knew that if I tried to sneak up on Urchin and his friends without being noticed, I would draw attention to myself so I strolled over to them.

They looked up as I approached. The two boys either side of Urchin prepared to make a dash for it. Urchin recognized me and put a restraining hand on their arms. "Hello, Keth," Urchin said. "Keth was the kid with the jacket," he told the other two boys, and they relaxed. "Keth, on my left is Grub, and on my right is Smiley."

"Are you wearing any food today?" Grub said. He had long, black, greasy hair that fell over his face, so the front of his head looked the same as the back.

"Sorry, no," I said.

"That's alright," Smiley said. "I'll never forget how it tasted." He had a puckered scar running from the left hand corner of his mouth up to his left eye, and it pulled his mouth up into a half smile.

"I thought you might be able to help me with

something, Urchin," I said.

Urchin leaned back against the legs of Prince Dorian's statue and looked at me for what seemed like a long time. His eyes were the palest blue I had ever seen, and his eyelashes were white. I met his gaze; neither of us blinked. At length, he smiled. "Keep an eye on things," he told Grub and Smiley. "Me and Keth are taking a walk."

Urchin climbed out from beneath the blanket. He was wearing a brown hessian sack with holes cut out for his head and arms. It was clinched tight about his narrow waist by a piece of frayed twine.

We walked together across the square.

"I want to steal some grain from the ships tonight, before they all leave," I said.

"Good on you," Urchin said. "It's about time we did something."

"Do you know any of the rebels who work on the water?" I said.

"I keep in touch with Punt," Urchin said. "Ash says we're not allowed to do that but Punt and me got talking after one meeting." Urchin's eyes slid away from mine, and he looked down at his feet, before he glanced back up at me. "We've been able to help each other out from time to time with things," Urchin said with a sly grin.

I knew about smugglers from 'The Pirate Prince,' one of the plays that the troupe performed. I guessed that Punt and Urchin might be running a little smuggling operation.

"And would Punt help us?" I said.

"We'll ask him," Urchin said.

15 THE PLAN

Urchin led me at a trot out of Dorian's Square and through the crowded streets. "This is Wharf Street," he said, as we entered a busy cobbled street that sloped down towards the river and ended in a wide stone archway in the city wall.

Carts travelling uphill were being pulled by horses, plodding along with their heads down, snorting steam from their nostrils into the cold air. Carts going downhill had boys hanging off the back, dragging their wooden clogs against the cobbles, slowing down the carts and making sparks fly. It reminded me of hanging off the back of the village cart as we returned to Mottle from the top field. I thought of Arky, Gumber, and Jenna and wondered what they were up to.

"Watch out, boy," a carter shouted.

Urchin grabbed my arm and pulled me clear of a cart. "This isn't the country, Keth," Urchin said. "You've got to stay awake." We queued to pass through the arch in the city wall.

"This is Wharf Gate," Urchin said.

A guard inspected us, and I tried to keep my face blank. He let us through. We walked a short way and the street emerged onto a stone quayside. I counted ten boats with their sails furled, moored along its length. Men bustled up and down gangplanks, either loading or unloading cargo.

"It's quiet this time of year," Urchin said.

"Looks busy to me," I said, "but I'm from the country."

Two narrow streets ran parallel to each other, sandwiched between the quay and the city wall. I saw the outline of buildings that had once backed on to the city wall but these had been pulled down. Sharp iron spikes topped the wall at this point.

"Dorian wanted to encourage people to use Wharf Gate," Ash said, following my gaze.

"I bet there are secret passages into the city," I said.

"There used to be," Urchin said, "but Dorian closed most of them off."

"But not all of them?" I said.

"No, he booby-trapped the remaining ones," Urchin said. "Punt says that one smuggler used a passage he thought only he knew about and fell into a trap. People heard his screams coming from the passage but no one knew how to rescue him; each day his screams got fainter until after ten days, they faded away to nothing."

I shivered.

"Unless he's working, Punt will be outside Stoutley's," Urchin said.

Shops and warehouses looked out onto the quayside. One shop had coils of rope hanging from hooks in the ceiling. Another shop stocked thick rolls of canvas, and three tough- looking old women sat on wooden stools with canvas on their lap, sewing it with long metal needles. A third shop sparkled with polished brass of all shapes and sizes.

"Those long thin ones are called telescopes," Urchin said, "and they let you see things that are far away."

They were beautiful. I gazed at them until Urchin tugged at my arm and we moved on.

We walked past what looked like a new two-storey sandstone warehouse with huge wooden double doors painted bright red to match a red-tiled roof.

"That's where Dorian stores his grain," Urchin said.

"Our grain, not his grain," I said.

"It's his at the moment," Urchin said, shrugging his shoulders.

"It's unguarded," I said.

"Only on the outside."

***

We continued along the quay until we saw a group of six boys standing in a line outside a door, above which hung a sign showing a stout man holding a steaming mug to his lips. The windows of this place were so grubby that I doubted that they let any light in.

"This is Stoutley's," Urchin said. "It's a coffee house. All the ship's captains and the merchants and their agents use it."

A fat man in a fur cap and a thick, brown, woolen cloak emerged from the coffee house. The boys in the line leaned forwards to catch the blast of heat coming from inside. The man raised two fingers, and the two boys at the front of the line followed him.

"Those lads work lighters, like Punt," Urchin said. "They queue for work here. Once Punt has finished whatever job he is on, he will join the line."

"What's a lighter?" I said.

"What Punt took you to the meeting in a couple of nights ago," Urchin said.

"It was dark," I said.

Urchin took my arm and we walked to the edge of the quay. "You see that big boat in the middle of the river," Urchin said, pointing it out. "And you see those little boats that have come along side of it, well, those little boats are called lighters."

The lighters were ferrying wooden barrels from the quayside to the big boat where the barrels were being hauled on board. They were small craft in length, maybe five times as long as me and about as wide as me. They had a flat bottom where the cargo was stored and a wooden platform at the back where the boy controlling the boat stood, making deft little flicks in the water with a single long oar. A cold wind was blowing in from the sea, rippling the surface of the water and making the lighters bob.

"Punt's just coming alongside the boat," Urchin said.

I peered across the water but he was too far away for me to see him properly. If I ever became rich, I would buy myself a shiny brass telescope.

We moved away from the edge of the quay and sheltered out of the wind behind a stack of wooden crates. The cold settled into my bones. Time passed, and I must have dozed.

***

"Here he comes," Urchin said.

I opened my eyes. A boy of about my age was approaching along the quayside. He wore black leggings and a dark blue, woolen smock. Pulled down almost to his eyes was a black woolen cap from which poked a fringe of black hair.

Urchin waved to him and the boy grinned at us and came over. My feet were frozen, and I stamped them back to life. "This is Keth." Urchin introduced me and Punt's grin widened.

"Nice to meet you in daylight," Punt said. "Are we up to something?"

He was so direct, it threw me for a moment, but I remembered how on the previous night, he'd said he was keen for action. "Do you want to help me to take some of our grain back, tonight?" I said.

"Does Ash know about this?" Punt said.

"We'll give him a full report afterwards," I said. "One at a time, with no interruptions."

"You're on." Punt's grin widened even further and his green eyes sparkled. "We'll talk to Bead to find out which is the best ship to plunder."

***

Urchin and I followed Punt along the quayside, stopping near a ship that was being loaded with wooden crates. Punt pointed out Bead near the ship's gangplank. She was a small girl with brown, shoulder-length hair, who looked to have seen no more than six or seven summers. She wore a gray dress with pockets at the side and a large pocket in the front.

She stood between two tall men, which emphasized just how small she was. One man wore a fur coat while the other had on a blue cloth jacket and a peaked cap. Bead held in her hands a wooden frame with wires attached across it. On the wires were wooden beads. The two men watched intently as Bead slid the beads rapidly along the wires, backwards and forwards.

"That's an abacus," Punt said. "Bead does sums with it, faster than anyone else on the wharf, and she never gets a sum wrong."

Bead said something, and the two men took a moment to look each other in the eye then shook hands with each other. Each man gave Bead an apple. She put them in the side-pockets of her dress then stowed her abacus in the pocket at the front.

As she left the two men, Punt waved to her, and she came over.

"This is Keth," Punt introduced me. "We're going to take back some of our grain, tonight."

"That's good," Bead said. "The last ship is due to leave on tomorrow's tide."

Bead was as relaxed about it as Punt was. I got the feeling they had been thinking about striking just this kind of blow against Dorian, and they had just been waiting for someone to give them permission to go ahead. I was being handed the role of rebel leader because I was the one who had said 'let's do something.'

"What's the best ship to go for?" I said.

"*The Sunrise*; they've just begun loading her," Bead said.

"How many will be on board tonight?" I said.

"The crew will be having a last night in the city," Punt said, "but they always have a guard on the ship."

"And it's moored close to Dorian's granary," Bead said. "If he calls for help then Dorian's guards will come running."

She walked back with us along the quayside and pointed out *The Sunrise*. It had three wooden masts: front, middle and back. The back of the boat was built up taller than the front, with windows in the side. The front of the boat came to a point and carried a wooden carving of a woman whose bottom half was a fish.

Dorian's granary was now a hive of activity. The doors had been opened and a line of men, bowed down by the grain sacks on their backs, shuffled across the quay and up a gangplank onto *The Sunrise*. They looked like a giant caterpillar.

"I know a couple of lads who will join us," Punt said. "We'll pick you up, Keth, at the meadow landing stage, soon as we can after curfew. That's the place I picked you and Silva up from before."

I nodded, hoping I remembered how to get there without blundering into the river by accident.

"How will we dispose of the grain?" I said.

"We've got a hideaway outside of the city," Punt said. I guessed this was part of their existing smuggling operation. "Can you, Grub and Smiley be at the usual spot," Punt asked Urchin, "and get Grist to meet us there?"

Urchin nodded.

"We'll drift down with the current and moor against the river side of *The Sunrise*," Punt continued. "We'll climb aboard, knock out the guard, fill the lighters up with grain, and be on our way."

Punt looked to me for approval. They knew the plan far better than I did but they needed me to act as the leader. "Sounds good," I said.

"What do I do?" Bead said.

"You've done your bit," Punt said.

"I'll watch from the quayside," she said. "I'll hoot like an owl if I need to warn you."

"But we don't want you getting into trouble," Punt said, looking uncomfortable. "You're just a little girl."

"I've got eyes, ears and a brain," Bead said. "I can use

them."

Punt looked at me, wanting me to take the decision. I admired Bead's spirit. "You're in, Bead," I said.

"Until tonight then," Punt said.

Punt walked off in the direction of Stoutley's Coffee House to pick up some more work.

***

"Little abacus girl," a commanding voice called from the entrance to the granary. "I need you to do some calculations."

We turned to look at the speaker and my heart missed a beat. I recognized the hook-nosed man in the black cloak, with the hood that was fitted tightly over his head. It was the grain collector. He had said that he was spending the winter in Russett, and where else would I expect to find the Prince's grain collector but outside the Prince's granary?

Bead walked over to the grain collector. I nudged Urchin, and we began to sidle away.

"Wait inside, little girl," the grain collector said. "You two, wait a moment," he called out to me and Urchin. His glance was as sharp as a peck.

Urchin and I looked at each other. Was this the moment to run? We had done nothing wrong. I held my ground, but Urchin scarpered.

The grain collector stalked over to me. He was wearing his black tights and his sharp, pointed, black leather boots. Did he just have the one set of clothes, I wondered, or did he have a chest somewhere filled with black hooded cloaks, black tights, and black boots?

"I recognize you," the grain collector said to me. "I saw you at Mottle and Brackford."

I nodded. I wished he didn't have such a good memory. "The troupe's here in Russett for the winter," I said.

"And where are you playing?" he said.

"Nowhere, yet," I said. "I thought we might get a gig at Stoutley's."

"I doubt it," he said. "Men need quiet to conduct their business."

"They wouldn't even let me in," I said.

"And why were you talking to the abacus girl and the timid, white-haired boy?"

"Local knowledge," I said. "The grownups, you excepted, won't talk to me."

He stared at me, as though he were weighing me up like a sack of grain and finding me a measure short.

"Where are your ravens?" I said, trying to change the subject. "Do they fly away for the winter?"

"They're here, keeping an eye on you," he said, giving me a thin-lipped smile. I heard a creak of wings and six ravens arrived and perched on the roof of the granary, looking in our direction. "I am a man with a destiny," the grain collector said. "Our paths have crossed three times now. That makes you significant. Does that frighten you?"

Man with a destiny, nonsense, I thought. More like an idiot with no friends to tell him black tights and knobby knees was a bad combination.

"I understand this land," he said. "At harvest time, my team of collectors travels through it, accompanied by my splendid ravens."

"What a responsible job you have," I said. "It sounds almost as much hard work as growing the grain."

His face flushed red and his gloved hand shot out and grabbed my left arm, just below the shoulder, squeezing it hard. I yelped with pain.

"I deserve to be recognized," he snarled. "I should be more than this." His eyes were wide, staring straight through me and out beyond the river. He wasn't upset with me; he had forgotten I was there.

The ravens hopped across the granary roof, their claws skittering on the tiles. The grain collector's face sagged, its red color seeping away. His eyes focused on me again, and he looked at his hand grasping my arm, as though he wondered how it had got there. He let my arm go.

"Change is coming," he said. "My ravens tell me it will arrive soon."

He turned and stalked back to the granary without a backward glance. I pulled a face at the ravens on the roof, but they just stared at me.

***

I made my way back to Wharf Gate, massaging my sore arm. It was the middle of the afternoon, judging by the position of the sun. Urchin fell into step beside me as soon as I'd passed through the gate back into the city. "Why didn't you run?" Urchin said.

"I hadn't done anything wrong," I said. "Besides, I know the man. He's the grain collector. He visits our village every year and takes away most of our grain, on behalf of Prince Dorian."

"Bet he's popular," Urchin said. "Are we still on for tonight?"

"Yes," I said. "This year, we're taking our grain back."

***

After leaving Urchin, I made my way back to the

lodging house. The sun was low in the sky by the time I slipped down the back alley and crept into the backyard. I was hungry, and I was hoping to eat something before I met up with Ma. He would be cross because I had missed rehearsals.

I snuck into the kitchen. A large pot of stew stood on top of the stove. I picked up a bowl and prepared to serve myself. I lifted the ladle, and it clanked against the side of the pot.

"Drop the ladle, laddie," Ma said. He stood framed in the doorway from the rehearsal room, tough and wiry like a string of gristle. I put the ladle back in the pot and put down my empty bowl. "Where have you been?" Ma said.

"I needed time alone," I said.

"I needed time with you here to rehearse," Ma said. "This is a troupe, Keth. We all work together."

"I'm sorry," I said.

"You can spend the rest of the day being alone in the stable loft," Ma said. "And don't bother coming in for supper because you have not earned it."

I slunk out of the kitchen, giving the stew pot a long pitiful glance. This did not win any sympathy, or stew, from Ma.

***

I lay on my back in the stable loft, chewing on a piece of straw, trying to keep my hunger pangs at bay. I moved as little as possible, conserving my energy for my night-time adventure, which I would now have to undertake on an empty stomach. Night had fallen, but I had no idea how long it would be until the curfew bell rang.

The stable door bumped open. "I just came to check on Thespian," Silva said.

"He's contented and letting rip the farts of the well-fed," I said.

Silva entered and hung her lantern on a nail by the door. She wore her black cap, and her silver hair spilled out from it and shone in the light. She was carrying something, and I smelled food. "I snuck you a bowl of stew and a hunk of bread," she said.

"Thanks," I said, touched that she had thought of me.

She reached up and handed them to me, and I began to wolf down the stew. "Where did you get to, Keth, after I left you?" she said, tilting her head up to me. Her wide cheekbones and narrow chin made her face look like an upturned triangle.

"I wandered around the city," I said. "I got lost and decided to stay lost for a bit."

"You're not planning to do anything stupid?" she said.

"Certainly not," I said. I was planning to do something brave and smart and not in the least bit stupid.

"Friends don't keep secrets from each other," she said.

The lump of bread in my mouth turned dry, and I struggled to swallow it. "No secrets," I said.

"That's good, because I'd be furious if you did," she said. "We wouldn't be friends anymore."

"Thanks for the stew," I said, handing her back the bowl.

"Goodnight, Keth," she said and left.

I wanted to tell her about the plan, but I thought that if I did she would put a stop to it, and then I would have let down Punt, Urchin and all the others. Once the plan had been successful, everyone would see things differently including, I hoped, Silva.

***

As I waited for the curfew bell, I wondered if Silva might still suspect me of being up to something, in spite of my denying it. I was upset by the thought that she did not trust me, even though she was right not to. I wished she was helping me.

The curfew bell rang. Perhaps she would slip out, follow me, and spoil what I was planning with Punt and Urchin, or I might persuade her to join us.

I slipped out of the stable and paused to listen. I heard voices coming from upstairs at the back of the house. I crept closer and strained to hear. Angry whispers were being exchanged between Ma and Silva.

"You're not going anywhere," Ma whispered. "Ragamuffin drank my cocoa tonight."

"Leave me alone," Silva hissed. "I've got work to do."

"Your work is performing in the troupe," Ma whispered. "And the troupe is neutral to Dorian."

"But, I'm not," Silva whispered. "I'm going, whatever you say."

"Then I'll start shouting and wake up the whole of Crib Street," Ma whispered.

"And what will you tell them?" Silva began to raise her voice. "That your daughter is a rebel? You're a great father; you let Rul go off and get killed, and now you're going to hand me over to Dorian for execution."

"I'll tell them you're slipping out to the stables to be with your boyfriend, Keth," Ma said.

Silva gasped. I hoped it covered the sound of my own gasp. "I hate you," Silva cried.

I heard something being thumped rapidly; possibly it was Silva beating Ma's chest. This was followed by silence. I winced. I felt dirty, because I'd listened to them hurting each other. I crept out of the backyard, no longer worried about Silva following me.

16 ROBBERY

I jogged through the city streets, making up for time that I had lost listening to Silva and Ma arguing. It was a clear cold night and the light from the splinter made it easy to see, but also easy to be seen. I found the spot where handholds had been chipped in the city wall. I climbed over the wall, feeling exposed in the splinterlight.

On the other side, I waded through the knee-high grass. The river reflected the splinterlight, making it look like a pale silver ribbon. My feet clumped on the planks of the wooden landing stage, and I trod more carefully to soften the sound.

"Is that you, Keth?" Punt whispered.

"It is," I whispered back.

I moved to the edge of the landing stage. Two lighters were moored there. Punt crouched on the platform at the back of one of the lighters. In the other lighter, a lad with ears that stuck out like handles sat on the platform, while a second lad sat inside. All three lads wore caps and smocks.

"That's Bilge on the platform," Punt whispered,

pointing to the boy with sticking out ears, "and Corac sitting inside."

I waved to the figures of Bilge and Corac and they waved back.

"He's too puny for this," Bilge whispered to Corac. His words carried to me on the breeze, and they stung. The boys who worked on the river were toughened up by loading and unloading heavy cargo every day, but farming the land was hard physical work and I'd grown up doing that. I'll show them I'm as tough as they are, I thought.

Picking a fight now would get us all captured. I boarded Punt's lighter, pretending I had not heard Bilge's whisper.

I tripped on something in the bottom of the lighter and almost fell over the side.

"Careful of the grapple," Punt whispered.

The grapple was a thin iron cylinder as long as my lower arm, with four big curved hooks of iron coming out of the top of it. Each hook pointed in a different direction to the others; looked at from the top, they made a cross shape. At the bottom of the cylinder was a ring with a long length of rope attached to it.

Punt pushed his lighter away from the landing stage, and Bilge and Corac in the other lighter followed us.

***

Punt stood on the platform at the back of his lighter. He let the current move the boat along, adjusting our direction with deft strokes of his oar that scarcely made a ripple. I gazed at the shoreline. The meadow gave way to a series of buildings with inlets between them, where the river made slurping noises.

"That's the Tannery Docks, where the rebels meet,"

Punt whispered.

Past the docks, there was a muddy section of riverbank that was then followed by a stretch of wooden wharf running beside the river. The water gurgled around the timber piles holding it up. Only a few boats were moored here.

The wooden wharf joined up with the stone quayside where more boats were moored, including *The Sunrise*. I was glad we had these boats between us and the quay, but at the same time, I was nervous, because we might be heard by their guards.

We came alongside *The Sunrise* and slowly travelled down its length. Its timber sides loomed above us.

Punt brought his oar out of the water. He picked up the grapple and positioned it so that it was hooked over the blade of his oar. He lifted up the oar, and the grapple was raised high into the air. He maneuvered his oar so that he placed the grapple over the rail of *The Sunrise*, two hooks on one side of the rail and two on the other. He removed the oar and stowed it in the lighter. The rope attached to the end of the grapple now hung down the side of *The Sunrise*. Punt took it and tied it to an iron ring at the back of the lighter. Doing all this, he had not made a sound. We were now moored to the big ship.

Bilge and Corac had moored their lighter just behind us, using the same method.

Punt climbed up the rope. I followed him. I hauled myself over the railing just in time to see Bilge and Corac creep up behind the guard. Bilge was drawing out a cudgel from his belt. I knew it was Bilge from the way his ears stuck out. Corac bent down, and Bilge jumped on Corac's back to gain extra height then swung his cudgel and smacked the guard on the top of the head. I winced. The guard's knees crumpled and Bilge and Corac together lowered him to the deck without a sound.

Bilge had brought rope and a cloth with him. He bound the guard's hands and feet while Corac gagged the guard with the cloth. I followed Punt across the timber deck and around the base of the central mast. We stopped at a wooden trapdoor, which was secured with an iron padlock.

"Entry to the hold," Punt whispered.

Bilge and Corac dragged the guard over to where we were.

"Is he alright?" I whispered.

Bilge shrugged. I knelt down and patted the guard's plump cheeks. His piggy little eyes fluttered open then closed again. At least he was alive.

"Who's brought the lock picks?" Punt whispered. The boys looked at each other. They looked at me. I stood up shaking my head. "Search the guard," Punt hissed.

Bilge and Corac searched him, but they did not find any keys. "Let's smash the lock," Bilge whispered.

"Too loud," Punt whispered, shaking his head. "If we just had a nail or something."

"Would a needle work?" I whispered, remembering that I had my mum's needle pinned in my jerkin.

"We can try it," Punt whispered.

I unpicked the needle and handed it to Punt. He knelt down by the lock and worked on it. We held our breath. If this did not work then the entire trip had been wasted. We heard a click and the lock sprung open. I breathed a sigh of relief. Punt grinned and handed me back the needle. I pinned it back in my jerkin and sent my mum a silent thank you.

Bilge and Corac raised the trapdoor. Punt had a lantern attached to his belt. He lit it and shone a narrow beam down into the hold, illuminating sacks of grain, piled one on top of the other.

Bilge and Corac descended into the hold. I moved to join them, but Punt stopped me. "We need you to drag the sacks across the deck to the rail," Punt whispered.

It made sense, but I had the feeling he thought I was not strong enough to lift a grain sack out of the hold.

Bilge and Corac lifted the sacks up to Punt, who piled them on the deck. I dragged the sacks over to the rail. They were heavy and awkward, and it was exhausting work. The pile of sacks beside Punt grew faster than I could drag them. When Punt thought we had enough sacks to fill both lighters, he, Bilge and Corac helped me move the remaining sacks.

Corac and Punt pulled tightly-wrapped canvas packages from beneath their smocks.

"These are slings," Punt whispered. A sling consisted of a length of rope that at one end split into four, and each of these four ends was knotted into a corner of a square of canvas.

Corac climbed down into their lighter. Bilge put a sack on the canvas square of his sling. He pulled the rope tight, and the corners of the canvas curled up, holding the sack in place. He then lifted the sling over the side and let the rope out, lowering the sack down to Corac in the lighter. Corac took the sack, and Bilge pulled the sling back up.

Punt climbed down into our lighter, and I began lowering sacks of grain down to him using our sling. It was a simple process but it was hard work, and my arms ached, especially my left arm where the grain collector had grabbed me earlier in the day.

Bilge and Corac finished loading their lighter with sacks. I still had several sacks to go.

"Do you want me to take over?" Bilge whispered.

The sensible answer was yes, but I'm not always sensible. "I'm fine," I whispered back. I wanted to prove I was as tough as they were.

Bilge shrugged, clambered over the rail, and boarded his lighter with Corac. Punt, with a wave of his hand, suggested they should be on their way. Corac slackened their mooring rope then used his oar to lift the grapple from off the rail. They pushed away from the boat and left us.

***

I continued lowering the sacks to Punt. I was on my second last sack when disaster struck. I lifted the sling over the rail of the boat ready to lower it down to Punt, and the muscles in my left arm cramped.

I yelped in agony and clutched at my left arm with my right hand, letting go of the rope. Punt cried in alarm as the heavy sack of grain plummeted towards him. I heard a loud thump and a splash. I stuck my head over the rail. Punt had been knocked unconscious, but he had been lucky and fallen inside the lighter. The splash must have been the grain sack going over the side after it had struck Punt.

We had made a lot of noise and we needed to get away as quickly as possible. I clambered over the rail. One handed, I climbed part way down the mooring rope then jumped the rest of the way. I wobbled as I landed on the platform of the lighter and almost fell over the side.

The cramp in my left arm was starting to fade. I raised the oar to lift off the grapple from the rail. I slipped the blade beneath the hooks of the grapple and pushed hard. The grapple did not move. The mooring rope was taut; I needed to slacken it off first.

I stowed the oar then flung myself on the iron ring at the back of the lighter and scrabbled at the knot. My fingers gouged at it, but it remained tight.

I forced myself to take a deep breath and calm down. I studied the knot in the splinterlight. I saw how the rope wound around itself, and I saw the bit I needed to pull on to loosen the knot. I tugged on it, and, sweet relief, the knot unraveled.

The rope slid swiftly through the iron ring as the tension in it slackened. The back of the lighter drifted away from the side of *The Sunrise*. I reached out over the water, towards *The Sunrise*, and grabbed the rope with the idea of pulling us back. Bad mistake. In the blink of an eye, I found myself suspended over the water with my hands clutching the rope and my feet on the back of the lighter. The water would be freezing and my clothing would drag me down. Swimming was not an option, but drowning was.

My feet slid from the lighter and I was left clinging to the rope against the side of *The Sunrise*. In the splinterlight, I saw the current pick up the lighter and draw it further away from me, with Punt laid out across the sacks of grain, unconscious.

"Too-wit-too-woo, too-wit-too-woo." It sounded like a little girl, trying to hoot like an owl. Bead was giving us a warning. Someone on the quayside had heard us, and we were in trouble.

I hatched a desperate plan of escape. I scrambled up the rope and flung myself over the rail of *The Sunrise*. I heard shouts from the quayside.

"Are you okay, Jem?"

"He's not answering."

"Get a boarding plank."

"Too-wit-too-woo, too-wit-too-woo," Bead sang out.

"That owl gives me the creeps, sounds almost human."

I added my voice to the shouting. "Help, help," I screamed at the top of my voice. "Save us, robbery."

I ran across the deck of the boat. The guard, Jem, was struggling with his ropes. I waved to him as I dashed by, and his piggy little eyes filled with hate. I heard the thump as the end of the boarding plank landed on the deck, and I sprinted in that direction.

I skidded to a halt at the head of the boarding plank just as the first man prepared to step on board.

"Robbery, robbery," I gasped. "They knocked out poor Jem."

"It's alright, lad," he said. "You're safe now."

I wished that was true. He moved past me, followed by two other men.

"Poor Jem," I blubbered. "Poor, poor, Jem." I wrung my hands as I hurried down the boarding plank.

Several men had gathered by the foot of the boarding plank. They had lanterns, so I put my head in my hands to stop them seeing my face. They patted me on the shoulder as I passed among them. I began to walk in the direction of Wharf Gate.

"That dratted boy is one of them." The cry came up from the boat.

Poor Jem must have had his gag removed, and now the game was up.

***

I ran. Behind me, I heard whistles and shouts and the footsteps of several men running after me. I looked over my shoulder to see how close they were. Bad mistake. I tripped. I went from running full tilt to lying flat on my face.

Four men were pursuing me. In unison, they roared in triumph as I fell over. The next moment, a small head poked out from behind a wooden crate. It was Bead. She threw something. Wooden beads rolled across the quayside into the path of my pursuers. One moment the men were upright, grinning and with arms outstretched, ready to grab me, and the next they were flying through the air, arms flailing, before landing on their backs with a series of satisfying thuds.

I got to my feet and ran on. I planned to dash through Wharf Gate and lose my pursuers in the city alleyways but as I reached the gate, I saw that it was closed. I kept running along the quayside and once more, I heard the men in pursuit begin to close on me. This time I didn't look back.

In the splinterlight, I saw the stone quay end and become a wooden wharf, just as it had at the other end of the quay. The slap of my feet on stone turned to a clatter as the timber planks of the wharf bounced beneath my feet.

I had a bad feeling I was going to run out of wharf soon, and the only way to avoid capture would be to jump in the river and drown.

"Ahoy." A shout came from ahead of me on the river.

I glanced in that direction and saw the outline of Punt, who had regained consciousness, and now stood on the platform of the lighter, working his oar. He had turned the lighter to face into the current, a little way ahead of me, and was bringing it into the piles of the wharf.

The breath of one of my pursuers tickled the back of my neck; his fingertips brushed my back. Fear gave me acceleration and I pulled away from him.

I closed on where Punt now nestled his lighter against

the side of the wharf, next to a wooden ladder, but I would be caught when I had to slow down to clamber onto the ladder.

I put on one last spurt of speed, and instead of going for the ladder, I dived from the side of the wharf, aiming at the lighter.

I hung in the air for a long moment, frozen in the splinterlight, then I plummeted. The lighter seemed to rush up to meet me. I landed on the grain sacks with a thud, and I heard a ripping noise beneath me. I had a horrible thought that I'd torn my stomach open, but although I felt bruised and winded, I didn't feel any sharp or jagged pain.

I struggled to my knees and felt about with my hand. The top-most grain sack that I had landed on had split at the side and was leaking grain. I positioned the sack so the tear was on the top, and we would lose no further grain.

Punt rowed the lighter out towards the center of the river. Shouts carried across the water to us from the wharf.

"They're getting away."

"Get some boats searching the river."

"Hurry, I can still just make them out."

"The grain collector won't be pleased." This last voice sounded frightened.

A large ship anchored in the middle of river loomed up, and Punt navigated us around it. We were no longer visible from the wharf.

***

Punt made for the opposite bank of the river, working hard with his oar to speed us along. Instead of landing when we reached the other side, Punt directed the lighter into a creek that emptied into the river.

We went along this creek for a few minutes then Punt turned into a smaller side creek that would have been hard to spot in daylight, and in the splinterlight seemed to appear from nowhere.

This creek was shallow and twisted and turned. The bottom of the lighter scraped against the creek bed. Trees and bushes grew thick on the banks of the creek and cut off the splinterlight.

"We'll have to drag the lighter, now," Punt whispered after a while.

I got out. The water was knee deep and cold. I waded energetically to the front of the lighter, trying to keep my feet from going numb.

"Quieter," Punt whispered.

I realized someone might hear my splashing, and I moved more carefully. We guided the lighter along the creek in the darkness, and I lost all sense of time. We had just worked the lighter around a tight bend, when our path was blocked by the branches of a weeping willow that swept right across the creek. I ducked beneath them.

"Over here," a voice whispered from the bank in the shelter of the willow tree. We were illuminated by a thin beam of light from a lantern. I shaded my eyes. Someone hung the lantern from a branch of the willow, and it produced a small pool of light on the bank, where six kids were waiting for us. I recognized Urchin, Grub, and Smiley, as well as Bilge and Corac from the other lighter. The final kid was a squat girl, a summer or so younger than me, with a square chin and a flat, squashed nose. She introduced herself as Grist.

We dragged the lighter in their direction. Punt moored it to the trunk of the willow, where it nudged against the lighter of Bilge and Corac that was moored a little further along the bank. They had already unloaded their grain sacks.

"What happened to you?" Bilge asked.

"We got delayed," Punt said with a shrug. "I'll tell you later. We'll work in pairs to unload the sacks."

Punt and I lifted up the top-most sack and passed it to Urchin and Grub. Grain from the split side spilled on to Urchin and pattered down on to the river bank.

"Careful with this one," I said. "The side has split." I didn't want to waste any of the precious grain that we had risked so much to steal.

Urchin and Grub carried their sack up the bank. I thought I heard a trickle of grain striking the grass. Punt shrugged at me. What could we do? We handed a sack to Corac and Bilge then another one to Smiley and Grist. The hiding place for the grain must have been a little way from the river, as once a pair had disappeared up the bank with a sack then we had to wait a bit for them to return. At last the lighter was empty.

"We'll rejoin Pit Creek and head upstream," Punt whispered. "We'll pick up a load of stone from Waggett's quarry at first light and return to unload at the quay as though nothing had happened."

I thought about this and the stir that I'd created at the quayside. "I don't think I can come back with you," I whispered to Punt. "People might have seen what I look like when they chased me."

"Can you get Keth back into the city?" Punt whispered to Grist.

"No problem," Grist whispered back.

"Good work," Corac said and shook my hand.

Bilge patted my shoulder. He and Corac were grinning as they waved goodbye to us and walked over to their lighter.

"We've done it," Punt whispered, clenching his fist and punching the air. "We've hurt Prince Dorian." He moved to the trunk of the willow tree to unmoor his lighter.

I was elated. I wanted to yell for joy but of course, we had to be silent, and we were still in danger.

***

The branches of the willow rustled as the lighters departed. Grist took the lantern down and shut off its beam. She led the way up the bank. I followed next, with Urchin behind me.

"There's an old ruined farmhouse here," Urchin whispered. "It's got a hidden cellar, where we've put the grain."

"But it will get damp," I whispered back in alarm.

"Punt stole some waterproof skins a little while ago," Urchin whispered. "We've wrapped them in those."

We walked across muddy fields and ditches in the dim splinterlight. The others had been this way before and knew where to tread. After I had tripped and fallen several times, we worked out a system where I held on to the back of Grist's belt, and she whispered instructions.

"Aren't you going to show me the ruined farmhouse?" I asked, after we had been walking some time.

Grist stopped so suddenly, I walked into the back of her. "Why?" she said. "Don't you trust us?"

"Of course, I trust you," I said.

"You can be too trusting," Grist said. "I don't trust you, yet."

I had just assumed everyone involved with the rebels was trustworthy. Grist set off again, and I followed, clutching the back of her belt. We continued walking until Grist called a halt, and we crawled beneath a hedge to rest. I closed my eyes, and I must have slept.

17 THE MORNING AFTER

Urchin shook me awake. I crawled out from under the hedge where we had spent the rest of the night. The sky was starting to lighten with the approach of dawn. I was cold and stiff so I did the stretching exercises that Grunter had taught me. Slowly, my body began to loosen up and feel as though it belonged to me.

"Do you live in a house?" Grist asked me.

"Well, I sleep in the stable," I said. I didn't want her to think I was stuck up.

"But you go inside the house," she said.

"Yes," I said. I was not sure what she driving at.

"You need to wash your clothes," she said. "I won't watch."

She was right. I had done a lot of falling over, and it now looked like I was wearing mud instead of clothes. In Mottle, it would not have mattered; we would have been glad of the extra layer of warmth. Here, someone at the lodging house would ask questions.

We stopped at a ditch that was knee deep in water and I washed my jerkin and pants. The water was clean as long as I was careful not to stir it up. The grain that had stuck to my clothes from the split sack floated away. I wrung out as much water as I could then put my damp clothes back on.

After the ditch, we crossed a field and picked up the road that ran beside the river. I recognized it from when the troupe had first arrived in Russett, which seemed like ages ago. A clump of trees stood by the riverbank, bare except for a few individual yellow leaves fluttering in the breeze.

"I'll see you in a few nights' time," Grist said. "It's good to know the rebels finally have a leader."

I was going to ask her who it was then I realized she meant me. My stomach knotted with fear. I had been playing with the idea of being a rebel leader and all of a sudden, it had become a reality. I had not planned any further than stealing the grain, and my fellow rebels had done most of the planning for that.

Grist waved to us and set off away from the city.

***

Small groups of people with their heads down were shuffling towards the city, and we followed them.

"Does Grist not live in Russett?" I said.

"She lives in Fledge," Urchin said. "Her family used to own the watermill there. Dorian took it but they still run it. She can get the grain ground into flour so we can pass it on."

"She's a bit bossy, isn't she?" I said. "Why isn't she the rebel leader?"

"No one likes her," Urchin said.

"And they like Ash?" I said.

"No, but we're scared of him," Urchin said.

I was scared too. In the space of one night, I had become an alternative rebel leader, and I wondered how Ash would react to that. I decided not to let my worries about the future put a damper on our triumph. "We've struck a real blow against wicked Prince Dorian," I said.

"That's right," Smiley said, with a proper smile, not just his scarred half smile.

"We're the best," Grub said.

We lifted up our heads and strode down the road, filled with pride. People were staring at us. "Stop looking cheerful," I whispered. "We look out of place."

We joined a crowd of people and a line of carts queuing on the bridge into the city. The bell for the end of curfew sounded somewhere inside the walls and a moment later, the gates at the far end of the bridge creaked open. A tide of people flowed into the city. The sweaty guard and the guard with the lazy eye were on duty. They did not give us a glance.

We arrived in Dorian's Square.

"You can contact me at number 37 Crib Street in an emergency," I said. We shook hands and I left them nestled at the foot of the statue of Prince Dorian. I had no idea what to do next except return to the lodging house and eat breakfast.

***

I opened the backdoor of the lodging house and entered the kitchen. The rest of the troupe was already at the table eating breakfast. Ragamuffin lay in front of the stove snoring and Madame Patwig was leaning over the stove, stirring the porridge pot. She shivered and pulled her red woolen shawl tight around her shoulders.

"Close the door, dear," she said. "The draught is

tickling me."

I did as I was told then lumbered over to the shelf and picked up a bowl. I licked my lips as Madame Patwig filled it to the brim with porridge.

"You look tired," she said. "I think Ragamuffin must have got your share of sleep last night."

Silva glanced at me sharply. I avoided meeting her eyes. I joined the others at the table and shoveled the hot porridge into my mouth, eating as fast as I could swallow.

"Would you pass the milk please, Silva?" Ma said, breaking the silence that had settled over the table. Silva ignored him and glared down at her bowl. I remembered that Ma and Silva had had a massive row the previous night.

Elba pushed the milk jug towards Ma. "Thank you, Elba," Ma said, "but I asked Silva."

"Yes," Elba said, "but I thought it might have curdled by the time you got it."

Crag got up from the table. "I need to visit my barber," he said, flouncing his blonde locks.

"If you could all stay in the lodging house first thing this morning," Ma said. "I may need to call on you."

Crag pouted but nodded and left the kitchen. Elba and Grunter exchanged a look then got up from the table and left as well. Ragamuffin woke up, stretched, mewed then strolled over to the back door. Madame Patwig went over and let him out. I kept spooning porridge into my mouth.

"It's no use sulking, Silva," Ma said. "We have to talk."

Silva continued to glare down at her bowl. I was surprised she had not burned a hole through the bottom of it and at any moment, the table would start smoldering. Talking was going to be a Ma-only activity.

Ma sighed and got up from the table. "Give Keth his reading lesson, Silva," Ma said. "I will be in the parlor if I have callers, dear Madame Patwig."

Ma left the kitchen. I licked the last of the porridge from my bowl. Madame Patwig approached the table, her black dress rustling as she walked. She patted the pale violet curls above her pear-shaped face.

"If you need to confide in a more experienced woman friend, Silva dear," Madame Patwig said, "I'm sure Keth would like an extra bowl of porridge to eat outside in the backyard."

It was a bribe but I was still hungry. I stood up, clutching my empty bowl.

"That's very kind of you to offer, dear Madame Patwig," Silva said, with her sweetest smile, which meant she was furious inside, "but I must give Keth his reading lesson."

"I understand, dear," Madame Patwig said, smiling just as sweetly as Silva. She snatched the bowl out of my hands and began clearing away the breakfast things.

Silva got up from the table and knelt in front of the stove. She spread the ashes and began writing the letters of the alphabet. I knelt down beside her and called out their names.

"You can rely on me to keep a secret," Madame Patwig said, and left the kitchen.

"But only for as long as it takes you to waddle down Crib Street and blab it out to the first person you meet," Silva muttered under her breath.

***

As we knelt in front of the stove, its heat made my damp clothes steam. "Damp wool," Silva said, wrinkling her nose. "Why are your clothes wet?"

"Perhaps the stable roof is leaking," I said.

"We need to fix that straight away," she said.

I knew my lie would not stand up to close scrutiny. "I got caught in a sudden downpour," I said, "while walking between the stable and the back door this morning."

Silva raised her left eyebrow.

I wanted to tell someone about my adventure, and Silva was my best friend. The only problem was that she had told me that we would not be friends at all if I did something exactly like what I had done last night.

The grain robbery has been a success, I told myself. Silva might be upset but she would soon cheer up. Once she had got over her anger, she might be prepared to help us and smooth things over with Ash. I decided to plunge in and tell her the truth. "A few of us rebels went out last night, and we robbed a grain ship," I said.

Silva's eyes went wide and this time both her eyebrows raised. The color drained from her face. "Did Ash approve of your little adventure?" she said in a tight little voice.

"No, but we'll give him a full report at the next meeting," I said. "He'll approve of it once he hears how much grain we stole; two lighters filled with grain sacks."

"Ash will kill you when he finds out," she said.

"He'll be a bit cross at first," I said, "but I can weather that. I'm used to people being cross with me."

Silva grabbed the front of my jerkin, knotting the wool between her fists and shook me so hard I thought my teeth would come loose from my head. "I'm not joking," she hissed. "He will kill you."

She let go of me and shoved me away from her. I lay on my back on the stone flags. Her reaction scared me. I thought she would have been upset that I had kept it secret from her, but she was so worried about Ash's response, she had not mentioned it

"You'll have to flee," she said. "Pack your things right now and get out of the city."

We jumped as someone rapped hard on the door of the lodging house.

"Ash wouldn't use the front door," I said, relaxing. "He's more likely to come down the chimney."

We heard the door open then voices in the hallway. If it wasn't Ash then perhaps it was the grain collector.

"Flee now, Keth," Silva said. She leaped up and began to drag me to the back door. She looked so desperate on my behalf, I struggled to my feet, ready to make a dash for it; I hesitated. If I ran out now, I would be saying goodbye to both the troupe and the rebels.

"I've started something here and I need to see it through," I said. My voice was meant to sound heroic but it came out as a hollow squeak.

An insistent inner voice was whispering inside my head. "The grain collector is in the parlor laying out his thumbscrews, and Ash is in the chimney sharpening his knife. Run, Keth, run."

I stood rooted to the spot with my hand on the backdoor.

"Can I have you all in the front parlor?" Ma's voice echoed through the house.

The moment to flee had past.

***

Silva and I trotted down the hall of the lodging house. I wondered who would be waiting for us in the parlor. At least I was not being summoned alone.

"Act as though nothing has happened," Silva whispered. "Try not to appear scared or jittery."

We entered the front parlor. Ma and another man

were standing in front of the fire warming their backsides, watched over by the late Colonel Patwig hanging above the fireplace. The logs in the fireplace were blazing, and I cheered myself with the thought that if Ash had been hiding up the chimney, waiting to slit my throat, he would have been roasted by now.

Ma's visitor was short and wide, with a round chest the same width as his waist, short bandy legs and arms bulging with muscles. He looked like a barrel on legs. He wore a black leather jerkin, and on top of his head sat a circular leather cap. His face looked as though it had been sewn together from scraps, it had so many scars on it.

Crag was already in the room; perhaps he had been listening at the parlor door. He was standing by the window where the drab winter light did its best to light up his profile as he gazed out at the street, doing his best moody but soulful look.

Silva went over and sat in one of the two armchairs, and Ma moved away from the fire to take up position behind her. She scowled up at him.

Elba and Grunter entered together. Elba sat in the other armchair opposite Silva, looking relaxed and gracious in spite of all the uncomfortable lumps in it. Grunter took up position behind the armchair, his hands resting lightly on Elba's shoulders.

I loitered near the parlor door. I might need to make a quick escape.

"Are you coming or going, Keth?" Ma said to me.

Doing my best to look relaxed and at ease, I strolled further into the parlor and perched on the edge of a small table. It toppled over, sending me crashing to the floor together with its contents, a glassy-eyed porcelain doll in a white silk dress, a carved wooden pig painted purple and a collection of toothpicks in a circular brass jar. I righted the table, put the doll, the pig, and the brass jar back on top, and began picking up the tooth picks.

"If I could have your attention," Ma said. "Your attention, Keth."

I looked up sharply and upset the small table again. The ornaments fell, and one of the doll's glass eyes bounced out and rolled under the cabinet filled with stuffed birds. I put the small table back upright then crawled in that direction.

"Get it later, Keth," Ma said.

"Keth's our fool," Silva said to the visitor.

"Everyone thinks he's acting when he's being an idiot on stage," Crag said.

"That' enough, Crag," Ma said. "Keth, if you'd be kind enough to pay attention." I sat up straight and kept still; that way I wouldn't knock over anything else. "I'd like to introduce you all to Master Bircher, who is the landlord of the highly esteemed Anvil Inn on Forge Street," Ma said, indicating the visitor.

"Pleased to meet you all," Master Bircher said and smiled at us.

I gaped. His teeth were made of wood. He caught my stare and grinned. "Finest mahogany," Master Bircher said. "I lost the originals when I swallowed a patron's fist. I'm a hard bloke with even harder teeth."

"Master Bircher is going to employ us as the entertainment every evening at the Anvil Inn," Ma said, "so let me introduce you all."

"This is my daughter, Silva," Ma said, patting her shoulder. Silva shot Ma a dark look.

"And sitting opposite her is Elba and her husband Grunter," Ma continued.

"I remember you, Grunter," Master Bircher laughed, flashing his polished wooden teeth. "You beat me in an arm wrestle three years ago, and my wrist still twinges on a cold morning." Grunter and Master Bircher grinned at each other, two strong men sharing a memory.

"That's Crag over by the window," Ma said. Crag and Master Bircher exchanged a nod.

"And Keth has introduced himself in his own unique way," Ma said. "He's our new fool."

"Better a new fool than an old fool," Master Bircher said.

I was not sure what he meant by that but we all laughed anyway because he said it in a jolly voice, and he was paying us.

"Would it be possible to have a look at where we're playing, before this evening, Master Bircher?" Elba asked.

"If you can come now, the inn will be quiet," Master Bircher said. "It's about the only time when it is."

"We'll all go," Ma said, "and we can work out our running order."

The meeting seemed to be over so I knelt down to peer under the cabinet filled with stuffed birds to locate the doll's eye.

"Careful, Keth," Silva said. "You might find Ash hiding under there." I leaped back in alarm and smacked into the small table, which turned a somersault and landed on the porcelain head of the doll with a loud crack. "Ash from the fire," Silva said, smiling sweetly, while everyone else stared at me as though I had gone mad.

"Don't worry about finding the doll's eye," Ma said, looking down at what remained of the doll's head. "If I was paying you anything, this would be coming out of your wages."

As the others filed out of the parlor, Silva stopped to help me pick up the table and the ornaments. "Take your chance and run," she whispered to me, "or you'll end up with a head like that doll."

I shuddered but I gritted my teeth. I refused to be frightened away.

***

Silva and I brought up the rear of our party that morning as we made our way along Forge Street to the Anvil Inn. It was a drab chill day with gray clouds promising rain later.

"Slip away, Keth," Silva said, "before Ash finds you."

"Wonderful, isn't it?" I whispered to her. "Ash never thinks of taking action against Dorian, but as soon as someone on his own side does something, he wants to murder them."

I had decided I was staying. I believed that, whatever Silva might say, Ash would give me the chance to explain myself.

Forge Street was where most of the blacksmiths had their smithies. The air was filled with the sound of banging and hammering and the hiss of steam as red hot metal was quenched in tubs of water. Groups of people clustered near the doors to the smithies. The hot blast from the forges made this the warmest street in the city.

Everyone who worked here seemed to have been built on a bigger scale than other people in the city. The blacksmiths were huge brawny men who carried massive hammers as though they were as light as twigs.

The Anvil Inn was situated midway along the street. It was built of whitewashed stone that had turned gray under the onslaught of soot from the forges. The roof was slate; thatch would have soon gone up in flames with so many sparks flying about. A battered wooden sign showing an anvil with a tankard of ale on top of it hung above the door and creaked in the breeze.

Inside, light trickled through the grimy windows, revealing a single large room filled with wooden tables and benches. I looked up and saw smoke-blackened rafters and a dirty ceiling. A bar ran down the right hand wall and in the far corner, on the side opposite the bar, was a small triangle-shaped wooden stage, partly covered by a set of wooden stairs leading to the upstairs rooms.

"This is the troupe providing the entertainment tonight, Smeggle," Master Bircher said to a boy in an apron. Smeggle had a lick of sandy-colored hair falling over his forehead, and he was busy walking between the benches, strewing fresh sawdust on the floor. "Helps soak up the ale and the blood," Master Bircher explained.

"Where does that door go to?" Silva asked, pointing to a door halfway along the back wall.

"That leads to the kitchens and the backyard," Master Bircher said.

Silva gave me a look that suggested she wanted me to take careful note of possible escape routes.

"How are we going to manage costume changes?" I asked Ma, trying to distract myself from thinking about running away.

"We're not doing plays," Ma said. "People at an inn are coming and going all evening, so they won't sit through a whole play. We'll sing songs and do comic sketches."

"And I'll challenge any man to an arm wrestle," Grunter said.

"We'll make that the climax of the night," Ma said with a grin. He sat on the edge of the stage. "I reckon we've got enough space to do the 'Unsuitable Suitor' routine."

Elba climbed on stage and sang a series of notes. Silva walked around the room listening intently to her. "The sound carries okay," Silva called to Elba.

I jumped when someone tugged at my sleeve. It was Smeggle, the boy in the apron. "There's a white-haired kid outside asking to speak with you," he said.

It sounded like Urchin. Why did he need to speak to me so soon? Everyone else in the troupe was busy and they did not notice me slip out of the inn.

18 THE RAVENS

As I emerged from the Anvil Inn, I saw Urchin hopping from one foot to the other, anxious to speak to me. He hurried over and grabbed my arm. "Your landlady told me where to find you," Urchin said. "Bead's gone into hiding. They found the beads from her abacus on the dockside."

My stomach turned to jelly. She must have tossed her abacus beads at the feet of my pursuers to make them fall over and buy me time. Bead was in big trouble, and I was the one who had told her she could be involved. I felt guilty, and I dropped my eyes from Urchin's face. I was looking at the dirty brown sack he wore, and I noticed little golden chunks stuck to it.

Without thinking, I picked one off him and examined it between my fingertips. It was a grain of wheat. Urchin brushed at his sacking, knocking off bits of grain and dirt.

"KWAA." A bird squawked above us. We looked up. A raven perched on the inn sign.

It flew down and pecked at the grain at Urchin's feet. "KWAA," the raven cawed and stared at us with beady eyes.

"Stupid bird." Urchin kicked at the raven, who hopped away from him. The raven cocked its head to one side and stared at us. "Those birds are all over the city this morning," Urchin said, scowling at it.

"I hate them," I said. "They used to fly around our village when the grain collector came. They knew if you were hiding any grain."

How had Urchin managed to get grain on his clothes? In a flash, I thought of the grain sack that had split when I had landed on it. Grain had spilled on to Urchin when he and Grub had carried that sack from the lighter to the hidden cellar.

My blood turned cold. If the raven had pecked me, I would have bled ice.

We had left a trail for the ravens to find. Grain would have spilled from the split sack into Punt's lighter. A trail of grain would run from the creek where we moored to the entrance to the hidden cellar. The only reason I didn't have grains on me was that I had washed my clothes in the ditch, because I was going back to the lodging house where mud would be noticed.

I had to warn Punt then try to clean up any grain lying near the hidden cellar, before the ravens found it. I thought about getting Urchin and his friends to help, but I suspected that the raven was following him.

"Walk back to Dorian's Square," I said. "You, Grub and Smiley need to find a place where you can wash any grain from your clothes. Don't go near the hidden cellar, I think the raven is following you."

Urchin gulped and glanced at the raven, who stared back at him. Urchin set off down the street and the raven flew up to the roof of the inn and hopped across the slates, following Urchin's progress.

I hurried in the opposite direction, making for the lodging house. If I just turned up on the wharf, I might be recognized so I needed a disguise.

***

I turned into Crib Street. Garrick, from a few doors down, was standing in his doorway looking up at the rooftop. I followed his gaze and saw a raven perched on the roof edge opposite the entrance to the lodging house. Garrick turned to me and doffed his black felt cap in greeting.

"Mysterious creatures," Garrick said. "Harbingers of doom."

"Has it been there long?" I said.

"Best part of the morning," Garrick said. "Has someone fallen ill at your place, Keth? People say a watching raven is supposed to be a sign of imminent death."

I shuddered at hearing Garrick, with his rich actor's voice, rolling out words like doom and imminent death, especially as they might be mine.

"Everyone's fine," I said. "We went over to Forge Street. We've got a gig at the Anvil Inn."

"That's a rough and boisterous tavern," Garrick said, scratching his blotchy red nose. "Get the blacksmiths to make you some armor."

"I'll catch you later," I said to Garrick and entered the lodging house.

***

I trotted down the hall. The door to the parlor was open and I heard Madame Patwig trilling inside. I peeped in as I passed and she was singing while dusting the ornaments. The remains of the doll had been swept away.

In the rehearsal room, I rummaged around in the troupe's costume hamper, looking for a disguise. I came up with a blue woolen coat that I put on over my jerkin and a wig of tight golden curls. Silva or I used the wig when we were playing palace messengers or the woodcutter's baby. I shuddered as I put the wig on. It made me look such an idiot, I imagined that my brains were gurgling out from the soles of my feet.

I slipped through the kitchen and out into the backyard. If the raven at the front was keeping watch on me then I intended to give it the slip. A sleek, fat raven perched on the fence near the stable. It was plumper than the one in Crib Street, on the other side of the lodging house. The raven eyed me as I walked over to it. I stopped just over an arm length away from it. I stared at the raven, and it stared back at me. Fly away, stupid bird, I thought.

I leaped back as the raven seemed to explode in a cloud of black fur and feathers. Had my own thoughts been so powerful, they had blown up the bird? I looked down and saw Ragamuffin holding the raven in its mouth. I must have distracted the raven, and Ragamuffin had taken his chance to pounce.

The raven's wings twitched once then fell still. Ragamuffin dragged the raven's carcass away, keeping a watchful eye on me. He was not planning to share his prize with anyone.

I grinned at him then slipped out the backyard gate.

***

I ran, dodging through the crowds. I wanted to talk to

Punt as soon as possible. As I turned into Wharf Street, leading down to Wharf Gate, I saw that traffic was queued up. The guards on the gate were searching all the carts and looking hard at all the people passing through. On top of the gate were perched six ravens.

I slowed to a walk and joined a line of people filing through the gate.

One of the guards was wearing what looked like a white linen cap on his head. As I got closer, I realized it was a head bandage, and the fat cheeks and piggy eyes below the bandage belonged to Jem, the guard on the boat, who we had knocked out. He had been stationed here to see if he recognized any of his attackers.

My first thought was to run for it, but I controlled my panic. The worst thing I could do was to draw attention to myself. I stayed in line, sticking close to the back of the man in front of me.

"Oi, Goldie, what do you want here?" a guard said to me. He had a flat, pulped nose and his breath stank of stale beer.

"Meeting my uncle," I said. "I'm late."

"Have a look at this kid, Jem," the guard said. I tensed, ready to run, but the guard put a hand on my arm. Jem turned to look at me. "If you had curls like this kid, the cudgel would have bounced straight back off your head," the guard laughed.

"The light from those curls would have blinded the attacker," another guard sniggered.

Jem was annoyed by the teasing and he was looking at my hair rather than my face. He turned away and spat.

"Some folk can't take a joke, Goldie." The guard laughed, let go of my arm and shoved me through the gate.

***

I jogged along the quay to Stoutley's Coffee Shop. Punt was not in the long line of boys outside waiting for work. I walked to the edge of the quay. *The Sunrise* and several of the other ships had left on the early morning, outgoing tide. Traffic on the river was quiet. I studied the ripples on the surface of the water. The tide was now coming in.

I spotted Punt a little further along the quay. He had his lighter moored against the quayside, and men were unloading heavy, lumpy sacks from it and piling them on to a cart.

I waited until the last sack was unloaded and the men stood on the quay dusting their hands.

"My master wants a word," I called out to Punt.

For a moment, he did not recognize me. He was looking at my golden hair. He grinned, as he realized who I was. "Come on board," Punt said to me. "We can talk on the water."

I climbed down a ladder set into the quayside and boarded his lighter. "Less chance of being overheard on the water," Punt said, untying his lighter and pushing away from the quayside. "Do we have a problem?"

The floor of the lighter was covered by thin wooden slats running crossways. Between each slat was a gap about two fingers wide. Grains of wheat were scattered in the gaps.

"This is the problem," I said, picking up one of the grains and showing it to Punt.

Punt stowed his oar and knelt down to have a look. We drifted, and the incoming tide pushed us beyond the stone quay. "How did they get here?" Punt said

"The grain sack that split when I landed on it," I said.

"I didn't spot them because I was taking on board those sacks of stone from the quarry at first light," Punt said.

"We need to clear up any grain spilled near the hidden cellar," I said.

"KWAA." A raven landed on the side of the lighter, making it wobble. I waved my hands at the bird while Punt looked for something to throw at it. "KWAA, KWAA, KWAA," the raven cawed, its call slicing the air.

We heard the creaking of wings from the quayside as ravens took flight and headed towards our lighter. "KWAA, KWAA, KWAA," the ravens cawed. The noise was like a cudgel smacking my ears. They landed on the lighter, all on the same side, tilting it towards the water.

Punt picked up his oar, ready to use it as a weapon.

"KWAA, KWAA, KWAA." One side of the lighter was now a throbbing sea of black feathers as more and more ravens arrived, and the lighter tipped closer to the water.

"Watch out, Keth," Punt shouted, raising his oar, ready to strike the ravens.

"KWAA, KWAA, KWAA," the ravens cawed, rising up together and hopping over to the other side of the lighter.

The lighter rocked wildly and Punt yelped as he overbalanced and fell off the back into the river.

"KWAA, KWAA, KWAA," the ravens cawed, launching themselves into the air. The lighter rocked violently then capsized. I plunged into the river, and the ice cold water dragged me down.

I had been too surprised when I fell in to grab a breath, and already I was desperate for air. I fought to free myself of my heavy woolen jacket. It clung to me like a murderer's embrace. My lungs were bursting. I got a shoulder then my left arm clear. Purple spots were flashing in front of my eyes. I shook my right arm free and shed the jacket. I felt dizzy, and I wanted to open my mouth and scream.

Something grabbed me under the armpits. We were rising. My head broke clear of the water. I spluttered and gasped for air. I took a deep breath. I opened my eyes. It was dark. A hand grasped my right wrist and guided my hand up out of the water until it touched a piece of wood. My fingers curled around it and I clung on. I raised my left hand to join it.

"We're beneath the capsized lighter," Punt whispered into my ear.

Things began to make sense. Punt must have rescued me, and we had surfaced beneath the lighter. The wood I was clinging to was one of the slats on its floor. Overhead I heard scratching sounds on the wood. The sounds moved along the length of the lighter. Ravens were walking up and down the upturned hull.

We waited. I imagined the ravens scouring the water, looking for signs of life. Eventually, we heard a creaking sound that might have been wings flapping, and the lighter wobbled. "KWAA, KWAA, KWAA." We heard the caw of the ravens growing distant.

"They've gone," Punt whispered.

"It could be a trap," I whispered back.

We waited a little longer.

"I have to know where we are," Punt whispered. "The current is tricky when you get close to the bridge. You have to line up your lighter right.

I heard the splash as he ducked his head out from beneath the lighter, and I ducked my head out as well.

I gaped. The pillar of one of the stone arches of the bridge crossing the river was hurtling towards us. I ducked back under the lighter. "What do we do now?" I said.

"Cling on," Punt said. "Wood floats better than we do."

We heard a huge crunch as the lighter smashed into the pillar. A shockwave ran through the lighter, making the wood ripple. It juddered our bones and rattled our teeth. We heard a ripping sound as timbers splintered. The lighter spun round and moved forwards with the current again. A beam of light entered from a hole punctured in its front right hand side.

Punt was about to duck out from under the lighter and have a look at the damage.

"Don't move," I whispered. "They might have bowmen from the gate tower on the bridge."

We stayed where we were, and let the current drag the lighter onwards.

***

"We've rounded Pulletts Reach," Punt said, after a while.

"Is that good?" I said.

"It means we're out of sight from the bridge," Punt said.

Punt ducked out from underneath the lighter, and I followed him. We were in the middle of the river and, judging by the speed of the passing banks, we were going faster than walking pace.

"Bad news, Keth," Punt said, looking at me, downcast.

"What?" I said.

"You've lost your wig," Punt sniggered. I burst out laughing, and we both howled with laughter. After a while, we subsided into snorts and sniggers, as we regained control of ourselves. "Better check the damage," Punt said.

He pulled himself along the side of the lighter until he reached the hole near the front. I followed him. The timbers around the hole were bent and twisted. "I can get that patched," Punt said. "We'll hang on until we reach Fledge. Grist's uncle worked the river for years and still looks after a couple of boats. As long as the tide runs steady, we'll be there in an hour."

I looked back towards the city. The black flecks of ravens hovered over the dock area. More alarming, I saw birds flying low over the fields. "We don't have time," I said. "We've got to pick up the grain we spilled near the hidden cellar."

"I can't abandon my lighter," Punt said.

"But if the ravens find the grain…" I said.

"A river lad never deserts his craft," Punt said.

"Maybe we can land, clean up the grain then come back and take the lighter," I said.

"And if someone saw the lighter from the road," Punt said, "or saw us go under the bridge and is following us?"

"What would they want with a busted lighter?" I said.

"Firewood," Punt said. "Might be the difference between surviving the winter and freezing to death."

"What's more important, your lighter or the grain?" I said.

"My lighter," Punt said straight away.

I realized I was not going to persuade him to abandon his lighter. If I was the alternative rebel leader, I would command him to do it and he would obey, but he had saved me from drowning, and I was not going to order him about. Perhaps I was not cut out to be a leader.

We were approaching a bend in the river. I recognized the clump of trees, with the few tattered yellow leaves, where we had struck the Russett road with Grist. It seemed ages ago but it had only been first light today. The current was taking us away from the middle of the river and close to that bank.

"I'm going to swim for shore," I said. "One of us should try and hide the grain."

"I'll tell you when to strike out," Punt said. "Swim across the current, don't fight it."

The bank loomed closer. "Now," Punt said.

I took a deep breath, kicked away from the lighter and swam for the shore. My muscles were numb and my clothing dragged at me, sucking me down. I rolled on to my back and kicked. My face broke the surface, and I snatched a breath before I went below again.

I looked at the sky through the water. It was a mass of low black cloud. I had no idea what direction I was pointing in. I panicked and rolled back on to my front. I snatched another breath. The bank was passing me by. The current was going to sweep me beyond the bend and back out into the middle of the river. I began thrashing my arms. The bank drew only a little closer. I was not going to make it this way.

I snatched another breath and dived hard for the bottom. My hands hit soft mud and hard stones on the riverbed. I clawed my way along the bottom towards the bank. I was too buoyant, the current tumbled me, and I lost my grip on the stones. I surfaced and gasped more air. The bank was nearer but I was running out of time.

I dived down again and clung to a large stone on the bottom, working it loose with my hands. I lifted it and held it to my chest, cradling it with my left hand. The extra weight secured me to the bottom. With my right hand, I groped my way towards the bank. My lungs were bursting but I forced myself to keep going.

Purple spots flashed in front of my eyes, and I let go of the stone and thrust for the surface.

I was in water that reached up to my chest. I coughed and spluttered then sucked in a lungful of air. The bank was close now and I lunged for it, floundering through the water. I hauled myself up the bank and lay on my back panting.

"Good luck, Keth," Punt shouted.

I raised my head. Punt had almost disappeared around the bend in the river. I waved my hand. I didn't have the strength to speak, let alone shout.

19 LOSS

Having clambered out of the river, I wanted to lie on the bank and sleep but it looked like it would rain soon, and I would freeze to death. I staggered up the bank and stood on the road, flapping my arms and stamping my feet to try and get warm.

I needed to find my way to the hidden cellar, but I faced two problems. First, could I find it, and second, I did not want to attract the attention of the ravens. It was no use my concealing all the spilled grain if a flock of ravens was watching me do it and reporting to the grain collector.

On the previous night, Grist had led us straight across the fields, but this time I stuck to the hedgerows that marked the boundary of each field. This kept me out of sight of the ravens, and it also gave me shelter from the bite of the cold wind.

The last time I had made this journey, it had been dark. Travelling in daylight meant that I didn't fall over in the mud, but it did not make it any easier to find my way. The fields had stiles and gates between them, and I tried to remember details about them from the previous night, to reassure myself I was going in the right direction; the trouble was I had been exhausted by that stage and everything had been a blur.

I paused part way across a stile and scanned the sky. A flock of ravens continued to circle over the docks, while individual ravens, almost lost in the dark, bruised rain clouds, flew above the fields. I ducked down from the stile.

A fat cold raindrop hit my head. I heard the patter as heavy drops struck the hedges and the duller thud as they pelted the muddy field. The sound grew louder like an approaching stampede as the rain became torrential.

Great, I thought. If we can't drown poor Keth in the river then let's see if we can do it on land.

A happier thought struck me, and I smiled. If I was getting rained on then so were the ravens. The rain might be so heavy that they would have to land and stop their search. An even happier thought arrived. Suppose the rain washed away all the spilled grain around the hidden cellar.

I scurried along beside the hedgerow, willing the rain to keep falling, and fall even harder if it could. I kept my head down and concentrated on trying to stay upright as I slithered through the mud. Suddenly, the hedgerow ended and so did the ground in front of me. I skidded down a muddy bank on my backside and shot into a creek filled with freezing water.

I staggered to my feet. Had I fallen into the creek that led to the willow tree where the lighters had moored? I had a moment of doubt, but we had crossed no creeks on the journey from the hidden cellar to the road last night; ditches yes but creeks no.

Was I upstream or downstream of the willow tree was

the next question. The only landmark I remembered was the tree itself. I thought about the route I had taken across the fields. I guessed I was downstream of the tree, and so I set off upstream, slogging through the water.

The rain came down like a wall of water, churning the surface of the creek. I moved to the side of the creek where it was shallower and each step took a little less energy. I no longer had any sense of time passing, I just put one foot in front of the other.

I rounded a bend in the creek and saw the willow tree. Its branches drooped down even further with the weight of the rain as though it wanted to shut the world out.

***

I waded over to the spot where Punt had moored his lighter the previous night. I peered at the creek bank and saw little golden flecks of wheat trapped in the wet grass.

I climbed out of the creek onto the bank, and began picking out the grains from the grass, one by one. It dawned on me that I had forgotten to bring a sack or anything to put the grains in. I folded up the hem at the bottom of my jerkin and used that as a temporary pocket for the grain.

I worked my way slowly up the bank, taking care to pick up every grain. At the top of the bank, a weak shaft of winter sunshine broke through the clouds and struck my face. I had been so intent on spotting the grain that I had not noticed the rain had stopped.

The trail of spilled grain cut across the corner of a field. The rain had not washed the grains away but had left them, like little flakes of gold, embedded in the mud. I crawled across the field, picking up each grain and storing it in the fold of my jerkin.

"KWAA." With a creak of its wings, a raven landed in front of me. It eyed me then pecked at a grain.

I lunged at it. It hopped away, and my hands closed on thin air. I lay face down in the mud.

"KWAA." The raven launched itself into the air. "KWAA, KWAA, KWAA." It circled the field, calling to its friends. Black specks in the sky grew larger as other ravens approached. They landed in the field and pecked at the grain. I staggered to my feet and ran at them, screaming and waving my arms. I chased them along the trail of spilled grain, and they hopped and flapped ahead of me. More and more ravens were arriving. I looked towards the city. The flock that had circled the docks was now heading in my direction.

At the edge of the field was a sunken lane, overgrown with brambles. Grains, like golden bugs, clung to the earth and marked out a narrow path between the thorns.

I followed the path, and the ravens flew ahead of me, as though they were an advance guard, announcing my arrival. The path emerged into what would once have been a small clearing although this too was now choked with brambles.

I followed the trail to the center of the clearing where the remains of a ruined farmhouse stood. Its stone walls reached to knee height. Inside had been a single room with a timber floor. The wood was now rotten, and thick weeds sprouted in the gaps between planks. By looking at the spilled grains, I knew where the split sack had been lifted over the wall and the position of the secret trapdoor down into the hidden cellar.

I clenched my hands into fists and thumped my thighs with anger. I should have started picking up the trail of grain here instead of at the creek bank; that way when the ravens arrived, they would not have been led straight to where the grain was hidden.

"KWAA, KWAA, KWAA." The ravens squawked in triumph as they swarmed in the sky above the ruined farmhouse.

I sank to my knees on the wooden floor. We had stolen the grain, but the grain collector was going to take it back. No one would enjoy a single extra morsel of bread because of my efforts. I had failed, and I had endangered the lives of other rebels. I had no more energy left to fight the ravens or the grain collector or Prince Dorian. I would wait here until either I died from the cold or the grain collector's guards came to arrest me.

I stared up at the seething, black feathered cloud of ravens, above me. "I hate you," I screamed, shaking my fists at them.

This was the moment the ravens chose to poop on me.

***

Raven poop, believe it or not, is a terrific morale booster.

I had been ready to spend the rest of the day collapsed on the floor of the ruined farmhouse, wallowing in despair and defeat, shouting my frustration at the ravens. But now, with my eyes streaming and my nostrils clogged with the vile stench of the raven poop, I staggered to my feet and ran from the ruined farmhouse.

A cloak of white and brown raven poop sat across my shoulders so I carried the foul stink with me as I blundered down the sunken lane, ignoring the brambles that ripped at me.

I stumbled up out of the lane and slithered across the corner of the muddy field. I hurled myself down the bank of the creek and plunged into the water. I submerged myself and scrubbed at my hair and face. I surfaced and took a deep breath of wonderful, cold, clean air.

"KWAA." A single, smug raven called as it watched me from a drooping branch of the willow tree.

In the distance, I heard the cackling of its friends, I guessed, still circling above the ruined farmhouse. My despair had passed. The action of getting the toxic poop off me before it either choked or dissolved me had brought me back to life. I stood up, shivering in the cold water. "So your job is to keep track of me," I said to the raven.

"KWAA."

"I'm going to call you Squawk," I said.

"KWAA," Squawk said.

"I've lost the grain for the moment, haven't I?" I said. Squawk didn't reply to this. He probably thought it was so obvious it wasn't worth the effort. "And the best thing I can do is head back to the city and try and avoid capture," I said.

Once again Squawk was silent.

***

I climbed up the creek bank and set off across the fields in the direction of the road. Squawk followed me. I no longer needed to stick to the hedgerows; the ravens had found what they wanted.

I reached a wooden stile and sat on it a moment. Looking back, I saw the buzzing, black cloud of ravens marking the spot where the grain was hidden. Squawk pecked at the ground then stared at me. "I'm not yet defeated," I told Squawk, wagging my finger at him.

"KWAA," Squawk said. This was probably raven for

"who are you kidding?"

***

I carried on until I hit the road near the clump of trees by the river side. The earlier torrential downpour had removed the last of the yellow leaves, and the trees were bare. It began to rain again as I set off in direction of Russett.

I had been walking a short time when I heard, from around a bend in the road ahead, marching feet.

"Left, right, left, right," a man's deep voice barked. "Keep up, peasants, or you'll be whipped."

Guards were approaching, and I guessed they had been sent to retrieve the grain that the ravens had discovered. I wondered about hiding in a ditch, but my new companion Squawk would no doubt do his best to hop about and give me away. Whatever I did would have to involve him.

I had a plan but I was exhausted, and I needed to appear confident and in command to carry it off. My muscles were telling me that my body needed to rest in a warm, dry place for several days. I summoned all of Grunter's training, clenching and relaxing my muscles, breathing deeply and stretching, so that I was supple enough to shape my body to fit the role I wanted to play.

I pulled back my shoulders and straightened my spine. Puffing out my chest, I strode forwards, an important young man on a vital mission. Squawk fluttered along behind me.

I met the guards coming in the opposite direction.

In the lead was a burly man with a chest plate, beneath which he wore a leather jacket with three white stripes sewn on to its arm, indicating he was a sergeant. Behind him marched two guards followed by a shaggy gray horse pulling a cart. Sitting on the cart holding the reins was a gray-haired man, dressed in a gray smock. Behind the cart were a dozen scrawny men dressed in rags walking with their heads down, and bringing up the rear marched two more guards.

"Halt," the sergeant shouted and raised his hand.

My guess that this party had been sent out to collect the grain was spot on.

The sergeant spotted Squawk hopping along behind me, and his eyes narrowed. Having a raven in tow made me suspicious. The sergeant looked the sort who liked to arrest first then ask questions later, perhaps fitting in a beating, between the two. I needed to take control.

"Corporal," I called out. "You're late."

"Sergeant," he gasped, looking offended.

"It will be corporal if you don't buck your ideas up," I said, striding up to him and rapping him hard on his chest plate. It hurt my knuckles but I did not show it.

"The best spot to stop is a few minutes further on," I said, "just beyond a clump of trees by the river side. Isn't that right, Squawk?"

"KWAA," Squawk said, hopping from foot to foot, unsure of what was going on and looking a little less smug than before.

"Exactly," I said, nodding to Squawk.

"Who are you?" the sergeant said.

"I'm the grain collector's nephew," I said. "And this is Squawk, my personal assistant. I've known him since he was an egg."

The guards, who had clustered behind their sergeant, now shuffled to attention. I gave them my best stern gaze.

"I've got my orders from the grain collector," the

sergeant said, folding his arms. "He didn't mention his nephew." His guards thought this was a good point, and they relaxed and rested their hands on their cudgels.

"I'm here to advise you, not give you orders," I said. "The ravens are over there." I pointed to the cloud of ravens still swarming in the distance above the ruined farm house.

"I can see that," the sergeant said.

I now spoke in a slow clear voice, to give the sergeant the idea that I thought he was an idiot. "Squawk and I have checked it out," I said. "You won't be able to get that cart over the muddy fields. You'll need to stop at the spot I mentioned and carry the grain to the cart on foot."

"I know that. I'm not an idiot," the sergeant snapped. A deep red color was rising in his face.

"That's what I told my uncle," I said.

The red color drained back out of his face as he chewed on the idea of the grain collector thinking he was an idiot and discussing it with others.

I raised my hand, pointing my finger to the sky. "It's raining," I announced in my most dramatic voice.

The carter sniggered but turned it into a sneeze as the sergeant looked sharply in his direction. I used the distraction to stride past the sergeant and his guards, placing myself in front of the scrawny men, who were huddled together, shivering in the rain.

"What happens to grain when it gets wet?" I addressed them.

"Doesn't keep," a cross-eyed man at the front of the group mumbled.

"Doesn't keep." I turned back to the sergeant with my eyes gleaming with triumph and wagged my finger at him. "It turns rotten."

"We've brought waxed goat skin covers for the sacks,"

the sergeant snapped. He glared at me with his hands on his hips. "I'm in charge of this operation, and if you have a problem with that then I suggest you talk to your uncle."

"Did you hear that?" I said to Squawk, sounding offended.

"KWAA," Squawk said, hitting his cue, spot on, without knowing it.

"I've delivered my advice, Sergeant," I said. "If you mess up this job then you're on your own."

I stalked off in the direction of Russett. I didn't look back. I guessed that Squawk would have to follow me because that was his job. Instead of getting me into trouble, he was helping to make my story ring true.

No one came after me. I guessed the sergeant was relieved to see the back of me. He would now be so anxious for the job to go smoothly that he would not think to question who I said I was until all the work was complete.

***

I strode along the road, buoyed up by my satisfaction at having talked my way out of trouble, but as I neared the bridge crossing over the river into the city, my strength left me. I was so weary I thought I might fall asleep on my feet. This was what my mum called bone tired.

It was late afternoon as I shuffled across the bridge. Squawk hopped along the parapet full of energy. Entering through the city gate, I almost got crushed when I wandered into the path of a cart.

"Watch where you're going lad," the angry carter shouted at me.

I waved him an apology then struggled on. By the time, I reached Dorian's Square either I was weaving from side to side or the buildings had taken up dancing. I slumped down exhausted at the foot of Dorian's statue, resting my back against his stone legs. I saw no sign of Urchin, Grub, and Smiley. I hoped they were safe. Squawk, with a single flap of his wings flew to the top of the statue and perched on top of the crown, looking down on me.

Since dusk the day before, I had clambered up and down boats, lugged grain sacks, tramped through mud, slept under a hedge, almost drowned, and spent an unhealthy amount of time in freezing water. I was exhausted. Keeping my eyelids open was like lifting two heavy sacks of grain. Why bother?

I closed my eyes and thought of my mum. I was walking through the huts of Mottle on a cold night. I found our hut. Mum stood framed in the doorway. A cooking fire burned behind her, and its light cast a glow about her red-gray hair. I've got stories for you, Mum, I thought, but first I need to sleep. She smiled and held her arms out wide in welcome. She smacked me hard on the back of the head.

My eyes jerked open. I had fallen asleep; my head had lolled back and I had cracked it against Prince Dorian's stone knee. If I stayed here, I would sink into sleep and die. I struggled to my feet and staggered off in the direction of the lodging house.

From time to time, I saw Squawk perched on a roof edge peering down at me.

***

I didn't want anyone on Crib Street to see me looking

so wretched. When I got there, I slipped down the back alley and into the backyard of the lodging house.

It was dusk, and the backyard was filled with shadows. As I trudged towards the backdoor, I heard Squawk hopping along behind me. I turned and flapped my hands at him.

"Go away, Squawk," I said. "You're in danger." He cocked his head to one side and gave me a questioning look. "I'm sorry about this, Squawk," I said.

Ragamuffin pounced, and for a brief moment, I saw only a flurry of fur and feathers then Ragamuffin held Squawk in his mouth. The flapping of Squawk's wings grew weaker then stopped.

I turned back to the lodging house. Ma stood, arms folded, leaning against the frame of the kitchen door. "I didn't expect you to come back," he said.

I remembered how I had left the troupe at the Anvil Inn without saying a word to any of them. "We've got a show tonight," I said.

"What makes you think you're in it?" Ma said.

"Don't you want it to be funny?" I said.

I tried to take a step towards the warmth of the kitchen but I did not have the strength to lift my feet. I tried to shuffle forwards; instead, I sagged to my knees.

"We'll leave out the dancing," I said. "Dorian's banned it anyway."

Ma and the kitchen seemed to billow in and out.

I slumped forwards and passed out.

20 THE ANVIL INN

I lay with my eyes closed in a warm room. I remembered talking to Ma in the backyard of the lodging house then things went blank. I tried to move my arms and legs but something was binding them. I've been captured, I thought.

I opened my eyes and looked up at a whitewashed ceiling. I tilted my head and looked down the length of my body. I was swaddled in blankets. To my left was a roaring log fire blasting out wonderful heat, and to my right were the spindly legs of a small table on which sat a china dog with sad eyes. They must have carried me into the parlor of the lodging house, I thought.

"Thank you," I said. My mouth felt stiff, and my words were slurred. Ma leaned over me. The lines on his face were deeper, and he looked older. "How long have I slept?" I said.

"Only a couple of hours, lad," Ma said. "It's early evening now."

I experimented, wriggling my body, inside the blankets. My muscles howled in protest. I needed two days' rest, not two hours.

"We've been turning you like a roast," Silva said. Her face appeared, hovering over me. "You're cooked all the way through." Her eyes were red and puffy, as though she had been doing a lot of crying.

Ma and Silva unrolled me from the blankets then helped me into an armchair pulled close to the fire. I thought the chair had grown extra uncomfortable lumps until I realized it was my aching muscles.

"Ask Madame Patwig for some stew, and ask her to prepare the Colonel's tonic," Ma said to Silva, and she left. Ma arranged blankets across my lap and around my shoulders.

Silva returned with a tray on which were a bowl of hot stew and a hunk of bread. I gobbled down the food, pausing only when I needed to breathe.

Silva took the tray from my lap, looked for a table to put it on that was not covered with ornaments and settled for laying it on the floor. She sat in the armchair opposite me while Ma pulled up a carved wooden chair and sat beside her.

"Silva and I have been talking today," Ma said.

"Talking?" Silva said, raising her left eyebrow.

"And shouting, bickering, crying and stamping our feet as well," Ma said.

"Ma stopped me leaving the house last night," Silva said, "which meant I was not around to prevent you doing something stupid."

"Silva and I have been arguing ever since we arrived in the city," Ma said. "We have a problem."

"Me?" I said.

"Does everything have to be about you, Keth?" Silva said, giving me a sharp look that hurt me enough to make me forget my aching muscles.

"I believe that the troupe must be neutral towards Prince Dorian," Ma said, "but Silva believes we should fight him."

Was Ma wavering in his principles? Could Silva and I persuade Ma to throw in his lot with the rebels? "Dorian's a bad man," I said. "We must oppose him."

"It's not that simple," Ma said. He sat back in his chair and folded his arms.

I wondered if that was why the rebels were all kids. A kid saw that it was a simple choice to fight Prince Dorian, but an adult found it more complicated.

"My son, Rul, thought it was a simple thing to fight Prince Dorian," Ma said, "and he died."

"So did my father," I said. "That doesn't mean they were wrong. They just picked the wrong way to fight him."

Silva got up and stood in front of the fire. She picked up a poker and stabbed at the burning logs. "And you think your adventure last night was the right way?" she said. "Is Prince Dorian going to be overthrown because you succeeded in stealing a few sacks of grain?"

"I'm not sure," I said, "but I think we have to show people that they can stand up to him."

"You give them a story to believe in," Ma said, resting his hands on his knees and leaning forwards in his chair. "One in which they are not downtrodden and defeated."

Were stories the lever that would move Ma over to the rebel side?

"You told me all stories were sacred because they were threads plucked from the land," I said. "This battle with Dorian will become a story. It will be a thread woven into the land that future performers will pluck to show people who they are. It's too important for any of us to be neutral."

"But you won't be part of that story, Keth," Silva said, "because Ash is going to kill you." Sparks flew up the chimney, as she split a log with the poker.

"When you left us at the Anvil Inn today," Ma said, "Silva told me you had fled the city, so we were a bit surprised when you turned up in our backyard."

"And upset," Silva said. She gave the fire a last hard jab then put the poker down.

"It's unsafe to leave you at the lodging house, so you're coming with us to the Anvil Inn," Ma said.

I grinned. I was going to perform with the troupe again.

"And the idiot laughs." Silva shook her head. "Do you have any idea how much danger you are in?"

Someone knocked at the parlor door. "Come in," Ma called.

Madame Patwig entered, carrying a steaming mug. "Colonel Patwig's patent reviver," she said. "It helped raise him the morning after a battle and many other mornings as well."

She handed me the mug. I sniffed it. It smelled worse than raven poop. "Hold your nose and down in one was the Colonel's advice," Madame Patwig said.

I followed the Colonel's suggestion. Everyone was watching me. Nothing happened. I shrugged at them. A few seconds later my stomach exploded in flames, my toes shot off the end of my feet and my eyeballs bounced across the parlor floor. I'm exaggerating, but only a little.

"It does take a moment to have an effect," Madame Patwig said.

I felt like myself again. I felt more like myself than I had ever felt before. Other Keths had been pale imitations of this one.

"What are we waiting for?" I said, jumping up from

the chair. "We've got a show to put on."

***

Ma put on his makeup, ginger wig, and red polka dot dress, while I dressed in my sailor boy outfit. We then returned to the parlor where the rest of the troupe had gathered. Grunter and Elba greeted me warmly, but Crag gave me a sour stare. "Oh look, it's Mummy's favorite," Crag sneered.

"Drop it, Crag," Ma said.

"No," Crag said. "It's not fair, and someone needs to say it. If I kept wondering off and missing rehearsals like Keth did today, I would be booted out of the troupe, but Mummy's boy does it all the time, and when he comes back, we're all meant to fall over ourselves to be nice to him. He needs a kick up the backside and a few lessons in starvation to teach him he's not so special."

I had a terrible feeling that Crag was making a fair point. "It's a good point," Ma said, rubbing his chin. The room filled with silence. I hoped Ma was not going to leave it at that. Ma slowly paced the parlor floor.

"The thing is, Crag," Ma said, stopping and turning to him, "you're in this business for whatever you can get."

"And Keth isn't?" Crag said.

"No," Ma said. "Keth performs because he can't help it. It's part of who he is. I knew that the moment I discovered him in the hamper at Brackford."

"And that means he's allowed to skip rehearsals?" Crag said.

"No," Ma said, "but I will be patient when he breaks the rules because he's young and foolish, and I know he'll always come back and do better."

Ma and Crag were talking about me as though I was

not there. I wanted to say something, but Ma's last speech had left me with a lump in my throat as big as the ones in the armchairs.

"It's going to be a demanding audience tonight," Ma said. "The patrons of the Anvil Inn are tough people. Just remember, they are people first and tough second. They laugh and cry just the same as anyone else. Let's give them a show."

***

We left the lodging house and made our way to the inn. I was bursting with energy and I wanted to stride on ahead, but Ma insisted I stay in the middle of the troupe. He was taking the rebel threat to my safety seriously.

When we arrived at the inn, it was already packed. It wasn't just that a lot of people were there but all these people were huge and brawny, even the women. It was like walking into a wall of solid flesh. We squeezed our way through to the stage.

"Go over to the bar," Ma said to me, "and tell Master Bircher we'll start in a little while."

I inched my way between people, ducking beneath the tankards of ale they wielded, and trying not to get my eyes poked out by the metal studs they wore in their leather clothes. Eventually I made it to the bar. Master Bircher was at the other end, and I leaned over to wave to him.

A raven landed on the bar, right in front of my face. "He won't hurt you, yet," the man standing on my right said.

I looked up and saw the hooked nose and thin-lipped smile of the grain collector. He wore his black cloak but had taken down its hood. Strands of oiled black hair were scraped across his pink scalp.

"Hey, no animals on the bar," Master Bircher shouted.

The raven hopped on to the grain collector's shoulder. I glanced up and saw more ravens perched silently in the rafters of the inn.

"Who do you think should be Prince Dorian's chief advisor?" the grain collector said to me. "A clever man who commands two hundred splendid ravens or a deformed twerp who carries a toad head on a stick."

I gaped. The grain collector was mocking Twist. "Men with special talents should be running this kingdom," he said, "and I've known all along that you're a cut above the rest. You're the first person in ten years who has tried to steal grain from me."

He took a long swallow from the tankard in front of him. "I want you to be my personal assistant," he said and smiled. "My real assistant, not just a pretend one to fool my idiot guards. Together, we can get rid of Twist."

My mouth went dry. Getting rid of Twist was an important step in getting rid of Dorian, and this man, who was my enemy, was offering to help. Working with the grain collector, I could achieve a lot more than working with the rebels.

I looked into his face. I saw the thin-lipped, cruel smile that did not reach his hard brown eyes. I remembered his last visit to Mottle, and what he had said to Scour when Scour had pleaded for us to be left more grain. "You should let the weakest among you die, so the rest can eat their share."

Mum would be ashamed of me for even thinking of working with such a man. "The answer's no," I said.

"Think again," he hissed, grasping my wrist with his gloved hand. "If you have not changed your mind by the end of the show then I will have you executed."

"Is there a problem?" Master Bircher said. He was

now standing across the bar from us, baring his wooden teeth in a smile. "We don't want any unpleasantness," he said to the grain collector, "but we know how to deal with it if we have to."

The grain collector released my wrist and downed his drink. "Another ale," he said, pushing his empty tankard towards Master Bircher.

"Ma told me to tell you we're going to start in a little while, Master Bircher," I said, "and that was a little while ago." I turned to go. "About your two hundred splendid ravens," I said to the grain collector. "It's two less now, because the cat ate them."

I made my way through the press of people towards the stage. Smeggle came in through the doors to the back yard, carrying a tray of steaming hot meat pies. I watched in awe as he weaved through the crowd, distributing the pies without a wobble. He had left the door slightly ajar, and I felt a twinge of fear as a pair of ravens hopped inside. I glanced up at the rafters. The ravens stared down at me.

Elba strummed her lyre, and Silva shook her tambourine as the troupe stamped on stage, making enough noise to turn heads in their direction. I pushed my way through the crowd, anxious to join them.

***

Things started well, with all of us singing 'The Tinker and the Jolly Farmers' Wife' then Ma, Grunter and I did 'The Unsuitable Suitor' routine, and the audience laughed so much, it took twice as long as when we rehearsed it. Elba and Silva then sang a sentimental ballad about a heroic dog pining for his master by the wall of the dead garden. This had grown men blubbering into their tankards. Ma and I then did our 'Ma and her Little Lad' routine, and the bit where he pulled out a frying pan from under his skirts and smacked me on the head with it almost brought the house down.

Everything was going well, until Crag went on stage to sing his song. Elba was accompanying him on the lyre and she took up position off to one side of the stage, sheltered beneath the stairs.

Crag's song was all about how handsome he was, and how difficult that made his life, because he had to choose between so many women chasing after him, but that was all right because he chose all of them.

The rest of us were standing just off stage. "Why are you letting him sing that song?" Silva groaned.

"He insisted," Ma said. "He'll have to learn the hard way."

Crag strutted along the front of the stage, singing about how irresistible he was.

"Last time I saw something strut like that was in a barnyard," a slab-faced woman called out.

"And it was trying to lay an egg," an old man with no teeth and an eye patch shouted out. He did a chicken impression, and the people around him laughed.

Crag winced. He tried to pick out the women in the audience and get them onside by giving them simpering looks.

"Are you flirting with our women?" a beefy man bellowed. He was bald with a tattoo of a green and red serpent coiled on his scalp and tattoos of wolves on his bare arms.

Crag had had enough. "Are you kidding?" he sneered. "You lot are so ugly, I can't tell the women from the men."

The beefy, tattooed man pushed back the bench he

had been sitting on and stood up. It was like watching a mountain rise up.

Up until that moment, the inn had been noisy. It now became so quiet that I heard the small scrape of Master Bircher bringing out a cudgel from behind the bar. Grunter leaped on stage and in one smooth movement hoisted Crag over his shoulder.

"Sorry I'm late," Grunter said, saluting the audience. "I'm the troupe's health officer, and I'm afraid this act's gone off. Not to worry, I'll dispose of it." Grunter bounded off the stage, still holding Crag, shoved through the crowd to the door leading to the backyard, kicked it open, and tossed Crag out.

"You've gone soft, Grunter," the beefy, tattooed man called out.

"Come off it, Bovis," Grunter shouted back. "I chucked him out the door."

"Yeah, but you opened it first," Bovis bellowed, and the crowd roared with laughter. It was a harsh sound, as if it had splinters of wood mixed in it.

The stage was empty, and the crowd was turning against us. I jumped up on stage and bounded into the center. I arrived having nothing to say so I said the first thing that came into my head. "Have you seen all those ravens in the rafters?" I called out.

The audience looked up.

"They're tomorrow's meat pies," I said. This got a small rueful laugh from the audience and a few glances towards Master Bircher. "We're going to cook them live with their wings sticking out of the pie crust," I said, "so they can fly direct to your table."

This got a bigger laugh. The audience liked the image of the flapping pies.

"Do you see that bloke at the bar with a raven on his

shoulder?" I said. The grain collector put down his tankard and glared at me, as the audience turned to stare at him.

"I was talking to him before the show started. He said to me he was a raven trainer. I thought he sounds more like a raven lunatic. I said what tricks do your ravens do? He said they fly up into the rafters, and when no one's looking, they poop in the ale. I said, don't folk notice? He said yes they do, they all think the ale tastes better."

The audience was laughing.

"That's the truth, Master Bircher," Bovis bellowed.

Master Bircher gave me a wide mahogany smile. He preferred a laughing audience to one that was hitting each other with the furniture.

"Mind, I don't want to bite the hand that feeds me," I said. "With teeth like Master Bircher's, if he bites back, I'll lose my fingers."

This got enough of a laugh to keep me going.

"Anyway, I asked the raven trainer what the hardest part of training ravens to poop into ale was, and do you know what he said?" I paused to build up the tension. "It's showing them what to do; I've fallen from the rafters six times already today."

The audience gave me a huge laugh. I mimed a man with his pants round his ankles, falling from a rafter into a tankard of ale. The audience shrieked with glee. Bovis was laughing so hard, tears were streaming down his face.

The grain collector had gone bright red. He shoved his empty tankard across the bar and called for more ale. His ravens skittered along the rafters.

We'd got the audience back on our side. Elba ducked out from beneath the stairs and strummed her lyre. Ma, Silva and Grunter joined us on stage, and we sang 'Bang My Anvil Heartily.' The audience joined in the chorus, whacking their tankards against the tabletops and sending ale spraying everywhere. I hoped Smeggle had put down plenty of sawdust.

"Crag's scarpered," Grunter whispered to me, during the applause at the end of the song. "And the backyard is full of ravens."

With all the ravens hanging around, I wasn't going to be scarpering like Crag.

***

The audience now loved us, and they joined in with every song and laughed at every joke. As the final act in our show, Ma came on stage with Grunter.

"Grunter here is willing to arm wrestle the strongest man in the room," Ma said. "If you win, Master Bircher will give you a barrel of ale, and I'll give you my hand in marriage; if you're rich and handsome, I'll give you the rest."

Bovis stood up and strode on stage. No one challenged whether he was the strongest man there, which probably meant he was. The audience cheered. I helped Smeggle carry a table on stage, and Elba and Silva brought on two chairs that they put either side of it.

Master Bircher left the bar and came on stage to act as referee. Grunter and Bovis sat opposite each other and locked hands with their elbows on the table.

"On the count of three," Master Bircher said. "One, two, three."

Grunter and Bovis sweated and strained, pushing at each other's arms.

"Elbow on the table, Bovis," Master Bircher called out, keeping a sharp eye on things.

I thought Bovis might be getting the best of things. I

glanced over at Elba, and she seemed relaxed and confident. Perhaps Grunter was giving a performance.

Bovis had driven Grunter's hand almost down to the table, but Grunter still resisted him. Bovis strained and swore but could not move Grunter's hand the final small distance that would give him the victory.

Grunter gave a mighty grunt that shook the rafters and made the ravens hop. His hand rose slowly and inevitably, driving up Bovis's hand until they were back to the position they started in. With another grunt, Grunter drove down Bovis's hand to the table, winning the contest.

The audience clapped. It had been like watching a play.

Grunter and Bovis shook hands and patted each other on the shoulder then Bovis left the stage.

***

We cleared the tables and chairs from the stage then gave the audience a final burst of "Bang My Anvil Heartily,' the most popular song of the night, and that was the end of the show. The audience applauded wildly.

I looked over to the bar. Master Bircher was back behind the bar, but I saw no sign of the grain collector. I hopped off the front of the stage, thinking I would slip through the crowd and out the front door while the ravens were watching the back of the inn.

"Have you changed your answer, laddie?" The grain collector loomed over me and grabbed hold of my wrist. He stank of ale.

"No," I said. I'd run out of clever words.

"Then you're under arrest," the grain collector said, "and you'll hang."

"What's the matter, friend?" Bovis said, placing his massive hand on the grain collector's chest. "Can't you take a joke?"

Bovis must have thought I was being arrested for having teased the grain collector earlier on. He gave the grain collector a hard shove to the chest, sending him staggering backwards. The grain collector tripped over someone's leg and fell over, flailing his arms and sending other people flying.

The grain collector was flat on his back, with the angry people he had sent sprawling standing over him.

"KWAA, KWAA, KWAA," the ravens in the rafters screeched. As people looked up, the ravens plunged at them, smacking into their chests and heads and knocking them over.

Bovis drew his cudgel, but a raven swooped down and pecked his hand, making him drop it. Another raven scraped its claws across his bald head, leaving red scratch marks across his serpent tattoo. Bovis howled with pain and fear.

Panic swept through the audience as the ravens buffeted people's heads with their wings and pecked at their faces. Smeggle flung open the door to the backyard, looking to escape. He was knocked back by what looked like a wall of black feathers as all the ravens who had been keeping watch outside flew into the inn.

A desperate crush formed at the Anvil Street entrance to the inn as people struggled to get out. They were barging and shoving each other as the ravens circled above them, flying low and pecking at their eyes.

"KWAA, KWAA, KWAA," the ravens screeched.

I crawled back towards the stage and crouched down low at the foot of it. The cries of the ravens drilled into my skull, making it hard to think.

Bovis was cowering beneath a table, as ravens took it in turns to swoop and peck at his bum.

Master Bircher had waded into the crowd to save the fallen Smeggle, who was getting trodden on.

Ma and Silva were helping wounded people across the stage and into cover underneath the stairs. Grunter was trying to protect them from the attacking ravens, wielding a broken chair leg. Elba was protecting Grunter's back, using her wooden lyre case as both a shield and a club.

A space had cleared around the grain collector. He sat up in a circle of overturned tables and benches. The strands of hair that he had scraped across his scalp now dangled from the side of his head. His eyes were bloodshot, and his mouth was no longer thin and cruel, but wide and laughing with glee. He's enjoying this, I thought with horror.

"You're going to be pecked to death, Keth," the grain collector said, looking at me and grinning.

A raven flew at my face. I jerked my head back. The raven smacked into the side of the stage and fell to the floor with its skull crushed.

I looked at the chaos around me and racked my brain for a way to stop it. I might have inherited a talent to see wraiths, but what use was that? I was a peasant not a wizard. I only knew about cows and soil and crops and being hungry. An idea flickered into life in my head. I knew about birds. When I was a little boy, two summers old, my father had taught me a dance to frighten away the birds from our freshly planted seed.

I climbed on stage and began to dance the spring dance.

Elba saw me and started to clap out the rhythm of my dance.

Tendrils of mist rose up out of the sawdust on the

floor of the inn.

A raven struck me on the back. I staggered but kept dancing.

Another raven grabbed at my hair, scraping at my scalp. I saw a brown blur as Grunter smacked it from my head with the chair leg.

As I danced, Grunter moved around me, swiping at the ravens who tried to attack us.

A raven flew straight at my eyes; a tendril of mist, like a wagging finger, reared up between me and the raven. It squawked in fear, veered to my right and crashed into the wall of the inn.

From the corner of my eye, I saw Ma and Silva come up beside me and join in the dance. From beneath upturned tables and chairs, people beat out the rhythm of the dance, following Elba's lead.

Mist filled the room but I knew only I saw it; the wraiths were taking form. Sending bright shafts through the mist were threads of light that whizzed around the room. For a moment, the threads just added to the confusion then the picture became clear. Every thread connected the head of the grain collector with the head of a raven. I was witnessing how he communicated with his birds.

The ravens wanted to get as far away as possible from the wraiths. They tried to fly out the doors or smash through the windows, but patches of mist floated in front of these exits, and the ravens veered away at the last moment. A swarm of panicked ravens circled the room just below the ceiling, squawking wildly as fingers of mist prodded them.

Ma, Silva, and I continued our dancing. Grunter and Elba joined in.

The grain collector stood up and staggered, his head in

his hands.

Three ragged, fluttering, human-shaped figures of mist rose up behind him. They peered over his shoulder, and one of them smiled at me, a smile that was a twisted rip in the mist that formed its face.

The eyes of the wraiths were no more than holes in the mist, but they still appeared to examine closely the point on the grain collector's head where the threads from the ravens entered. The grain collector began to tremble. I knew he could not see the wraiths but perhaps he felt their presence.

With a ripple, the three wraiths merged into one. This new wraith cupped its mist hands around the threads where they entered the grain collector's head, squeezed them tight then yanked them hard. All the threads snapped and disappeared.

The wraith looked at me. The hole that was its left eye shut then opened again. It had winked at me. The wraith's body split up and drifted apart, mixing with the rest of the mist, which was beginning to fade.

The ravens landed on the rafters. They thrust out their chests and fluffed their feathers, as they stared down at the grain collector with concentrated fury. In a flash, I understood that those threads had been chains, binding these proud birds to the grain collector and making them his unwilling slaves.

I stopped dancing. The grain collector looked at me bewildered, with tears in his eyes.

"I've lost touch with my splendid ravens," he said.

"Run," I screamed at him.

The ravens swooped on him. He threw up his hands to protect his eyes leaving his pale white throat unprotected.

I turned away, not wanting to see his end.

21 TRIAL

A little while later, we were re-establishing order amid the chaos of the Anvil Inn.

A dressing station for the injured had been set up on stage. Master Bircher had brought down bed sheets from upstairs, and Grunter was tearing these into strips that Silva and Elba were using as bandages to bind up people's wounds.

The only person who had died was the grain collector. What was left of his body had been covered with a blanket.

The surviving ravens had all flown from the inn as soon as they had finished with the grain collector, except for the one that had flown into a wall and knocked itself unconscious. Smeggle, who had suffered nothing worse than bruises, was tending the dazed bird.

Ma and Master Bircher were sitting on the edge of the stage. I loitered close by to overhear their conversation. I wanted to know what they were planning to do, and whether I needed to flee.

"Did you know this man?" Master Bircher gestured

with his foot at the body beneath the blanket.

"He looked familiar," Ma said, "but I didn't see him properly, before the ravens got to him."

"I know him," I said, jumping in. "He was a nasty piece of work. He used to go round the villages every year after the harvest, taking most of the grain we had grown and leaving us nothing to live on. He trained his ravens to search for hidden grain and peck out the eyes of anyone caught hiding it."

I wanted Ma and Master Bircher to realize that while the grain collector had met a horrible end, they should not feel too sorry for him.

"Popular man then," Master Bircher said. "What happened with his birds tonight?"

"He lost control of them," Ma said. "He started a fight, his birds became over-excited, and they turned on him."

"I did a village dance we used to do in the spring, before Dorian banned it," I said. "It's meant to scare the birds away."

"But this is an inn, not an open field," Ma said, "and the birds went mad instead."

I was going to add to Ma's explanation but Ma gave me a look, and I shut up.

"He started the fight and it finished him," Master Bircher said. "Rough justice, but it is justice of a sort."

"Are we going to tell Twist about this?" Ma said.

"I don't think so," Master Bircher said. "He'd only use it as an excuse to hurt people. And if he finds out about the dancing, we'll all be hung."

"What about the body?" Ma said.

"My brother works at the dead garden," Master Bircher said. "He can slip it in with the other 'unknowns' first thing in the morning. From what young Keth said, I don't think he's got any friends to mourn him."

"Won't Dorian investigate when he finds out his grain collector has disappeared?" I said.

"By then the trail will have gone cold," Master Bircher said. "And no one from these streets will talk to him. We have our pride."

"My poor pecked bum." A pitiful cry came from beneath a table. "I'll never sit down again." Bovis crawled into view.

"Who's going to bandage his wounds?" Elba said.

"My turn to heroically volunteer," Ma said, standing up with a sigh. "Have we got some of that ointment that really stings?"

Smeggle popped out into the backyard with the raven he had been tending, which was now stirring against his chest. I was glad it was not going to end up in a meat pie tomorrow evening, although the ones Grunter had hit with chair leg would.

So that was it. The grain collector had been defeated, and we were going to clean up and hide the evidence. I sat on the edge of the stage feeling a little sad but mostly feeling tired. The effects of Colonel Patwig's patent reviver were wearing off.

Smeggle came back in from the backyard. He had released the raven. He sidled over to me. "Can I have a quick word outside, Keth?" he said.

The others were all busy tending to the injured. I nodded to Smeggle and followed him out into the backyard. "What is it, Smeggle?" I said then choked as a pad of damp material was pressed against my face. It smelled foul.

I slumped forwards and passed out.

***

I woke up when someone dashed cold water into my face. I tried to protest only to discover that I had been gagged.

I sat on a wooden chair in a pool of light. My legs had been tied to the chair legs, and my hands had been tied behind my back. I craned my neck and saw that the light came from a lamp hung from a ceiling beam. I looked down, and saw the floor was made of gnarled wooden timbers in a fishbone pattern.

The pool of light extended no more than a body's length around me; just beyond I saw the outline of rectangular piles of what smelled like animal skins, reaching from the floor almost to the ceiling. To my right, I heard water gently lapping, and every now and then, something wooden tapped against a wall.

I guessed I was in the warehouse where Silva had taken me for the rebel meeting, but this time I was on land rather than on a lighter in the basin.

A loud hacking cough broke the silence then someone spat. I heard the splash as a wad of phlegm hit the water. Ash must have organized my kidnapping. Marvelous, I thought. Ash does nothing to bring about Dorian's downfall, and when he does take action, it's against another rebel. If Ash didn't exist, Dorian would have to invent him.

"Turnip has been brought here on trial for his betrayal of the rebel movement," Ash announced.

Rubbish, I thought. I was on trial because I'd put Ash's snotty nose out of joint by actually doing something rebellious. Hands up who stole the grain? Is your hand up, Ash? I didn't think so. Okay, maybe the grain was taken back, but who then defeated the grain collector and set free his ravens? Hand still down, Ash? I'd have my hands up if you hadn't tied them behind my back, you useless bag of tar. And I'm called Keth not Turnip, because I don't need a stupid nickname to make me feel important.

I chewed on my gag but could not make a single sound.

"Turnip organized an unauthorized and poorly planned raid on a grain ship," Ash said. "Several previously trustworthy rebels were drawn into his scheme. As a result of this, Bead, Corac and Bilge are all in hiding, and we will no longer benefit from their observations of river traffic. Punt is drowned."

I hoped Ash was wrong about that last bit of information.

"Although a small quantity of grain was stolen, it was soon recovered by the grain collector and returned to the grain warehouse," Ash said.

A little splinter of doubt pricked me. Had my actions harmed the rebels and achieved nothing? Did Ash have good reason to be angry with me?

"Turnip is a danger to the rebel movement, and we must execute him," Ash said.

"Don't you dare," a voice called out. A boy detached himself from beside a pile of skins and walked into the pool of lamplight. It was Smeggle. He still had his apron on. He pushed his lick of sandy-colored hair out of his eyes and stood in front of me, facing my accusers.

"Don't be silly, Pot," Ash said.

"I'm not being silly," Smeggle said, "and I'm not called Pot; I'm called Smeggle and this lad in the chair is called Keth, and he drove a flock of ravens into a frenzy, and they pecked a bad man to death, and that is more than any of us have done in the last year, and you shouldn't kill him just because he does stuff when you don't, and if I'd known that was what you were going to do, I'd never have got him to go out into the backyard. I'd have told him to run away."

Smeggle stopped speaking. I thought he had run out of breath. Instead, he reached into his apron pocket and pulled out what looked like a small circular metal blade with a flourish.

"This is a potato peeler," Smeggle said, "and I know how to use it."

"But only for peeling potatoes," Ash said.

Other rebels laughed in the dark, but I was touched by Smeggle having the guts to stand up for me.

I heard small splashes and wood bumping against the basin wall as people got out of a lighter. Another boy stepped into the circle of lamplight. It was Urchin. His shock of white hair seemed to glow in the light.

"I agree with all that stuff, Pot, I mean, Smeggle, just said," Urchin said, "and I don't have a potato peeler, so I'll just have to use my teeth."

Grub and Smiley joined Urchin in the circle of lamplight. The four of them made a semi-circle around me, facing my accusers. I wished one of them would think to turn round and remove my gag. I'd seen enough bloodshed at the Anvil Inn, and I wanted to tell them to stop it. The only good that could come of rebels fighting each other would be if Dorian choked to death while laughing about it.

"All traitors will be executed," Ash said.

"Do we have to?" a prim girl's voice said.

"Yes, Pin," Ash said. "The rules are clear."

I detected a note of impatience in Ash's voice. A tall lanky girl about my age in a black pinafore dress with her dark hair in braids walked slowly into the circle of lamplight. "Sorry. I'm no good at fighting," she said.

"It's good you're with us anyway, Pin," Smeggle said,

and he made space for her between himself and Urchin.

The two opposing groups faced each other, and I had no idea how to stop them coming to blows.

***

The standoff was interrupted by a series of short, sharp splashes growing louder as something approached us from the direction of the river. A lantern beam cut across the water of the basin. Had we been discovered by Dorian's soldiers?

The other lighters bobbed in the water as a lighter shot into the basin, powered by Punt standing on the back. Ma, still in his costume of red polka dot dress and ginger wig, stood at the front, thrusting out his bosom and holding a lantern. Silva sat in the middle.

It looked as though the lighter would plough into the wall of the basin but at the last moment, Punt dug his oar hard into the water and swung the lighter sharply sideways, sending a wave of water splattering across the wooden floor and leaving the lighter resting placidly against the side of the basin.

"Sorry we're late," Ma said, stepping gracefully from the boat. He spoke in his lady's voice. Silva hopped out of the lighter and stood beside Ma. "You can always spot an actor," Ma said, glancing at me. "Keth makes sure he is well lit and center stage every time. And you've put a gag on him. I wish we'd thought of that."

"Shut up, you stupid old woman," Ash said. "Only rebels may speak and only when commanded."

"I'm Silver Fox," Silva said. "This lady is actually my father, and he has something to say that's worth listening to."

"He is not a rebel and must be silent," Ash said.

"How can she be her dad?" another voice, not as quick on the uptake as Ash, whispered in the dark. "Shouldn't she be her mum?"

"If you respect me, you will let him speak," Silva said.

"Let him speak." A chorus of whispers came from the dark.

"Or is it her?" a confused voice added.

"He must be silent," Ash said.

"If you don't let him speak, I'm leaving the rebels," Silva said.

A long silence followed. It was broken by Ash coughing then spitting.

"Your father may speak," Ash said.

"I wanted to say a few words about Keth," Ma said, now speaking in his man's voice. My heart swelled and once more the lump came to my throat. It would be just like in the parlor of the lodging house, when Ma stood up for me against Crag.

"Keth is the biggest idiot I've ever met," Ma said

I choked on my gag. I'd been expecting praise. Ma might as well hang me from the rafters himself if he was going to say things like that.

"I lead a troupe of players," Ma said, "and Keth is my apprentice fool. The idiocy he brings to life, he also brings to the stage, and he makes folk laugh."

"Get on with it," Ash said.

"Fools have always been vital members of troupes," Ma said, "but they belong to a much older tradition. In bygone times, fools were employed by kings to tell them truths that their courtiers were afraid to speak. Keth, although he may not realize it, is part of that tradition."

Was I part of some ancient tradition or was Ma just spinning words?

"I spent many years believing I could be neutral to

279

Prince Dorian," Ma said, "until Keth said, he's a bad man, and not to oppose him is to support him."

"And we rebels thought all we could do was watch Prince Dorian," Silva said, "until Keth said, let's do something."

"They're right," a voice whispered in the dark, to murmurs of agreement.

Ash was losing the support of the meeting. "We'll let the fool speak," Ash said, "and listen to his words of wisdom. Remove his gag."

Ash was gambling on me saying something stupid that would contradict what Ma and Silva were saying about fools speaking the truth.

***

Urchin loosened my gag; I had only a little time to think. What truth would one of these ancient fools have delivered to his king in this situation? If I was the fool then I was not the king. The thought was like a lantern being lit in my head. It cleared away so many shadows.

The gag slipped from my mouth.

"Water," I croaked, playing for time while I got my thoughts straight. I had just this one chance to get my words right and stop the rebels from attacking each other.

Urchin knelt by the edge of the basin and soaked the gag. He returned and squeezed the water from the gag into my mouth. I swallowed and coughed.

"I'm proud of all my friends who have stood by me," I said. My voice caught, and for one awful moment, I thought I might start blubbing. I took a deep breath and steadied myself.

"But rebels must never fight each other," I said. "The rebels divided cannot defeat Prince Dorian.

"Hear, hear," Ma said and nodded his head so that the ginger curls on his wig bounced.

"We can't just collect information on Prince Dorian without using it to take action against him," I said, "but the action we take has to be guided by as much information as we can get. Taking action and collecting information fit together."

Murmurs of agreement came from the shadows.

"I want to play my part in overthrowing wicked Prince Dorian," I said, "but I don't want to be the rebel leader. I'm the fool, not the king."

"You could be king," Urchin whispered. "We'd follow you." Smeggle gave the smallest nod of his head in agreement.

"Ash is the rebel leader," I said. "He's built up this group who harvest information about Dorian. I want to use that knowledge to do things that will bring Dorian to his knees. And someone like Silva, I mean Silver Fox, can act as the link between Ash and me."

I had made my offer. If Ash chose to reject it, the rebel movement would rip itself apart and be finished before dawn. A silence fell over the rebels. They digested my words. Would Ash compromise with me to hold the rebel movement together?

"Release Keth," Ash said. "And don't cheer, remember last time. We will meet tomorrow night to work out the new arrangements. This meeting is closed."

***

Smeggle scraped through my bonds with his potato peeler. I shook hands with him, Urchin, Grub, and Smiley and thanked them for being so courageous and standing up for me. I tried to shake hands with Pin as well but she kissed me on the cheek instead, which made me blush.

I went over to Ma and Silva and hugged them. "We've room for one more," Ma said.

As I climbed aboard the lighter, I tapped the planks at the front.

"Good as new," Punt said. "Grist's uncle did a grand job."

Ma put on a dark woolen cloak with a hood. "I don't want to look conspicuous," he said, "but I had to make an entrance at the meeting, so they'd want to listen to me." Ma snuffed out the lantern and we were in darkness.

"How did you know where I was?" I said.

"When you and Smeggle disappeared from the inn, I guessed," Silva said. "The rebel meeting was due tonight anyway, and we met up with Punt at the meadow landing stage."

"Hush now," Punt said, and he pushed the lighter away from the side of the basin.

We were soon out on the open water. It was a clear night and the splinterlight danced on the river.

***

Punt dropped us off at the meadow landing stage. We crossed the meadow, and Ma astonished me by how nimbly he climbed up and over the city wall.

"I can do the same things I did when I was a young man," he whispered, "but I'll be too stiff to do anything tomorrow except grumble."

We scurried through the deserted nighttime streets and returned to the lodging house, slipping in at the back gate. We crossed the yard, and Ma tried the backdoor. "Locked," he whispered. "I don't fancy waking everyone up."

Silva pointed to a ledge she used when climbing up the back wall of the house.

"Now, that's just a bit too much," Ma whispered. "We'll have to bunk in with you, Keth." It was a tight squeeze in the stable loft. "It's cozy," Ma said.

He lay on his back, and Silva and I lay on either side of him, resting our heads on his costume breasts. "Why didn't Ash just slit my throat?" I whispered.

"He probably wanted to," Silva whispered, "but you're too popular. He needed to get the other rebels to agree with him to do it."

I jumped as a rattle began in Ma's chest and emerged from his nose as a snort.

"Relax, Keth," Silva said. 'It's just Ma snoring."

We went to sleep.

***

We were woken in the morning by the ringing of the curfew bell.

We emerged from the stable to find Madame Patwig crouching by the back door examining Ragamuffin.

"Good morning, dear lady," Ma said. "Please forgive our unusual entrance, but I bumped into an old family friend last night, and we got talking. We were caught out by the curfew."

I expected Madame Patwig to leap on this piece of potential gossip, but she just nodded.

"Poor Ragamuffin is unwell," she said. "All those nasty birds he ate yesterday have upset his delicate little tummy."

Ragamuffin raised his scarred face to us, belched, and then mewed pitifully. We traipsed inside and sat around the kitchen table. Elba and Grunter entered the kitchen, arm in arm, and joined us at the table.

I was halfway through a bowl of porridge when Crag appeared. He sidled over to the table with his eyes lowered and cut himself a slice of bread.

"What happened after I left the inn last night?" Crag said, nibbling on his bread and examining the table with interest.

"Nothing much, a little bit of a brawl," Ma said. "Keth got the audience back on side, and we finished the rest of the show."

"Thanks, Keth," Crag mumbled; he found the edge of his slice of bread fascinating. "I stuffed up last night, didn't I? Do you want me to pack my things and go, Ma?"

"I'm not going to boot you out of the troupe for making a mistake," Ma said, "although I might if you don't learn from it."

"But you've got the gig at the Anvil Inn," Crag said. "They hate me."

"We'll put you on at the back as chorus," Ma said, "and get you to lead out on 'Bang my Anvil Heartily.' In a few days, they'll have forgiven you."

"Thanks, Ma," Crag said. "Must dash, things to do." He left the kitchen with his eyes still lowered, clutching his slice of bread.

"Did I really just see Crag being humble?" I whispered to Silva.

"It won't last," she whispered back.

"I need to get the case for my lyre repaired today," Elba said. "It took quite a pecking last night."

"We can go to Master Chipley," Grunter said. "He'll do it for free if I give him a hand with some lifting out the back." They left the kitchen, hand in hand.

"I'm off to the markets," Madame Patwig said, "and I

need to get a tonic for poor Ragamuffin."

***

Ma, Silva, and I were left alone in the kitchen. We moved our chairs to sit in front of the stove. "What happened last night, Keth?" Ma said.

"You were there." I shrugged. When I'd talked about what I'd seen after the performance at Crouchers Hollow, no one had believed me so I was not going to start now.

"True," Ma said, "but I don't think I saw as much as you did."

"When you dance, Keth, you look as though you're in a trance," Silva said. "Are you somewhere else?"

"I'm in the same place as you," I said.

"Did you see mist and wraiths?" Ma said.

"You saw nothing, so if I open my mouth, I'm a liar," I said. I got up and stalked over to the backdoor. I had not realized until now, how much it had hurt me that no one had believed me after our performance at Crouchers Hollow.

"Mum told me never to talk about it," I said. "She was right."

I flung open the back door and stormed out. I stomped across the backyard and returned to the stable loft. I lay down in the hay, waiting for Ma and Silva to pursue me. They didn't. After a while, I fell asleep.

***

It was late afternoon when I was woken up by Ma and Silva knocking on the stable door. They had brought me the traditional peace offering of a bowl of stew and a hunk of bread.

"The world is full of stories and legends," Ma said.

I spooned down the stew, wondering where this was leading.

"Some of them get forgotten," Ma said, "but they don't die, they bide their time below the surface of everyday things then choose their moment to reappear."

I chewed on a lump of meat.

"I think old legends are stirring," Ma said, "and your sight will be part of their retelling."

I mopped up the gravy in the bowl with my bread. Ma had piqued my curiosity. I swallowed the last bit of bread and took a deep breath. "I saw the mist and the wraiths," I said. "If I tell you about them will you in turn answer my questions?"

Ma rubbed his chin. It rasped. He had not shaved since yesterday. "Alright," he said.

Ma and Silva listened rapt as I told them all about the wraiths I had seen at the Anvil Inn, and what I had seen at Crouchers Hollow, and the first time I saw a wraith when I danced the harvest dance the previous harvest time.

After I had finished, a silence fell as Ma and Silva digested what I had said. At length, Ma took a deep breath. "Your turn to ask questions, Keth," he said.

"Who is Dawyn, the boy from Grindle with the soft hands?" I said. "The one who collapsed when he put the crown on?"

Ma hesitated. "I promised to keep it a secret," he said.

I held his gaze. "And you promised to answer my questions," I said.

Ma sighed. "Dawyn is the eldest son of Prince Gawain, who was overthrown by Prince Dorian," he said. "He's the legitimate heir to the throne of Russett."

"But he's a slimy ratbag," Silva protested.

"And our noble lord and master," Ma said, with a half smile on his lips.

"Did Gawain have any more children?" I said. I was hoping we could get one of them to replace Dorian instead. I hated the idea of handing the throne to such a grain-weevil as Dawyn, especially as I'd insulted him on stage.

"Prince Gawain had three children," Ma said. "Merrian, a daughter, the eldest child, Dawyn, the eldest son, and Pluck, the youngest son. By law the title passes to the eldest male child. Gawain was not confident of winning the battle against Dorian, and he had his three children hidden among his people.

"I hid Dawyn in the peasant village of Grindle, before travelling to join Prince Gawain at Crouchers Hollow," Ma continued. "Dawyn was supposed to blend in with the villagers, but the spoiled brat refused to do any work. The head man of the village was afraid that if he forced Dawyn to earn his keep then later, if Dawyn reclaimed his throne, the village would be punished. Dawyn has been allowed to grow up with soft hands and a weak spirit."

"What happened to the other two children?" Silva said.

"I don't know," Ma said. "I only know about Dawyn. Gawain believed it would improve their chances of survival if no one but him knew the complete story."

"Does the nightmare crown you carried in the costume hamper belong to Gawain and his heirs?" I said.

"No one owns the crown," Ma said. "By tradition this land is split into territories ruled by princes. In times of great peril, one among them is chosen to be king, and he wears the crown of all the lands."

"But it looks so tatty," Silva said.

"It wants to stay hidden," Ma said, "or at least it used

to."

"Is this crown what the old legends are about?" I said

"I don't know," Ma said.

"So how do we find out?" Silva said.

"We listen," Ma said, "and when they are ready, the legends will talk to us."

I shivered. Legends that told themselves to you in their own good time were like dances that did not want to be forgotten or crowns that chose when they wanted to be seen; they were spooky.

"So what do we do next?" I said.

"This evening we perform at the Anvil Inn," Ma said, "and tomorrow we plot the downfall of Dorian and Twist."

I grinned. A performance at the Anvil Inn was as real and solid as Master Bircher's mahogany teeth; nothing spooky there.

***

Silva shaved Ma then we changed into costume and joined the rest of the troupe assembling in the parlor, before heading off to the Anvil Inn. Madame Patwig wished us good luck. She was in good spirits as Ragamuffin had regained his health.

At the inn, Master Bircher welcomed us with a wide mahogany grin, and Smeggle gave me a cheery wave as he weaved among the crowds of people with a tray of meat pies on his shoulder.

The chairs and tables looked battered with chips and splinters pecked out of them by the ravens. Many of our audience looked in even worse condition, still wearing their bandages from the previous night. Bovis was now sitting on a straw cushion to protect his sore bum. He was looking rueful as he pulled a black feather from out of his meat pie.

"If this is the result of a bit of a brawl, I'd hate to be here when a real fight breaks out," Crag said.

We took a few minutes to set up then launched into our show. The audience loved us. They even put up with Crag, who stayed in the background. I was standing by Ma at the side of the stage as we listened to Elba and Silva sing once more about the loyal dog pining for his master by the wall of the dead garden. Tears ran down the faces of hard men.

"It doesn't get better than this, Keth," Ma said and smiled at me.

I nodded and grinned back.

I was now an accepted member of the rebels, and we had defeated the grain collector. Tomorrow would be a new day in the battle to overthrow Prince Dorian, and I would be fighting with Ma and Silva by my side.

But best of all was being here, right now, in this room. Elba and Silva were winding up their song and in a moment, Ma and I would burst on stage and give the audience our 'Ma and her Little Lad routine.'

Ma was right. It didn't get better than this.

ABOUT THE AUTHOR

Aldred Chase is the author of the Nobody's Fool Quartet and the Sinister Sydney Series. His first experience of fantasy fiction was reading 'The Hobbit' at school, and he has been hooked on the genre ever since. His favorite places for writing are cafes and park benches, but he does most of his work sitting at his desk. His best ideas come to him when he is traveling by train or walking by the sea.

To keep up to date with all his latest news visit his website at www.aldredchase.com.

NOBODY'S FOOL QUARTET
Apprentice Fool
Royal Fool
Prince Of Fools
Dragon's Fool

SINISTER SYDNEY SERIES
All Things To Everyone